# PROVINCETOWN FOLLIES
# BANGKOK BLUES

# PROVINCETOWN FOLLIES
# BANGKOK BLUES

## RANDALL PEFFER

BLEAK HOUSE BOOKS

MADISON | WISCONSIN

Published by Bleak House Books,
an imprint of Big Earth Publishing
923 Williamson St.
Madison, WI 53703

This is a work of fiction. Any similarities to people or places, living
or dead, is purely coincidental.

ISBN: 1-932557-19-9
LOC: 2005936205

## Dedication

For Gail N, Barbara LC, Meddie, Ben, Alison, Derek & Susan ...
who believed

For Bobby E, Linda & Graeme, Becky & Elwin, Temba & Vuyelwa
and all the folks at Community Affairs and Multicultural
Development ... who know the score

For Joey L, Lamont, Peggy H, David Z, Richard TEB. and Tuki ...
who walk the walk when Paris is burning

For Varat, Harit, Claire, Shay & Sumida ... khawp khun khrap

For the Amerasian Foundation ... angels at work

For Ken B, Bob P and their brothers in arms ... who
fought the fight

For the Provincetown Police and Fire & Rescue ... who
keep the peace

For the men at the leather bar, the women at Vixen & the Pied, the
two-steppers at The Boatslip, the singers at the Governor Bradford
... and ESPECIALLY the fabulous girls at the Crown & Anchor,
the A-House, the Post Office Cabaret, Club Euro, Esther's and
Jacque's ... who party on

For Noah & Jacob ... The dudes abide

For Jacqueline, as always ... my sun, my moon, my Venus

# PROLOGUE

The night they arrest Tuki Aparecio, she is not picturing *Shawshank Redemption;* more like *Dead Man Walking.* Two cops escort her into the Barnstable County lockup in handcuffs. A dozen men are hanging on the bars of their cells hooting and shouting, grabbing their crotches, licking their index fingers. It smells like cigarettes and the burning scent of ammonia masking something worse.

With death grips on her upper arms, the cops rush her down the corridor, swinging their billy sticks at the outstretched hands, rapping the bars of the men's cages.

"Back off, outlaws!"

She still has on her makeup and a little black spandex dress from Frederick's. Five gold tummy bracelets encircle her waist. White lace pantyhose go with her red rhinestone box-toed pumps. The guys are foaming at the mouth. But what else would you expect? The police took her down the second she came off stage.

"Come to daddy, baby girl." One of the inmates has his face to his bars, his tongue flicking in and out of cracked, bloody lips.

A guard presiding over the scene rolls his eyes and spits.

"How about we just leave you with these tomcats, lollypop?"

But he's not serious. He's just having a little fun with her. When he gets her in an empty cell at the far end of lockup, he looks her up and down, stares at her hips. Finally, his eyes drift back up to her breasts. Stares some more.

She wants him to go away. Wants to close her eyes and make tonight end. But she is too afraid of what he might do when she is not looking. So she watches him with dead eyes, nails ready to claw.

"Shoes and chains, doll face!" He holds out his hands, waiting.

She feels like she's being strip-searched. This is all part of the scene, right? Brandy and Delta have told her: First they snare you, then they treat you like *klong* water. When you are no longer an amusement for them, they send you off to the death camp.

Suddenly he turns, seems to vanish in the bright light of the jail. The iron gate slams shut on her.

"Sweet dreams."

She does not sleep or eat. Some thing—some force—just takes over there in the cell. The next thing she knows her nails are digging a half-inch deep into both of her wrists. Blood is spurting all over the place, and she is screaming at the top of her lungs in Thai. Maybe a man's name. The wail sounds like some kind of wildfire.

Bridgewater State Mental Hospital. August 2. Alone in a pink terrycloth robe, Tuki sits on the ledge of a window with a chain-link screen across the opening.

Her knees are pulled up under her chin, and her dark hair falls in a thousand wild braids and ringlets over her shoulders and arms. Her hair veils everything but her lashes, nose, lips, and chin. The room is in shadows so she is little more than a silhouette against the blazing summer sun outside. Her skin looks dark. It is not just from the lighting. The bandages on her wrists give off a silvery glow. Yesterday she turned twenty-nine.

She is not a woman like the others in the ward, the ones who shuffle around like shadows, the ones who drool or mutter or shriek at Jesus. There is something unexpectedly strong and slender about that left leg that has worked its way loose from the folds in the robe. And that face. Lashes like you cannot buy from L'Oreal. Lips of plum. The chin forms a vee with the cheeks ... the effect is a little catlike. Imperial even. But now, backlit by the sun, she could be a child.

She is watching a tractor mowing the lawn outside, wondering when the monsoon rains will truly begin. Suddenly up walks a man. A real man in this boneyard of women, trailing the scent of Canoe. He is middle height, late twenties or early thirties. His dark, razor-cut hair and shadow of a beard remind her a bit of Tom Cruise, but not Tom Cruise. He is too Latin, the hair too wavy, maybe even curly if it were longer. He is carrying a leather brief case and wearing a gray summer suit. His white shirt is loose at the collar. His pale pink lips are pursed. Something is bothering him.

He sits down in a chair facing her and says, "This must all feel like a nightmare."

She just stares down at him from the window ledge, can hardly believe he is talking to her. She wants to say something, but she has suddenly forgotten her English.

"I'm sorry, I didn't mean—"

She leans toward him.

He opens his mouth, but now no words come out. He just stares at her. She is a magnificent freak of God's and her own invention. The best-looking person he has ever seen. A siren and a killer. He knows those warm, dark eyes mask ten thousand secrets. Everything inside his head tells him to run as far and as fast from her as he can. But he stays, and doesn't know why.

She gives him a shy smile. She has found some words to break the screech of the lawn mower outside. "Tiger got your tongue too, la?"

"I guess so." The words catch in his throat. He rubs his eyes with the palms of his hands.

"Look ... I don't know exactly how to ..."

She slides her legs off the windowsill. They are right at his eye level. The columns of skin between her knees and ankles look made from honey. She puts her hands on her knees, bends down until she is face-to-face with him. When she has eye contact, she speaks.

"Buddha says it is not possible for you to make a mistake, if you speak from the heart."

He shifts in his seat, straightens his shoulders. Maybe he is getting his balance back.

"What would you like to be called?" He unzips the briefcase on his lap.

"Tuki. Always Tuki, la. You know, like TOO KEY?"

"It says 'Dung' here in your file."

She gives him a sad little look. He only makes eye contact for an instant. Still, she can see something—nerves maybe—clouding those gentle brown eyes. He does not want to be here. That must be it.

She sighs, pulls her knees up under her chin as before, stares out the window, thinks that any second the rain will come and turn the whole world to smooth, dark mud.

"Why does it say Dung? Who is Dung?"

"Dung? Dung is my long lost brother. If you know what I mean, detective."

He pictures a little kid with dark curly hair, golden skin. His body jerks a little, a shock running up his spine. He bites the inside of his lip, tastes the blood. Tries to refocus. Damn. He is screwing this all up. Find a common ground, establish a rapport, pal. You know the attorney-client routine. What the hell is wrong with him? He has not even introduced himself.

"I'm not the police, Tuki. I'm Michael Decastro. I'm your court-appointed attorney. It's the law. You get an attorney. I'm sorry."

"You're sorry?" An edge creeps into that soft voice of hers. "You are sorry it's the law? You are sorry you are my lawyer? I do not understand."

He waves his hands in front of him, trying to stop a runaway train.

"No, no, NO! I'm sorry for this confusion. I'm sorry for your troubles. Really. I'm here to help. Let me help you." Sweat is starting to run down his temples. "Arson and murder. These are pretty scary charges."

She buries her face in the pink robe covering her raised knees. Suddenly there are tears in her voice.

"Please, PLEASE, do not let them send me back to Thailand. I swear I did not kill anybody. I swear to Buddha!"

He wants to reach over to her, touch her hand the way his mother always does when someone has a problem. But then he wonders whether this would be appropriate. He holds back. She is not Filipa after all. Not even a little like his fiancée.

When the sobs stop, he clears his throat.

She is still on the windowsill, drying her eyes with the hem of her robe. Now she lifts her head and looks at him, sees the nerves burning in those brown eyes again.

"One other thing you should know," he says as if he is at Saturday evening confession. "I'm an experienced public defender. I've had murder cases before. I think I'm pretty good at my job. But you're my first—"

A little chirp escapes her throat. Suddenly she is grinning. Huge. It is an odd grin. Kind of inappropriate, coming out of the blue at this awkward moment the way it does. But it is quite a pretty grin. It starts with her plum lips and straight white teeth, then spreads to her proud chin. Two little dimples bloom on her cheeks as her eyes light up full of discovery. From a radio somewhere in the distance, Paul Simon sings about diamonds on the soles of her shoes.

"You have never met a girl like me, have you?"

He shakes his head no. Hell no.

## ONE

The next time they meet at Bridgewater, Tuki sees a stormy look in Decastro's eyes. As soon as he sits down facing her on that window ledge again, the words just explode from somewhere inside his chest.

"Help me out here, Tuki. What the hell happened in Thailand?" His voice sounds ripped. She feels afraid, does not like his swearing. She just wants a little bit of kindness. A little respect. A friend, maybe.

"What's wrong, Michael?" She cannot believe she has called him by his first name. She means no disrespect. The name just popped out of her mouth.

It catches him by surprise. Almost nobody calls him Michael except Filipa. Most people call him Castro. His family calls him Mo. He has to take a deep breath, collect himself.

"I got a message on my answering machine this morning from a guy who says he's with the Royal Thai Police. Says he's been looking for you for over five years. You want to tell me about it?"

*"You not a bastard, not freak. Your mother always say you very special baby. Holyholy child," says Brandy. "Never forget, la! You holyholy child like Buddha. Love child." She and Delta are Saigon queens, the ones who took Tuki, a toddler then, on the boat from Vietnam to Thailand. The ones who raised her in Bangkok. As always, they speak to her in the rough English they learned in Saigon's bars. They want her to look to her future. Learn this strange tongue. They tell her English is the one language everyone must know to survive the curry of races and nationalities in places like Bangkok's Patpong. New York City.*

*"When you get U. S., you tell people your daddy, U. S. Marine," sniffs Delta. Her voice gets loud and husky the way it always does when*

she is trying to be strong. "You tell people Semper Fi, la! He marry you mother. All legal. We had license. We had you birth certificate, Cho Ray Hospital. Tell them look up record. You American girl. American people keep good record. You tell them. They see!"

She thinks about the people in the refugee camp who stole her papers so long ago and wonders if they hated her because her daddy came from the U. S. With those papers she could have an American passport. American citizenship. She could go to America on the Orderly Departure Program for the children like her, the ones the GIs left behind. No shaky Thai passport. No problem with Immigration and green card. Maybe she can even find her father.

She remembers the end of the film M Butterfly when Butterfly appears for the first time as a man—so thin and sad and pale. Now she is that boy ... in the picture for her fake passport and here dripping sweat outside the airport. No makeup, man's suit and tie, long, curly hair tied back. Brandy and Delta think they are doing the right thing when they have her dress like this for the picture, and for the trip. They say she must match a boy's face to a boy's body ... because in places like Thailand, strip searches at border crossings are not out of the question. The passport even has her male Vietnamese name. "Dung"—courage. "Aparecio, Dung Tuki" it says on the passport, "male." But where is the boy in the picture? He does not even exist, except for this journey.

"You worry too much," says Delta. She is reading Tuki's mind. "We teach you have big dreams. We teach you be free. We teach you trust self, love self, count on own self to be happy. No wait for some man in big car. We teach you be princess. You pretty. You sing. You dance. You make lots of people happy. We teach you how fly. Remember that?"

"Now we push you out of nest," says Brandy. "Everything decided. No time left in Bangkok. You go before we have more trouble. This place finished for you."

She hands over an envelope with a ticket to New York on China Airlines. With it is the address and phone number of a drag restaurant in the city. The owner is an old friend of Delta's. He used to run a club in Saigon.

"It no theater—no sing and dance like here—but it something. It *fresh start. No Bridge Over River Kwai Death Camp for you," says Delta. The makeup runs down her cheeks in little streams.*

*And all the while Gladys Knight is singing a song in Tuki's head about leaving. About midnight trains to Georgia. She has not the faintest idea where that is, but it sounds like someone's home.*

# TWO

Michael Decastro is thinking things aren't looking too good for his client. The case, so far, is circumstantial. But the state police, who always get the call when there is arson and murder, have Tuki nailed for motive, opportunity, and means. They also claim to have a videotape from a security camera that puts the stolen murder weapon in the hands of the Diva Extraordinaire of the Provincetown Follies. They just cannot link her to the fire conclusively, nor do they have any eyewitnesses to the murder. Not yet. Maybe he can get a special hearing to reduce her bail and bust her out before anything else comes to the surface. Innocent or guilty, she will not last long behind bars. He can see that.

It's happy hour in the attic he rents over the liquor store in Chatham at the elbow of the Cape. The rain started before he got back to town from the mental hospital. Now it's coming down like a shower of marbles on the cedar roof. A drizzly gray light seeps in through the single window in the dormer. It will be dark soon.

Whiskey boxes full of law books and clothes are scattered around the room. His bed is just a mattress in the corner with an old sleeping bag for a comforter and an Elmore Leonard crime novel where the pillow should be. There is a metal garbage can, full of pizza boxes and soiled paper plates, next to the sink and the fridge in the corner.

He puts on his favorite Red Sox shirt to help him think, and then leans back on two legs of his folding chair to stare bleary-eyed at the mound of stuff before him—eight-by-ten, black-and-white photos, police reports, and old newspapers. All of this crowds the top of his Formica kitchen table, circa 1965, that he calls his office. A laptop is pushed to the side, playing a John Coltrane CD. The tenor sax moans about ecstasy, heaven, and hell ... "Naima."

What is he going to do about this case? When he got out of law school, he signed on with a legal aid group on the Cape because he thought he would be doing good deeds like tenant-landlord arbitration, representing the underprivileged in divorce and custody battles. Civil stuff. He liked the idea of being a sort of legal Robin Hood. But the public defender's office is chronically short of staff. And in the three years he has been practicing, the state has thrown him just about the whole range of criminal work. First, it was the DUIs, prostitution, drug possession charges. His boss said he was a natural. And after a year in court, he was already getting tagged for assault cases and B&Es. Pretty soon he was sitting second chair on homicide cases, watching the senior on the case pleading them out, one by one. The murders never went to trial. No way. It was too risky, and too expensive for everyone involved.

The writing was on the wall, so to speak. He knew his time was coming to get nailed with a murder case of his own. But he never expected this. You would think the state could come up with someone better suited for a high-profile murder one and arson case. Somebody with more homicide experience. Someone who does not feel twitchy about gays, Provincetown transvestites. Someone who can at least talk their language. But it is summer and most of the PD's top guns have other cases or have vanished on vacation. So now Tuki is all his. Perfect. He has a client who looks like a cross between Halle Berry and Miss Saigon, but who can pee standing up.

Sometimes he just plain wishes he had stuck with fishing. His father Caesar put the case to him one day a few years ago when they were having a slammer trip a hundred miles east of Nantucket.

"What the hell you want to waste all that time and money for on law school, Mo? You haven't heard enough lawyer jokes from me yet? You think the world needs another shyster? You got the world by the balls out here on Georges. Bright sky, blue sea, a good boat, a mess of fish for catching. Your old man and Tio Tommy. The Sox game playing on the radio. *Cristo Salvador!* Leave that legal crap for the weak and the angry. You're a Portagee. Your family comes from Sagres. You have the blood of Prince Henry the Navigator in your veins. We've fished out of Nu Bej for four generations. You were born to fish for king cod, *bacalhau.*"

He tries to picture his father and his father's brother, Tio Tommy, out there right now on the *Rosa Lee*. The rain is going to stay northwest of Georges Bank. The sky will be a fortress of crimson pillars at sunset. He can hear the winch cables as they start to haul back. Smell the pungent scent of struggling fish as they boil to the surface in the net. The birds wheeling and diving for a free—

A headline shouts at him from the heap of newspapers.

"Drag Queen Charged in P-town Blaze!"

The words rap him in the chest.

The cops already seem to have a read on the escort service she is hooked into. And from what he can tell, this is just a sideshow. The client is always hiding something. That is what he has learned in three years of criminal work for the PD. So, what *is* she holding back? How much is she lying? She left some kind of mess back in Bangkok ...

He takes the last gulp of beer, kicks out of the chair, heads to the fridge for another can.

He has to get his head on straight, has to remind himself that Tuki is no girl. She's a tranny, pal. Plain and simple. He does not know why he has started thinking of her as female. It's ridiculous. She looks like a woman. An amazingly good-looking one. Hell, maybe it's easier to think of her as a showgirl than as a gay guy in a dress. That is just too weird for him.

Gay is not a lifestyle he cozies up to. He wouldn't call himself homophobic, but he cannot help it. He gets a sour taste in his mouth when he thinks about the gay boys and what they do behind closed doors. It is not like many gays come out in the Portuguese fishing community of New Bedford. Good old Nu Bej. Where men are men; women are women. Or at least they keep quiet about it. He has only known about five gay people, only discovered their orientation after they moved away. And trannies? He has never even been to one of their drag shows out in Provincetown.

Still, there is something about her. He cannot just write her off as a perv. It's confusing. She is already starting to take up space in his memory. He already has begun to see pictures from her life in his mind. He sees her swinging in a hammock in a dingy room somewhere. He sees a toddler with dark, curly hair. Golden skin. A teenager dripping sweat at the outside baggage check, the airport in Bangkok. No makeup, a man's suit, hair tied back. The jets whine in the morning heat. Her surrogate mothers' makeup running down their cheeks in little streams.

He can tell she has been well loved. Maria, his mother, says that nothing matters more. And the name on her passport ... *Dung*, courage. With all that she has been through, from Vietnam to Bangkok, New York to Provincetown, she must have *dung* in spades. That is something you do not see every day. So who is he to judge?

On the fishing boat with his father and Tio Tommy, he has never spoken up when they bash the fags in P-town. Now he thinks it must be payback time. Fate has singled him out for some special kind of torture.

*Cristo Salvador!* Provincetown. He has seen it. Drove out there last year in the fall for a weekend with Filipa. Miles of the most beautiful beaches he could ever imagine, sweeping sand dunes, and an ocean that has some of the best whale watching and fishing in the world. It's a village that goes all the way back to the Pilgrims. It overflows with colonial cottages, cutesy guesthouses, millions of flowers, narrow streets. Commercial Street offers a long winding business strip of shops, clubs, and restaurants, all right at the edge of Cape Cod Bay.

The scene throbs with fishing folk and summer vacationers on a lark, all the while harboring the largest gay resort scene in America. P-town is the last place you might expect to find murder and a monster fire.

But he knows it is a place where you must always wonder where reality ends and fantasy takes over. It is a haven for an unbelievable collection of queens, cowgirls, calendar boys, dragons, vampires, and hoes. Tuki's world. Now it is about to be his. Jesus. Like it or not.

He hears her sob, *Please, PLEASE, do not let them send me back to Thailand ... I swear I did not kill anybody.*

He pictures the media circus that will be her trial. The protestors with placards. "Unnatural Sinners Burn in Hell!"

His stomach churns.

# THREE

The public loves Provincetown, quirks and all. It is a money machine for the Cape. The fire, coming at the height of the summer, feels like a death in the family. So at Tuki's initial arraignment, the court responds to cries for the queen's blood and sets her bail at a million dollars. It is a figure that guarantees she will rot behind bars until her trial.

But a week later, with the spotlight off the district court, the presiding judge is willing to entertain the notion of a hearing to reduce the suspect's bail. She has heard about how the suspect has tried to shred her wrists, and maybe she does not want a senseless death on her conscience. Careers crumble when someone dies from foul play behind bars.

The bail hearing is a botch job from the moment he calls his client "she." And it ends with the judge beckoning him to the bench and telling him in soft tones to get a grip.

The D. A. argues that Tuki is a runner, to keep the bail high, but he really has no hard evidence. And in the midst of the whole fiasco, Michael pulls a rabbit out of his hat. He manages to get a state psychologist to say that while Tuki's lifestyle is unconventional, she does not suffer any identifiable disorder. She is a transsexual, and comfortable with her gender role. It would definitely be in the best interest of her mental health if she could get back to work.

In the end the judge grits her teeth and reduces Tuki's bail to two hundred thousand dollars. Her employer, Provincetown Follies, Inc., posts the bond. They want her back. The Diva Extraordinaire is a cash cow.

"You saved me!"

Standing before the front entrance to the hospital, Tuki throws her arms around her attorney and rocks him in an enormous hug. She is just an inch or two shy of his five feet ten. The hospital has given her back her clothes so she is wearing the black spandex dress, the tummy chains, the white panty hose, the red rhinestone pumps. Her braids are in a ponytail, bursting like a fountain from the top of her head. And she has a mango scent. One of the inmates lent her skin cream.

He stiffens. People are staring at them. This is too strange. Getting hugged by a ... what the hell is she anyway? An illusion. Her body presses against him. Any instant he expects to feel a cock grinding against his leg. But the cock never comes. Just firm, pert breasts and soft lips on his cheek. It is so weird. She could almost be Filipa. God, would Filipa freak if she saw this scene.

He slides out of the hug.

"What's the matter, la? Are you afraid of me?" She is giving him a cockeyed look, trying to read him.

For some reason he hears the judge's last words echoing in his head. "Plead this case out, young man, or the D. A. will eat you alive. You have thirty days for discovery. We go to trial right after Labor Day." Christ, Labor Day. He is getting married on the Saturday of Labor Day weekend. Filipa has invited half of New Bedford. They're supposed to go to Sagres and Lagos, the old country, for a week on honeymoon. How is that going to happen?

"Look, Tuki. I'm going to drive you back to your friends in P-town. But we've got to talk." He nods to his green Jeep parked at the sidewalk. It has not been washed in months. The winter cap is still on it.

"If we are going to find out who set the fire, who really killed Alby Costelano, who is setting you up and why, you have to start telling me the truth, do you understand?"

She feels a jagged knife twist in her belly and stares out the window at the Cape Cod Canal below them as they cross the Sagamore Bridge.

"I do not know what you mean. What is wrong, Michael?"

That name again. It feels too familiar. He pauses, heaves a deep sigh. He says he needs to hear about the night the vampires went running through the streets shrieking, "P-town is burning!"

She remembers stories of Vietnam that she heard as a child. Stories about the *maw sa sum*—the monsoons of fire from the American jets. She pictures how the flames came sweeping across the rice paddies and everything seemed to freeze, the air cold as night. Time stopped for a few seconds, and the spirit of the fire sang her angry song. The night Provincetown burned, it was the same way. The fire screamed. The sky grew cherry red. Buildings turned into silhouettes. A whole neighborhood became a shadow ... then nothing at all. This is what she sees every time she tries to fall asleep now.

"But that night in Provincetown, Tuki. What happened?"

Her gaze returns out the window.

*The clubs and bars of Provincetown are just letting out. The boys go arm in arm. The girls go arm in arm. Someone is playing blues on a clarinet in front of Town Hall. Laughter bubbles from the crowd loafing on the patio of Spiritus Pizza. The bikers crank their Harleys in front of the Old Colony. Then they start to roll through the lamplights and the neon glow. Commercial Street is in party mode again.*

*But not Tuki. She's a girl beyond sad and angry. She needs to get away, slips down an alley to the harbor. The fog swirls in off the bay in cold waves. She does not know how much time passes. She just walks.*

*The next thing she knows she is alone on the beach in the fog, waiting for the storm that is sure to come.*

*She cuts her bare foot on a broken shell. "Let it bleed," she thinks. Wua hai lom khok? It is too late. Why build a cattle pen after the cow is lost?*

*This is the thought that is running through her mind when she smells the smoke and hears the sirens.*

*The air at her back makes a big rushing sound. In the time it takes her to turn and look, the sky turns the color of blood, the fog disappears. She can see everything on the beach like it is noon. From a half mile away she can see the fish piers, the little boats aground on the sand flats, a forgotten beach chair, all as if they have been magnified. Even from this distance the patios and back porches of the shops, restaurants, and bars look almost close enough to touch. And towering over it all is the Painted Lady with her turrets and widow's walks ... surrounded with a halo of fire.*

*"Burn baby burn. Just take it all away, la," Tuki screams. "The lights, the costumes, my faithless eff. Take him. Take the bastard. And take my miserable little luk sod self while you are at it!"*

*She is drawn back to the flames, back up the beach to the heat of the fire. Her eyes study the comets of burning gas that arch into the sky and leap from building to building. A wind whips her braids and red robe.*

*Fire trucks wail in the streets. Men in raincoats with hoses scurry and start to circle the beast. Sparks flare and fly. Police push back the gathering crowd of refugees and spectators on the beach. But she passes through them. An invisible moth fluttering closer.*

*"This is your destiny, la," she says to herself. "This is why you are always drawn to the water ... to find your balance. You are the fire. You are the flame. Feel the heat. Feel the power. The Evil Empire is burning."*

*Then she sees a figure burst onto the beach. It appears out of a wall of orange flames nearly surrounding the Painted Lady. He is burning, trailing feathers of fire from his legs and arms and head. He seems the only dark thing left of the night. He looks about as big as King Kong as he staggers across the beach toward her, flapping his arms, screaming, "You fucking whore!"*

*Something cold pierces her heart. She knows that voice. She loved it once. But in two or three seconds, its echo is all that is left of Alby. That and a heap of flesh with a knife in its belly, lying among the ribbons of seaweed near the high-tide line. Smoke rises from the body in little clouds.*

## FOUR

He sees the dunes of Provincetown National Seashore looming a couple of miles ahead and wishes he could have more time with her in the Jeep before he gets her home to the Follies. He is still just scratching the surface here. She is not really telling him the whole truth about Provincetown. Or Bangkok. Not close to it. He knows that. But she is talking now, seems to have lost her guile, dropped her guard. The trick is to keep her going.

"So you're not really Thai. You came from Vietnam?" He raises his eyebrows, pushes out his lower lip. Puts two and two together. "One of the boat people?"

She grins, just the ghost of a smile, maybe having another memory.

"Your mother was Vietnamese, but your father, American?"

"*Luk sod,*" she says. In Thailand they call people like her *luk sod.* Two races. Half-breed.

Out of the corner of his eye, he is catching a glimpse of her dark skin, her thick black hair and its fountain of braids. He cannot help looking at her. Something is not adding up here.

"Was he white?"

"Who?"

"Your father."

She gives a sudden shiver like she thought for a second maybe he was asking about someone else.

"No." Her lips purse as if she is holding back a secret. She cocks her head and gives him the eye. Wants him to take his best guess.

He considers her Latin surname, his own dark-skinned fisher-folk second cousins in Nu Bej. "Was he Cape Verdean?"

"No."

"Puerto Rican?"

"No."

"Indian?"

"Like Pocahontas?"

He nods, "Yes."

"Noooo!"

He closes his eyes and smiles that boyish smile again. "Black, right?"

"They call me the Tiger Woods of drag, la."

He gives a little chuckle.

"You sing your words."

"What did you expect?"

The notes of her voice go up and down like some kind of song. She says the song in her words comes from Asia, too, from her *mayuh*. In Vietnamese *me* means mother. It is the same word in Thai.

For just an instant an image flashes through his head. He sees an Asian woman in a red dress, clutching a child.

She is still explaining. Thai and Vietnamese people have many tones for their vowels. They talk as if they are singing even when they speak English. So it is not just Africa and America that he hears in her voice. There is a little Saigon, and a lot of Bangkok, too. She learned her English in Bangkok. Picked up the "la" thing from Brandy and Delta, and the other showgirls in the Patpong.

"My friend Nikki says I am a big sponge. I just soak up everything. I do not know about that, but I do know about all of this 'la.' It does not mean anything. Just an expression, an extra note in the song, I would not mind being through with it once and for all. It is not like I just got off the boat. For more than five years I have been totally an American girl. But Bangkok ... and all the rest ... maybe it never really goes away. It just hides for a while, waiting to surprise you."


Brandy and Delta are telling the story of her me and father, helping to put together Tuki's past.

*She was born in late July 1973, and for the first couple years of her life she lived with her me in a room in the Saigon Hotel on Dong Du Street across from the Saigon Central Mosque. Tuki never met her father because he finished his tour in Vietnam before she was born. He told her me that he would send for her to come to America. It was an old story ...*

*He vanished. They don't even have a photo of the man. But Brandy and Delta used to know him. They say he looked like Lou Gossett Jr. in* An Officer and a Gentleman, *so that is how she sees him in her mind ... an unsung hero in somebody else's war.*

*They were quite a couple. Brandy and Delta say her me was one of the most famous B-girls in the dance bars on the side streets off Dong Khoi in downtown Saigon.*

*"When she dance that Gladys Knight "Midnight Train to Georgia," la," says Delta, "everybody in Saigon thinking they must go get good lala quicky quicky. She was some sexy girl."*

*So, that is how she pictures her me. Dancing in the shadows at the far end of some GI bar to ease her heart, to feed her baby. They called her Misty in the bars, but her real name was Huong-Mei. She vanished, too.*

*At the beginning of 1975, the armies of the North broke the peace and invaded South Vietnam. Town after town fell to the communists— Quang Tri, Hue, Da Nang, Nha Trang. Refugees poured into Saigon on Highway 1. Delta says the whole city was, "crazy crazy back then." Everyone knew that the communists were coming. They were going to kill or arrest anyone who was friendly with Americans.*

*People in the government, the soldiers from the South, and the bar and the theater people were to be the first targets. So the owners of the bars and clubs, the dancers, the drag queens, the bartenders, and the whores put their money together to hire shrimp boats to take them to Thailand.*

*Everything was getting ready when the president of the country resigned and disappeared. Then the vice president quit, too. And the communists were right outside the city. Saigon was in chaos. Word up and down Dong Khoi Street was that everybody from the bars had to go to the boats. They had to leave that night.*

*But Tuki's me said she had to go to the bank to get her savings. There were thousands of people trying to do the same thing, crushing toward the building. Tuki was just about two years old and into everything, ready to run any direction and lose herself or get trampled. So Misty took her back to the Saigon Hotel to wait with Brandy and Delta. She said she would be back after she got her money. But she didn't come back, and everyone else was heading for the boats that waited at the Ben Nghe Channel.*

*It was dark, and Brandy and Delta could hear explosions and gunfire in Cholon. They left a note for Misty, wrapped the baby in a blanket, took her papers, and left. No makeup, no costumes, no nothing. "Goodbye, la."*

*Off they went with nothing but dark peasant clothes, straw hats, and a bag of Pampers.*

*"We escape. Go to Krung Thep," says Brandy. "City of angels. Bangkok, la."*

# FIVE

He is starting to get the picture. In his mind he sees the shadow of a woman standing in a small boat with her arms outstretched, beckoning or trying to catch something that has gotten away from her.

He is squinting, trying to make out the details of the figure in his brain, when he almost goes through a traffic light as the Jeep approaches Provincetown on Route 6. He jams on the brakes. The tires squeal. The Jeep skids to a stop at the red light.

"Heeey, sugar!" A note of alarm.

He shakes his head, seems in a fog.

"Aparecio, black?" he says almost to himself. "I'm not getting this. What aren't you telling me?"

Tuki is silent and looks out the window again. She is thinking that if he lawyers like he drives, the monsoon has hardly even begun. This is Alby's revenge. This cute wreck of a lawyer. She feels his eyes drift over her breasts, and she knows they look good. Maybe a little small, but perfectly symmetrical, with nipples that stand up and say hello under the black spandex.

The traffic light turns green. The Jeep seems to make the turn off the highway and head for the village on autopilot.

"You've got fabulous hair," he says. He is hoping a compliment can get the conversation started again. They are just blocks from her drop off at the Follies.

He is not just stroking her, she does have amazing hair. She tells him that she has been growing it out since she was just a whisper, and she can do a hundred different things with it. Sometimes she uses wigs in her show when she does a Diana Ross or Whitney routine. The sisters use lots of wigs themselves when they perform. But mostly she uses her own hair.

"You know, it adds to the illusion. Right now, I am doing it in funky long ringlets and braids like Janet Jackson. But in Bangkok my hair was usually straight down my back. When it is not pulled up like this in a pony, it still goes way long. Black and silky. With twisted ribbons of curls. But when I straighten it, I can do Tia Carrere with some of those songs she rocks in *Wayne's World*. And I have done serious opera in Bangkok."

He pictures her in a red-and-white silk kimono.

She says that the suits that came to the Patpong on the charter flights from Tokyo and Singapore loved it.

"Please ... please just tell me about the name Aparecio." He needs closure on at least one of her mysteries. How the hell did she come up with a Southern European surname? Aparecio? It sounds like something the mob gave her.

She reads his mind, and grunts softly. "Hey, la, you think I get it from *The Godfather* or something?"

He shrugs, sucks some air through his nose, rolls down the window the whole way. The Jeep suddenly feels like an oven, and the AC doesn't work.

"To tell you the truth, Tuki, I don't know what to think about you. You mystify me. Help me here, okay? How can I defend you when all I get from you are pieces of stories and a boat-load of contradictions, huh?"

The Jeep is in the traffic creeping toward the center of the village where the bulldozers are still scraping four charred blocks of Provincetown into piles. This client interview is almost over.

Her pretty face frowns, her lower lip trembles.

"What did I do to you? Why are you so mean, la?"

"I don't know who you are!"

She stiffens, pushes out her lower lip.

"It is my life! Not yours. Why do you care?"

"Because I don't have a clue where to start with this case. Jesus. Murder and arson? They could put you away for a hundred years! And we only have twenty-nine days to get ready for court. Maybe you should get another lawyer. Maybe I should have stayed a fisherman. I don't know."

Traffic stalls.

For a minute she looks like she is going to cry. Then she rises up in her seat, leans toward him.

"Go fishing. What do I care, la? I am home now. Tomorrow is tomorrow. I have a show tonight. *Suwat di ka*. Like *siyanara*, Joe!"

The Jeep door flies open with a loud crack.

*She is living with Brandy and Delta in the back room of a little theater in the Patpong. It's the kind of theater with live sex acts and women who shoot ping pong balls out from between their legs, and it's the only place Tuki remembers as home.*

*She got the name "Tuki" after the motorized rickshaws, the tuk-tuks, that zoom along Sukkumvit Road. She loves the tuk-tuks, loves to zoom.*

*Brandy and Delta take their acts from theater to theater in the Patpong, but they call this cramped little room home, a place they can hang their hammocks, songbird cage, and clothesline. There are little cooking stoves in the upstairs rooms that are too nasty to rent to the whores, so they use those to cook their meals.*

*It's really no place for a child, but it does not matter to Tuki. The theater is her playroom. She loves the music, the lights, costumes. But mostly she loves the fabulous girls, and she knows that this is what she was born to be. A showgirl. They come from all over the world. Olga from Sweden has real silicone breasts like pillows. Lili from Singapore gives Tuki candy and sips of her durian fruit shakes. She says "la" about a thousand times a minute. Passion from Indonesia is the first person to put lipstick and eye shadow on Tuki's face. Everyone speaks English mixed with Thai from the streets. When the girls are working, Tuki listens to the American music that the girls bring back for her from the cassette vendors in the night market.*

The next thing he sees after Tuki bolts from the Jeep is his client sashaying across the street in front of him. Her hips swing like a million dollars in that black spandex.

Ahead of her stands a rambling Victorian hotel, the Painted Lady, dressed in greens and gold and lavender. Miraculously, it has survived the fire intact. There are haunted-house turrets and widow's walks that look out on Cape Cod Bay. The drag shows are in a huge ballroom on the first floor. And in big letters at the top of the Provincetown Follies marquis are the words, **"WELCOME BACK, TUKI APARECIO, DIVA EXTRAORDINAIRE!"**

The traffic starts to move again on Commercial Street. From the steps in front of the ballroom she shouts at him as he grinds past in first gear.

"My name is no lie. My daddy is Marine Private First Class Marcus Aparecio, Inglewood, California. Some goat-footed Italian, or maybe Portuguese, danced a tango with his mama-san. They were in love, la!"

Great. After a two-and-half hour drive, he knows her racial history and some odd bits of her life in Southeast Asia. About three mysteries solved, only about 9,997 to go. He cannot decide whether to head back to New Bedford to catch the next trip on the *Rosa Lee* or stick around in P-town to see her show.

# SIX

During their first few weeks in Bangkok, Brandy and Delta sewed costumes, made wigs from human hair they bought on the black market, and fashioned falsies out of bags of bird seed. They liberated lingerie from clotheslines and stole women's shoes from the doorsteps of hooker hotels. All in preparation for their stage debut.

Like Tuki, Brandy is luk sod. Her father is French. She has creamy skin, Western, blue eyes, with shoulder-length chestnut hair. Onstage she often does show tunes. Numbers from Jesus Christ Superstar, Godspell, and—especially—the nastier pieces from Hair. For a while she does Barbara Streisand.

Delta is the opposite. She's one of the really dark-skinned Vietnamese. Chocolate skin with long, black, silky hair that she saves for the street or a date. Delta's act is strictly soul sisters. She uses a vast collection of wigs and falls for her acts as Dionne Warwick and Roberta Flack.

# SEVEN

Tuki has worked a lot of clubs, most of them pretty much zoos. Queens prancing around singing to themselves, practicing routines ... or lost in their own faces in front of makeup mirrors. Costume trunks everywhere. The smell of cigarettes, hair spray, eyelash glue, and the medical adhesive that some showgirls use to hold on their falsies.

But for the moment, things are quiet in the second-floor dressing room at the Follies. Tuki is showering in the plastic stall in the corner, soaking in needles of cold water. She is trying to free her head of dark thoughts of the murder, the fire, her trial, her lawyer. Trying to get her groove back for the show. But her mind is wondering whether it is someone from the club who is framing her, when she hears Richie, the manager, shouting at the door.

"Jesus fucking Christ. It's Friday night. We gotta get it the hell up tonight, ladies. The hungry hordes descend ... and it is only a month 'til the season ends. If you want your bonus at the end of the summer, you better start making it tonight, girls. I want the lightning to flash, and every cock and nipple in the house hard as a whore's heart."

Suddenly she is feeling dizzy.

Just then Nikki and Silver bust into the dressing room laughing. They have been rehearsing downstairs on the stage.

"My god, you little slut," exclaims a thick English accent. "Can't you close the curtain? You've got water all over the floor. And it hurts my eyes to see you in there practicing some kind of Chinese water torture on that pathetic brown body. Sometimes you look absolutely like one of those under-fed Asian gods. Really. You are too much!"

So much for the welcome home. The voice is Silver's. Even without looking, Tuki can smell that Silver is smoking weed because the dressing room reeks when she turns off the shower.

She feels a big purple towel fold over her shoulders and around her torso. A light pair of hands starts to pat down her back.

"Are you okay, *padruga*?" asks Nikki in her cute little Moscow voice. "You are freeeezing."

Tuki's back is still toward Nikki, so she takes Tuki's hair in her hands, gathers it together, wrings out the water, and wraps a spare towel around her head and hair like a turban with a tail. It's like she is back in Bangkok again.

*When Tuki is five, Brandy and Delta take her to an American missionary school in a church. It is a girls' school. That is what she is, because that is what she feels like. That is what her mothers are. Anyone can see that.*

*The other kids are mostly Thai and come from all over the city, but everyone speaks English in school. They wear little blue-and-white uniforms and sing songs like, "Amazing Grace" and "Swing Low, Sweet Chariot," her favorite. Every day she rides to school in a tuk-tuk with Ingrid who lives in the Patpong, too. Her mother is an exotic dancer from Denmark and makes enough money to have her own apartment. Ingrid has a big explosion of strawberry hair, and she loves to sing. She and Tuki sing songs by the Jackson Five riding back and forth to school like two little princesses. Sometimes on their rides she is so tired from staying up to watch the show in the theater, she falls asleep with her head on Ingrid's shoulder.*

*Growing up in the eighties, going to the missionary school with Ingrid, she feels like a flower in dark moist soil. But she is not stupid. In Thailand—or Vietnam—where the air is always wet and hot, children do not wear clothing very much until they are more than two or three years old. So, it is no mystery to her that boys and girls have different shapes between their legs. But when she turns six, she gets confused because Brandy and Delta are G-I-R-L-S ... and she had seen their* chaangs.

*So she asks if they are really boys. Her mothers sigh and tell her to pay attention. "This is a Buddhist thing, la. What is between a person's legs is not the only thing that makes a girl or a boy. They say that in this world many people are very 'young' souls. Like they were birds or animals in their past lives, and they are just learning what it means to live in the skin of a human. So those young souls still think a little like ducks or rats* or kratai—*rabbits*—*who believe male and female has to do with what is between the legs. But some people are much older souls, and they know that what makes a boy or a girl lies in the heart and soul of a person, not just the body ... and each person holds the power to be both male and female.*

*"Look at the Buddha, la—the oldest soul. A holy child. A love child. The Buddha shows that each human has shades of both male and female." They point to a carving they keep on top of their only dresser, a male-looking Buddha with big breasts. Proof. This is Asia ... where people seriously sit around for years wondering about the sound of one hand clapping.*

*"We very old souls, la," says Delta, and gives her a kiss. "You very old soul, too. Your mother always say you special child. Holy child like Buddha. Love child. Understand?"*

*Maybe, she thinks.*

*Now it's third grade. The end of the monsoon season. This year the school offers tai chi training for students to get some exercise and a little self-defense skill. Tuki and Ingrid are trying this. And while the rains have mostly let up for the fall, one afternoon there is a big storm that washes out the after-school tai chi training in Lumpini Park not ten minutes after it starts. Because they are far from a shelter, all of the kids are getting soaked. The teacher shouts for them to run back to the school to get out of the storm. But Tuki and Ingrid love the rain, so during all of the confusion they sneak off to slide in the mud like river otters.*

*When they are covered in dirt and finished with their otter play, they walk home to the Patpong. Tuki takes Ingrid to the club where she lives to dry off and get fresh clothes. Brandy and Delta are not home. Tuki gets a towel for Ingrid and herself, some clean underwear, a couple of extra school dresses. They are both laughing about being dirt balls and singing, "One, Two, Three" by the Jackson Five as they peel out of their soccer shorts, T-shirts, and panties.*

*Then they are standing there naked in front of each other. And Tuki is the only one still laughing.*

*Ingrid is staring at her body like she has just seen someone vaporize.*

# EIGHT

When she turns around, Nikki is still there. Her hands pull the towel more firmly over Tuki's shoulders, across her chest. Then she gives her friend a kiss on the cheek and smiles.

Nikki is four inches shorter, so Tuki dips her knees to return her kiss. Backstage, it is a rule: someone kisses you, you kiss them back. She can taste the salt and sunscreen on Nikki's skin. She has been swimming. The little sister is such the athlete.

Among the three queens in the show, Nikki is the least girlie. Right now—because she is wearing baggy shorts, cross-trainers, and a blue sleeveless tank—she looks like a twelve- or thirteen-year-old boy out of the L. L. Bean catalogue, especially with that two-inch-long pageboy cut that she parts on the left. A little choirboy. No chest at all. And she is young, maybe twenty-four. When Tuki first saw her, she thought Nikki was one of the light and sound kids.

But the crowds gather to see Nikki made up in a tangle of dishwater blonde hair and a skimpy cocktail dress ... bringing Janis Joplin back from the dead. So much energy and pain fuse in that tight little body. It looks ready to explode onstage when "Janis" screams out when the soundtrack wails, "TAKE IT! Take another little piece of my heart now, baby!"

People can't believe her eyes. She has these naturally thin, long brows that arch high and sharp over the outside corners of her enormous hazel eyes. A thousand grains of broken glass sparkle in them. And she always has this sort of cockeyed look that says, "Mischief."

This is exactly what Tuki is seeing right now as Nikki pats the towel along the sides of her head again, and says, "I miss you, girlfriend!"

*For months, Ingrid traveled back and forth to school with the other kids. And every time that Tuki tried to talk to her, she got quiet and* made up an excuse to go away. Tuki thought that if she told her what she knew about old souls she would maybe understand a little.

But Ingrid never gave Tuki the chance. Sometimes at tai chi she would trip Ingrid and make it look like an accident, but Ingrid still would not look at her face. Tuki stopped trying.

One day when Tuki is at home singing along to Delta's new Diana Ross tape, there is a knock at the door. When she opens it, she sees Ingrid, who shoves a bunch of yellow flowers into her friend's hands.

"I'm sorry," she says.

Then both of them cry like little crocodiles.

Later, they hike down to the water taxi dock by the Oriental Hotel and talk.

Ingrid asks Tuki if Brandy and Delta make her dress up like a girl. When Tuki tells her, "No, I AM a girl," Ingrid sighs.

"Then you were just born different, la?"

"Yes."

She wants to tell Ingrid all about old souls, but she is crying again. She knows that Ingrid is feeling sorry for her, confused.

"Yuu thi nai chaang," she snorts, puffs out her belly, gives a goofy smile, and waves her arms in front of her face like a trunk. "Have you seen my elephant?"

Suddenly, Ingrid stops crying and busts a laugh.

"You are crazy as a malaeng saap. Cockroach." Those words feel like a hug.

For some reason she pictures her favorite sweet. She sees sticky, red, coils of it.

"You are like licorice, la."


Tuki gives Nikki another little kiss on the cheek.

"You are sweet."

"What you doing?"

She is not exactly sure what Nikki is asking, but her voice blurts out. "Whitney. I am feeling her, so I guess I got to go with the mood, la."

"I mean, what's with you and the cold shower, padruga?"

"Some Asian craziness, I guess ... to wake up the blood."

Tuki is glad her wrists have healed. She does not want Nikki to notice the scars. Does not want to talk about the filthy men, the spilled blood, the shadowy women at Bridgewater ... or the cute lawyer who already wants to quit her case and go fishing. She does not want to wonder whether any of the people in this room killed Alby, set the fire, framed her. She just wants to get back in front of an audience.

"Wake up the blood? You lie."

Tuki shoots Nikki a look that begs. *Can we drop this?*

"Ah, the mysteries of the Dragon Lady," Nikki sighs. "You sooo compli—"

"Excuse me, but will you two fag hags stop with the Thelma and Louise routine, and help me dry the floor before every bloody costume we own turns up with water stains around the hem from Miss Tuki's little harlot bath!"

Silver is shouting over her shoulder through the open bathroom door as she drains—guy style—about a pint of what used to be vodka and seltzer into the toilet.

*"Please,* just once put the seat back down for rest of us," says Nikki.

"Yeeesss, dear."

Tuki can feel the smirk on Silver's face even before she turns around and walks across the dressing room, zipping her fly with one hand and offering Nikki a drag on the joint with the other. Nikki frowns, but takes the joint without looking at Silver. She smokes it dry as she stares out at Cape Cod Bay through the open door to the little deck. When she turns around, she is smiling again.

"Whitney will be nice," she says. "Don't you think, Silver?"

"Absolutely, darling, we can close with Whitney tonight. Let's see if the famous Miss Tuki can still wail ... after her little vacation in the Big House. How's the billing go, sweetie: 'Down, dirty, blue, and funky until the sister's voice just shreds the audience's hearts?' Did I get that right? Or was that just some jive a writer cooked up after you gave him a hummer?"

Tuki stares daggers at Silver. Says nothing.

The dressing room remains totally quiet for ten minutes. Nikki takes her shower. Silver rolls on platinum lipstick at the makeup table, Tuki files and paints her nails like she is making claws.

After Nikki is out of the shower in a robe, Silver kicks back her folding chair with a screech and crosses the room to Nikki and Tuki. She doesn't stop walking until she is so close you can smell the scent of Absolut Lemon on her breath.

Nikki steps back as if to get out of the line of fire.

Tuki takes a rat-tail comb in her hand and holds it like an ice pick.

"All right, girls. Let's make up. Give mama a big kiss. We've got a show to do." She puckers up her lips like she is some kind of pet bird. Nikki rolls her eyes, then leans forward and gives Silver the kiss she demands. Now it is Tuki's turn.

She hesitates, wonders what Silver knows about how Alby spent his last moments, then she smiles a bitter grin, stretches to those platinum lips, plants the smooch.

"On with the show!"

Silver sighs. "Friends again." She pulls her hair out of its pony-tail. It falls down to her shoulder blades like strands of white gold. Jean Harlow and Marilyn Monroe—with all the peroxide in the world—never had it so good.

Silver is the real thing. At thirty-two she is the reigning queen of the Follies. In guy clothes, like jeans and a crew-neck sweater, and with her hair pulled back in a ponytail cinched at the neck, Silver looks like David Bowie on the best day of his life. Thin face, high cheekbones, piercing blue eyes, six feet one, rugged, and macho, even, if you see Silver wearing cowboy boots and riding a black Harley. That is how you mostly see Silver by day. For her—or him—drag is theater; theater is illusion; illusion is pure power.

Put Silver in a white corset with six hundred dollars' worth of glue-on silicone tits stuffed into her D cups, a red mini, a pair of black tights, and her trademark silver pumps, and she will stop traffic when she takes on Commercial Street. Back in New York, Silver has been known to bring four lanes on Broadway to a halt. There is not a girl in the world with better legs. The total vamp—beyond Garbo or Madonna, both of whom she does onstage. But Silver is at her best when she is her own girl, lip-synching to show tunes from *Rent, Cabaret,* and *Chicago.* Her "All that Jazz," done in a silver bodysuit, which she peels out of onstage, gives new meaning to the word *babe.*

The girl is famous. She's played Honolulu, Vegas, San Francisco, Amsterdam. She had her own sitcom on NYC cable for two years, gigs in more than a half dozen music videos, a cosmetic ad, and— maybe—a part in an upcoming feature film. Silver Superstar, world-class runway filly. But she does not sing. She needs the other girls to put some heart and soul and rhythm into the show. Such the queen.

Michael would probably love her, thinks Tuki. Silver looks like she could kill her best friend for a new pair of stilettos. But then again, what would Silver know about friends?

# NINE

*Nobody, nothing, dares to come between Tuki and Ingrid. They are best friends. They ride the tuk-tuks together. Sit beside each other in school. Do homework in the park, sitting on their favorite bench like a couple of pigeons. Sing and dance at home with each other. Sometimes they put on their mothers' costumes when they are not around. Make up their own routines to songs like Tina Turner's "Proud Mary."*

*They watch American movies together. Love and musicals are Tuki's thing. Ingrid goes for space flicks. They are all over films like* Saturday Night Fever, Flashdance, Star Wars. *Sometimes they pretend that they are the African American sisters Celie and Nettie in* The Color Purple. *Other times Tuki pretends she is the jazz singer Shug Avery in the same movie, or Billie Holiday in* Lady Sings the Blues.

*Ingrid says she is Princess Leia from* Star Wars. *Out on the streets of Bangkok, she starts carrying a silvery umbrella found in a corner of Brandy and Delta's club; Ingrid says it is her light saber. It will kick butt.*

*That's good because they need something to help protect themselves. The Patpong has turned totally crazy. It overflows with porn tours from Japan, Taiwan, Singapore, and a lot of Western tourists, too, from Germany, Holland, Australia. Sex—lala—is big business. More and more young girls from the country, some no older than Ingrid and Tuki, start hustling on the corners. Pimps pack gangs of teenage girls four or five to a room in apartments. Even the girls in the live sex shows and the straight-out whorehouses, massage parlors, are hardly more than kids.*

*Ingrid's mother has quit dancing to be a bartender because these kids are becoming exotic dancers, too. Bangkok is selling its children, and it turns the world on. Heroin addiction and AIDS spread like fire. Skinny little girls and boys lie dead in the alleys. There are no more jokes in the Patpong.*

Their mothers tell them no way can they go out alone after dark. The problem is not the farangs, the foreigners, it is the junkies who rip you off to get a fix or pimps who kidnap girls, get them hooked on pung chao, make them turn tricks.

But Tuki and Ingrid do not worry much about what is happening in the streets. Not even a chance. They still live in their own little world of songs, dances, and movies. And they have also started reading books like mad, romance novels they find in the dumpsters at places like the Oriental Hotel.

Their favorite thing to do on a weekend is to go down to the water taxi stops on the river to get away from the Patpong. They talk and watch the boys dive off the piers. They compare their sleek golden backs and legs. They hold their breath when the boys boost themselves out of the water with muscles bulging like steel cables in those arms. Sometimes the boys shout things to them in Thai, and they wave back, but they are quiet as kwaang, deer.

One day Tuki and Ingrid are doing their kwaang thing, watching a group of older boys at a water taxi stop farther up the river from where they usually go. They are comparing these boys to the guys back at their regular stop and to the boys in their movies and books. These guys are way ahead in the buns department. The girls hardly notice that it is getting dark, that the boats on the river have begun to turn on their lights. Before today, they have always left the piers before the boys stopped their swimming, but this evening the boys are drying themselves with towels and walking down the pier toward them ... the girls are blinded by their golden bodies.

Before they can stand up, five or six of the boys are circling around them asking in Thai why the sexy little farang and her luk sod friend do not go swimming to cool off in this heat. Are they afraid of the river?

"I'm not afraid of anything," says Ingrid in a screw-you-for-asking voice.

Tuki just smiles and looks at the wet sheen in the boys' hair.

"Then show us. Take a swim," says one of the boys. The others cheer.

"Fuck off," says Ingrid. Then she gives Tuki this big-eyed look that says she knows of all the things she could have said in English, the F-word was absolutely, one hundred percent the wrong one.

*Here we go, la. Battle stations.*

*"Foak you," says the leader in English that sounds like he has learned in a fancy British school. "You stupid, little, Patpong slut!"*

*The boys begin laughing and pushing toward the girls. They are backing toward the river. And Tuki is wondering if she is going to meet with any rats or snakes when she jumps in.*

*But while Ingrid is looking for a safe place to jump in the river, Tuki suddenly grabs Ingrid's light saber with both hands and swings it like a golf club. It clips the leader in his* chaang *with a loud thwack.*

*He doubles over and falls to the ground screaming in Thai.*

*"Run!"*

*Her legs wheel into action. She does not know whether it is Ingrid's voice or her own that coaxes, "Warp speed, Mr. Spock!"*

*The boys are chasing them, but they stop when they enter the Patpong. Maybe the boys are the ones who are afraid here.*

*Ingrid is laughing, and so is Tuki ... when they finally pause to catch their breath outside her mothers' bar.*

*"Who do you love, Cheesecake?"*

*This is a favorite line from one of their trashy novels.*

*Ingrid throws her arm around Tuki's waist and gives her a kiss on the cheek. She says, "Friends forever."*

# TEN

Attorney Decastro is in investigator mode, cataloguing everything for his case. He's trying to orient himself to this brave new world.

As soon as he sees the inside of the Painted Lady, it reminds him of a speakeasy in a movie about Mafia kings during Prohibition. The ballroom is two stories high, at least eighty feet long, complete with glass chandeliers and a rotating disco ball. Ten golden columns hold up the ceiling, which has actual frescoes of ancient Greeks in their birthday suits.

There is a balcony around the second floor of the ballroom. The light and sound kids hang out up there in their shorts and T-shirts, working the spots and the soundboard.

Downstairs the wallpaper is red brocade, like the cover on a Valentine's Day box of chocolates. For the show, the waitresses—club kids in drag—pull black velvet curtains over the windows and the three sets of French doors that lead to a cafe deck facing the beach. So when the house lights are all down low and blue and the table lights are giving off a salmon glow, the place looks ripe for mystery and romance.

To top off the whole scene, there is a wide, semi-circular staircase sweeping down from the dressing room on the second floor. A landing branches off to the little stage and runway. This is how all the girls make their entrances, down these stairs. Queens of the night. Suspects. Anyone who works here might have lit the fire, might have killed Big Al Costelano.

Working the long marble bar is the manager Richie, who's in a backwards Red Sox ball cap and "Ring Pirate" muscle shirt. His partner Duke is a Mr. Clean type who is into no shirts, leather vests, Fu Manchu facial hair, and nipple rings.

The big digital clock over the bar reads 7:43. Upstairs in the dressing room the queens are going over their cues with the light and sound kids. Downstairs the crowd is already clustered at their tables. The dragon waitresses are flirting with the clientele and pushing tray-loads of drinks to the upbeat tempo of "Material Girl" while Madonna's music video flickers on a screen at the back of the stage. It's an eighties, retro kind of summer.

He can handle this. After three rum and cokes on an empty stomach, he is starting to think screw the D. A., screw the judge, screw the case. He is ready for his first drag show.

Tuki was wrong about his response to Silver. He watches her come and go with her Broadway show tunes routine without so much as a single stirring below the belt or a pitter-pat of the heart. He is just wondering how this queen hides her stuff in that silver, skin-tight jumpsuit. How did Tuki hide it in that spandex dress? He is thinking that maybe they use duct tape or something to pull their hardware back between their legs when suddenly Silver starts into a lip-synch of "Memory" from *Cats*. He almost gets up and walks out. He hates this karaoke-like stuff.

But then Nikki makes her entrance as Janis Joplin, Southern Comfort bottle and all, which he can see she is slugging on for real. She rips the club open with "Me and Bobby McGee" and then goes buck wild in her closer, the long version of "Piece of My Heart."

Maybe this is karaoke, he thinks, but Jesus ... are you sure she's really a guy?

The house lights go dim for thirty seconds while a waitress rakes the money off the stage. Then a blue spotlight picks up a figure in a red, filmy evening dress standing at the top of the steps. A diamond choker glitters at her throat. Slowly, her head starts to rise. She looks just like Whitney Houston. Her hands fall from prayer, her fingers begin a slow rhythmic snap, her hips pick up the beat, the mike rises to her lips, and she is singing "Exhale." Not lip-synching, really singing. "Everyone falls ... in love sometime ..."

"Holy shit!" thinks her attorney.

The background guitars and strings cut in. Her voice is a woman lost in a memory of love on a hot slow night in the delta. The Mississippi ... the Mekong ... or the Chao Prya, Bangkok.

Down the stairs she comes, three steps on the beat. She pauses. Her body does a slow burn to the pain of the lyrics. Then she takes three more steps in a kind of lazy shimmy, her voice gaining strength with each step like an approaching freight train. The audience is whistling and cheering, so loud that the sound and light kids have to amp up the volume on the speakers.

She strolls the runway with classic voguing—chin high, three strides, turn, smile, pose. Again. When she hits the chorus, she starts with the "Shoop, shoop, shoop, shoo be doop, shoop, shoop" then holds the mike out low at arm's length, a signal for the audience to pick up the refrain. As they do, she scans the crowd. People wave creased bills Whitney's way. Mostly singles, but fives, tens, twenties, too. She folds them into her free hand before she slips the green into her cleavage.

When the music stops and the applause rings, she sees Michael sitting alone at a table on the right side of the runway. She makes eye contact and gives him a little smile.

Richie shoots her two thumbs up from the bar, and a waitress comes up onto the stage with a huge champagne goblet that has a big red strawberry at the bottom of the glass. This is part of the act. It is Perrier, and it gives Tuki a chance to catch her breath and unload her tips into the basket on the waitress's tray. She takes a slow sip, holds the glass out in front of her, eyes it. Then she begins—*a cappella*—Whitney's torch of torches from the final scene of *The Bodyguard*.

"Bittersweet memories,
   That is all I'm taking with me,
   So goodbye, please, don't cry,
   We both know I'm not what you need,
   And I ... will always love you ..."

The sound system weeps with violins. Now she is dragging her sorry self back home across the room toward the staircase. Singing.

Sitting there tasting the last of his rum, he sees that she is unpacking her heart, her soul, for the crowd, for him if he will just pay attention. Closing her eyes, she sings so that she will not cry as she remembers.

*A girl in a secondhand red dress boards a water taxi at a big house on the* klong *in Thonburi, near the sheds where they keep the royal barges. She can still smell a man's lemon bath and fresh sweat on her hands and in her hair. The shadow of a man is standing there, watching her, in his white linen suit. Motionless. Overcome. The taxi breaks free of the dock in the current, and a raft of water hyacinths fills the void of brown water. She heads out on the swollen river downstream, toward the Patpong. She watches until she can no longer even see the bowed roof of the house she leaves behind.*

And she sings again, "I will always love you ..."

She does not even notice the money being shoved into her left hand.

At last, she slips out of her red pumps and starts up the stairs. They are the stairs at the Oriental Hotel dock near the Patpong, and they are the stairs from the stage back to her dressing room. She feels as heavy as the river. The music and the sound of her own voice cut her like a snare of piano wire. Her skin freezes in the blue beam of the spotlight. At the top of the stairs, she stops and holds the last note of the song until she is completely out of breath.

Twice she pauses and looks back around the room. Through her blurry eyes she thinks she sees a smooth Asian face with his eyes riveting on her. She is wrong. It is only a lawyer, a man who would rather go fishing than find out who really killed her lover. But he is also a man who seems unexpectedly struck with waves of emotion.

# ELEVEN

His client and the case keep tumbling through his mind for the whole drive south back to Chatham. He cannot shake the image of a woman in a red dress, dragging herself up a staircase. Singing. Closing her eyes. Was that all just an act or was there substance? It felt so real. So sad, really. How can you not be moved after such a show? There is a strange hollowness in his chest.

He remembers the voice of the Thai detective on his machine, "I understand you are Miss Aparecio's lawyer. More than five years I am searching for her. Please call me. Perhaps you do not know who you are getting into here."

*Who* you are getting into? What a Freudian slip. His head boils with questions. What is she hiding? If she did not kill Big Al, who did? Does she know? Who set the fire? Why? Why would someone frame her? What about this escort service he has read about in the police reports? How do Tuki and the victim fit into that picture? What does any of this have to do with Bangkok? And ... if you get really lucky, pal, and score some answers, can you be of any help here? Or is the judge right? Will the D. A. eat you alive?

The questions are still rattling through his head when he shuffles up the outside stairs and into his attic pad to find a body on his mattress. He can see its contours in the light filtering into the room from the cone of yellow fog around a street lamp outside. He stands in the doorway, stares, tries to focus.

Suddenly, the body sits up, tosses off the sleeping bag that she had wrapped over her to keep out the summer dampness.

"Hey, where you been?"

"Filipa?"

"Who did you expect?"

He says nobody, he thought she had to work tonight. She is

interning this year at a women's psych clinic in Cambridge, part of the practicum for her PhD.

She rubs her eyes, seizes a wine glass sitting on the floor next to the mattress, takes a sip. He can smell the Chardonnay.

"I got off. We were over-staffed. So I thought I'd surprise you. Traffic to the Cape was hell. Want some wine?"

He shakes his head no. He cannot understand why she never remembers that he really does not like Chardonnay.

"You don't sound too happy to see me."

"No. No. Of course, I am. I'm just really beat, Fil. This case is messing with my mind, you know?"

He dumps his briefcase on the table, tosses his suit jacket on the back of a chair, heads for the fridge. A pain is starting behind his eyes. Four rum and cokes. Maybe there is still some fizzy water left.

"Provincetown is more gothic than ever. I swear it looked like *The Rocky Horror Picture Show* tonight. And that's just on the surface. I can't even imagine what goes on behind closed doors. Guys dressed like girls, girls like guys. The whole lets-hold-hands gay thing. I saw a guy with a mustache dressed like Dolly Parton. And my client may be the biggest fruitcake of the—"

She grabs him around the chest from behind and hugs him while he is bent over staring into his fridge. He can feel her breasts warm his back, her pelvis presses against his hips.

"Do we have to talk about work?"

"Not if you keep doing that."

He turns around. They kiss. Long, slow. Grinding bodies. Her hand feels for him. His fingers slide up under her skirt, slip along the smooth curve of her hip. In thirty seconds she has his pants down around his ankles and they are screwing each other against the open door of the refrigerator. She is petite. Her short legs struggle to clutch his hips to hers. He sucks on her neck, lost in a secret garden beneath her mane of thick hair. It is naturally dark brown, but she has dyed it a coppery red for him. Now she does not look like all the other Portuguese princesses who he grew up with in Nu Bej.

He goes off before her, tries a long, probing kiss to sustain his vigor for her sake. But his legs are melting as he drives her harder with each thrust against the refrigerator door.

"Ouch."

"You okay?"

"Something's biting me in the ..."

He steps back from the fridge, eases her to the floor.

"Did you miss me?"

He rubs his open hands up under her jersey, feeling the peach fuzz as his fingers slide from the small of her back to her shoulder blades.

"You have no idea," he sighs.


Just as he is about to nod off, she spoons up against his back and whispers. "I tried to call you about ten times tonight while I was stuck in Cape traffic on Route 6. Why was your cell phone off?"

"Not a clue. Maybe it was out of juice. Sorry. Was there a problem?"

"It's my mother, Michael. She was calling me all day, bugging me with thirty different things about the wedding. Her latest thing is that the bridesmaids' dresses clash with the rugs in the church. She wants to buy a new carpet. Damn her. If the invitations hadn't already gone out, I'd ask you to elope with me, you know?"

The mattress muffles his response. He is trying to will himself into a dream about fishing out on Georges with his father. But his mind keeps picturing a girl in a red robe standing over a burned and bloody body on the beach.

# TWELVE

She finds him standing outside the screen door of her bungalow. It is ten o'clock on Monday morning. The sun is burning off the last of the fog. From her doorstep, here on a steep hillside, you can see Cape Cod Bay in the distance, spreading out to the west like a sea of sapphires. She lives in one of the studio-style guest cottages at a compound called Shangri-La in tony Truro to the south of P-town.

"I thought you were going fishing."

"I'm back," he says. It is true. Yesterday he and Fil went fishing for striper with some of her old friends from college who summer in Bass River. He hooked into a forty-five-inch monster. Landed it, tagged it, let it go. It's amazing the focus and high he can get from fishing.

"Are you still my lawyer?"

"You still need one?"

She is silent, thinking. Remembers all the raw emotion she saw on his face at the end of her show. Finally she opens the screen door for him to enter. She is wearing a deep blue kimono with little red and gold dragons stitched over the breasts. Her hair, with its sun streaks and kinky braids, is exploding around her face. No makeup. He likes the look. He thinks that if you put her in normal clothes like a pair of Calvins and a simple cotton top, no one would ever suspect her gender secret. Maybe it is just the wackiness of Provincetown that makes him feel all itchy inside, not Tuki at all. Or maybe he has just gotten used to her, started folding at least one drag queen into his vision of world order.

They sit at a little breakfast table that looks out through a picture window to the bay. He opens his briefcase and pulls out a tape recorder.

There is a delicate white chrysanthemum in a red fluted vase in the center of the table. She picks up the vase and lifts the flower to her nose and inhales. Then she pours them each a cup of green tea.

"Where do we start?"

He has been thinking about this since yesterday morning, wondering what his dad, the great fish hunter, might do. Now he has a little bit of a plan. He has decided to stay away from talk about the night of the murder and the fire for a while, avoid talking about her relationship with Al Costelano. He is not going to ask her again about the Thai dick whose call he has not yet returned. He wants her to trust him, drop her guard, tell him everything that crosses her memory. He knows that sometimes it is the most seemingly insignificant, peripheral details from way before the time of the crime that will make your case.

"Why don't you tell me some more about Bangkok?"

*Klaus, a sailor from a Dutch ship, reminded the girls of River Phoenix the first time they met him at a food stall in the park. He was all over her beloved best friend Ingrid. Between her thirteenth and fourteenth birthdays, she grew about five inches taller and ventured into wearing her mother's minis and makeup. She started going out on the town looking like a stand-in for Jodie Foster in* Taxi Driver. *Everyone was always looking for a piece of her candy. And as far as sailor boy was concerned, Ingrid was throwing a fire sale.*

*These days, she has all but disappeared. On the few occasions that Tuki sees her, the girl's eyes are rolled halfway back in her head like she has been smoking opium or something. So Tuki is alone for the first time in years. At first she hangs at home in the theater, rips through books like toilet paper, watches about two movies a day, listens to Lionel Richie tapes—doing her "Tuki the Sponge" thing big time.*

*And she's having body problems of her own, but not the good kind like Ingrid. The spaces beneath her arms and below her bellybutton are suddenly sprouting thick, dark hair like crazy. Shaving large parts of her body and plucking her brows has become a lifestyle. Brandy and Delta see what is happening, but they figure as long as she still has to wear a uniform to school, and students have a "no jewelry" rule, things cannot get too out of control with Tuki.*

*But at night when her mothers are performing, or on dates, she starts spending hours working on her eyeliner, lashes, and lipstick. She roots through her mothers' boxes of costume jewelry, but she cannot find big enough earrings to suit her or enough brass bracelets. She begins wearing Delta's black bras even though she has nothing to put inside except tissue paper. She tries on her mothers' clothes, puts her hair up in a French twist, steps into a pair of Brandy's pumps. At first, she just listens to Lionel Richie on the cassette player and practices walking in those shoes. Eventually, she is singing along and doing her own routines to Mary Wells, Diana Ross, Patti LaBelle, and songs from* Flashdance *in front of a dressing mirror. She imagines men falling in love with her, sending flowers, buying her presents after they see her perform.*

*Then one summer night before her fourteenth birthday, she decides to hit the streets. Yes, she is an Asian girl by day and just about everybody in the Patpong knows her. So it is time to try perfecting the skill that will keep American immigration agents guessing for five years. For her debut as a W-O-M-A-N, she goes black. She wants to be her own girl, not some hand-me-down thing from Brandy and Delta. So she goes shopping. As the Thais say,* Kai ngam phro khon. *A chicken is beautiful because of its feathers. But of course, she is as poor as a roach, so other means than Thai baht must be used to procure the costume to transform her into a sex machine.*

*For the first time in her life, Tuki wants things she cannot afford to buy. So she steals. It is not pretty. And you will not hear her making any excuses, except one: she only steals from the rich and she always leaves something beautiful in return.*

*This kind of stealing is actually quite easy. Walking home from school alone, she discovers that every day the Montien Hotel on Surawong Road throws out a lot of flowers. She takes the best and makes bouquets. Then she goes around to the fancy shops on New Road and offers flowers for sale. She is most successful in early evening when people are getting out of work and stores are very crowded with shoppers. She is a cute little* luk sod *with big round eyes and almost a meter of silk hair down the back of her school uniform. When she goes into a shop, smiles prettily, and offers her bouquets, the sales people usually say they* will buy flowers for their wives or girlfriends or husbands or mothers. But she must wait because they are busy with customers.

So she smiles a lot, wanders around the store. Eventually the clerks get so distracted by their business that they forget about her. That is when the size-four dress rack, the wig collection, and shoe display get a little emptier, and her school bag gets a little heavier. That is when she leaves flowers in a pretty place like the top of a jewelry case ... before disappearing in the crowd.

Pretty soon—with the stealing—she has her own wardrobe. Now she is dressing to kill in a little black silk dress, black hose, gold heels, plenty of jewelry, a light touch of dark makeup, and sassy ruby lipstick. Her own hair is pinned up under a stocking cap, and she is wearing a shag wig, teased up into a funky nest. The wig is streaked with blonde, like the one she saw Tina Turner wearing in a video. She grabs a little patent-leather purse, pulls on a pair of Wayfarer sunglasses, and sneaks out into the streets.

She has given herself a new name, "Tennille," as in the Captain and Tennille who sing "Do that to me one more time; once is never enough ..." Now she is going to show Miss Licorice Cheesecake what a real honey pot can do. Like, yeah, Big Mama, we cool!

When Tennille cruises Surawong and Silom Roads, men chase her like hungry rats. At first she pays no attention to the whistles and calls and funny noises. She hides behind her dark shades, keeps on trucking. But after a few nights, the glasses come off. Now she makes eye contact, smiles at cute ones, throws some body language into her strut when she passes women. Pretty soon everyone knows Tennille can strut her stuff. She even goes into some of the clubs on Patpong Road, Number One, Soi Superstar. But she does not stay long because men start getting the wrong idea, and the regular B-girls give her looks that singe her hair. Still, she is having fun.

Once she runs into Ingrid and her sailor boy coming the other way down the street. Tuki all at once hates Ingrid, and wants to be her. Girlfriend, then wife, then mother. Ingrid will have that life soon, Tuki knows. She turns Lionel Richie way up in her head, raises her chin, and walks on by.

*Ingrid tries not to notice, but she is checking out Tennille's new black leather mini out of the corner of her eye. After she passes them, she stops and turns halfway around. Sure enough, sailor boy is watching her over his shoulder, until Ingrid jabs him in the ribs. Tennille gives her a little smile, like gotcha back.*

# THIRTEEN

"Want to get out of here, la?"

He can tell from the scratchiness in her voice that she has had enough talking for a while. It will almost be noon. There is a hot southwest breeze blowing. The sky is powder blue.

"Sure."

"The beach? You have a swimsuit?"

He smiles. Man, is he prepared. When it is summer on Cape Cod, you should always carry a swimsuit and a beach towel in your ride.

It is only when he has slipped into the faded pair of red surfer's jams in her bathroom that he wonders what she is changing into for the beach. A woman's suit must be out of the question for a queen.

He is sitting in a hammock outside the bungalow, swinging, sunning himself, wondering if any of this Vietnam and Bangkok stuff is relevant to his case when he hears the padding of her feet and turns to look.

"Jesus!"

"Something wrong?"

She is standing in front of him wearing big tortoise-shell sunglasses, lipstick. Not much else. Yards of flesh are showing above, between, and below a lime-green Malia Mills bikini. It is high waisted like support panties, but the side panels are cut out so that he can see every inch of her long legs. On the top end she is wearing what looks like a sports bra. In one hand she swings a purple beach towel, and in other she dangles a Kenya bag with street gear folded neatly inside. Her hair is up off her neck in that outrageous ponytail again, a fountain of black and gold curls.

"You look unbelievable."

She smiles. It is a cute, almost bashful smile that he does not expect.

"I won't embarrass you?"

He shakes his head no. Hell no, he thinks. You look like a million bucks.

"Good. Then we can drive back over to P-town. I want to take you to the Slip. It only has a beach when the tide is out. But there is a great deck. We can talk more there, by the pool. I must be crazy, la. But I feel so ... so free today. You gave me this. You freed me, Michael."

Yeah, for about twenty-eight more days, he thinks.


During the ten-minute drive to P-town, he keeps quiet, but she feels his eyes flashing over at her.

"Okay. You are a little curious, am I right? You want to know how I hide my secret."

He feels himself blush. Well maybe, sort of.

She says that in places like Japan, China, India, Thailand, where males have been impersonating females for five thousand years in the theater, drag queens form closed societies. And there are certain tricks that the old queens pass on to the little princesses when they begin to reach a certain age.

"Old queens are always on the lookout for, you know, princesses—young boys who look like girls or little boys who wish they were girls or a little girl trapped in a boy's body."

He nods, guesses he can understand that.

The young princesses keep the family, the "house," thriving. It is the budding little princesses who bring the money into the house, either through traditional theater, burlesque like the Follies, escort services, or straight-out prostitution. And the children come. Some are street kids with no homes, some get bonded to the house by poor parents, some grow up in the house, like Tuki.

"Whatever. When the princesses' bellies begin to sprout hair, the queens teach them the trick of pushing their jewels back up inside their bodies and out of the way, la. Over the years this little trick becomes possible even after the princess's jewels have ... well ... you know. I do not think any more about getting tucked in the morning than I do about brushing my teeth."

For a second the Jeep swerves off the road, kicking up sand. He has a look of pain on his face. He is trying to imagine tucking his own ... *Christ!* He arches his shoulders back to clear his mind.

She says that the word on the street is that drag queens take female hormones—estrogen shots. That part is only really true for real TS, as in transsexual, types like her. She uses electrolysis and estrogen to slow the growth of face and body hair down to a trickle. After a couple of years of use, female hormones, taken in combination with an antigen to block testosterone, softened her voice, made her breasts and butt swell.

"But, here is the total truth: no safe amount of estrogen will shrink a princess's *chaang* back to the size it was before she grew up. The old Asian solution to all of this is string."

He squints his eyes, cannot picture what she is talking about. Not sure he wants to.

"We call it a gaff, la. You can make one or pick one up at any drag shop. The ones you buy look sort of like an eye patch of triangular black cloth with a loop of elastic cord around either side. You wear it like a G-string, and after you tuck the jewels and pull the pinky back between your legs, the cloth holds everything in place. Some girls make their own by threading a loop of old pantyhose—for the string—through the cutoff cuff from a pair of jeans—for the patch."

"Unreal," he says before he can catch himself. Suddenly, he wants to ask how in hell she pees in that gear. Of all the cases in the country, he has to draw this sideshow. Is anything what it seems?

She is smiling again. Damn. Does she like blowing his mind?

"The queens in Bangkok showed me how to use a leather thong as a gaff when I was just a little princess: goat skin. Very soft. Cord so thin most people cannot even see it through sheer panties. Anyway, whether you see me from front or back, you see G-I-R-L above and below the waist. Right, la?"

His eyes veer to that lime bathing suit then dart back to the road. They are in P-town now. The Jeep is creeping west in the usual throng of traffic on Commercial Street. A couple of college boys on bikes cruise up alongside, stare at her breasts, smile. Like life is good.

Tuki gives them a look. A bluesy little grin.

She sighs. "Some girls scrape together fifteen thousand dollars or more and get a total sex change. Doctors castrate you, peel the skin off your *chaang*, cut out the muscle, reposition the urethra, and make—"

"Jesus! Spare me the gory details."

She shrugs, gives a little sigh.

"Sometimes I think about this ... maybe save my money ... if you keep me out of jail."

He feels his stomach churning. "Are we there yet?"

# FOURTEEN

The Boat Slip is an upscale, weathered-wood, seventies hotel built in the style of a condo complex on the bay side, harbor beach. It has a big wooden deck around a shimmering blue pool. It's a total gay scene. If you just want to catch some rays for a few hours and check out the current selection of studs, the Slip is the place. They have tea dances at four, a dance club by night, theme parties. It costs you a few dollars to get in if you're not a guest, but the Slip is a cheap show.

With her lawyer in tow, she stands in the shade on the edge of the deck at the Slip, waiting for the blurs of tan bodies and bright fabrics laid out before her eyes to settle themselves into shapes. As her vision clears, she sees a dark bronze Tarzan type with wavy dark hair, blue eyes, a long nose, heavy beard shadow. He is sitting up on his chaise, twisted like a discus thrower, showing off the unbelievable vee shape of his upper body. One leg is on the deck, and even from here you can see the line of his hamstring beneath the webs of dark leg hair that seem to meld with his black boxer trunks.

Michael rubs his eyes. He guesses why she likes it here. But how the hell did he let himself get talked into this little adventure? Men are staring at him. One of them just winked. Damn.

"I'm out of here, Tuki."

"No. Wait. Stay. I want to talk ... please. I'll tell you how this all started."


It is Memorial Day weekend, the beginning of June. The start of the summer season in P-town. There is a party after the Saturday night show. Everybody from the Follies is going.

They take the bartender Richie's car. When the Range Rover crests a hill and comes out of the woods, she sees the reflection of lights in some kind of harbor or bay or river ahead at the foot of the hill.

*The road dead-ends in a driveway before reaching the water. There must be thirty cars parked around this traffic circle—Jags, Benzes, Porsches. And standing at an Asian-looking entrance gate are two guys in suits.*

*They know Richie because they wave the whole entourage down a curved, sloping walk to the house. Meanwhile, Richie is babbling on about the show. He tells her that she was un-effing-believable tonight, and just wait until the effing critics publish their effing reviews because everyone is going to get effing rich.*

*She is hardly paying attention because her mind is trying to take in a long, one-story, teak-looking house that stands at the bottom of the hill by the water. It has a really steep roof and a gallery of open French doors. Richie is suddenly grabbing her hand and squeezing it. He says he knew that she would like this place. "It's Shangri-La."*

*The house is not Thai style, but it is close. It is sort of a pavilion. One wall at the end of the room houses a glass case displaying swords and knives with curved blades and big handles. She does not know much about such things, but she knows they are called* dha *in Southeast Asia. Suddenly, she is remembering the klongs of Thonburi, the River House, and ...*

"What?" Michael feels like he is losing her.

"Forget it, la." She is looking around the Slip, smiling at the studs.

He feels his skin beginning to boil. She is driving him crazy the way she starts stories then cuts them off. Flirts with everything that moves. "Why? Why forget it, Tuki?"

"Not important, la. You want to know about the party?"

He is afraid she will clam up if he says even the littlest thing to hassle her. "Sure, the party. Tell me."

*When she gets to the entrance, she is back in Thailand for a second. Automatically takes off her sandals, leaves them by the door. Inside the music hits her. Brazilian jazz. It pumps from speakers all over a huge room with vaulted ceilings. One side of the room opens onto a deck over the water. Given her current company, she is expecting some kind of drag scene, but the room vibrates with a crowd of people who look like movie stars and models.*

*She is thinking she does not even begin to fit in with these people. Like, get me out of here. But she is loving the feel of the wooden floor against her feet. Maybe this place is not all that bad. There is a chef in a white suit and hat standing out on the deck grilling shrimp* satay. *She smells the ginger and onions and hot pepper and peanut oil and soy sauce. She cannot wait to get over to that grill for a few of those jumbo* kung phao. *And suddenly she is remembering long dinners on the deck of the Oriental Hotel in Bangkok.*

*Before she gets more than five steps into the room, the jazz cuts out. A horn sounds the call to post. Everyone turns to stare at her. She is really feeling embarrassed. Her clothes. After the show she dressed to blend into the crowd along Commercial Street. Her hair is pulled back in a barrette. She is not wearing anything on her face except a little cinnamon lipstick and eyeliner. Her clothes are total college girl—a ribbed, burnt-orange cardigan, a pair of baggy Guess jeans, sandals.*

*Someone's arm hooks through hers. It is a blonde Hollywood type, and she is raising a champagne glass in toast. Tuki looks around the room, sees Nikki, Richie, Duke, Silver, and a number of the dragon waitresses from the Follies among all the pretty faces. She lets out a little flash of laughter, a smile. Nerves.*

*The next thing she knows the woman who has her by the arm is shouting. "Everyone must welcome to Provincetown, Tuki Aparecio, diva of the first magnitude."*

*The crowd raises their glasses. Someone cheers.*

*She cannot help it, her smile blooms. A blush warms her cheeks. She does not know what to say. No one has ever thrown a party in her honor before. Her body takes over. She presses her hands together and bows respectfully as people do in Thailand. People clap. When she raises her eyes, someone has turned up the jazz again. Richie is standing there with a big goblet of Perrier with lime for her.*

*The blonde introduces herself. She is clearly the hostess—very slinky and rich, with serious gold around her neck and an aqua-colored* silk sarong from Malaysia. But for some reason, Tuki has the feeling that this is not her house.

The hostess is stroking her forearm with both of her hands. She says Richie will show her around. There are a lot of people here who are hoping to meet Tuki.

Then the blonde is gone in a flash of color.

She does not know what to do. She feels dizzy. But Richie hands her a linen napkin, a skewer of grilled shrimp. He tells her to relax. Pretty soon these people will be her new best friends.

One night she comes home in her street drag. When she turns on the light in the dark room, there sit Brandy and Delta. Do they beat her and call her a street-sweeper slut? Beat her? No. They never touch her in anger. Call her names? Like she cannot believe.

They screech at her in Vietnamese for about an hour. She does not understand a word except the references to her mother and father. But she gets the message, because before the two of them finish with her, Delta has spit on her wig and ripped it into pieces. Brandy has thrown the whole mess out of the window.

"You want be beat by man, hook on pung chao, die with AIDS? Then you go in streets like cheap ho, la."

"You young. You princess. You want respect. You start work in show. Tomorrow. Sleep now. Then make choice. Street or show. No both."

When the light goes out, she hugs herself and thinks Luang kho ngu hao. Now I put my hand in the cobra's throat.

# FIFTEEN

*Even though it is early June, the night has gotten warmer instead of colder. The stars are out, a fingernail of a moon sends a silver trail across the water. From the deck she can see that Shangri-La is on some kind of inlet. She does not hear any surf so it must be on the bay side of Cape Cod, not the ocean side. She cannot leave this deck. It is better than being at the river's edge in Bangkok. No disturbing lights from a city on the far bank, no scents of charcoal from the cooking fires in the peasants' houses up the klong, no whining of long-tail boats and water taxis drag racing through the night.*

*She stays out on the deck, back against the railing, eating* kung phao, *meeting amazing looking people who Ruby, the hostess, parades by for introductions. She starts to have fun. The men are right out of GQ. The girls are high as kites and funny. Some are trannies, most are not. But no sooner do they move away to dance indoors—where the light has been reduced to a few candles and subtle spotlights—than she forgets their names.*

*To her pleasure, the gods grant small favors and thankfully nobody asks her to dance. She is beginning to feel more than a little tired.*

*Tuki drifts to the far end of the deck and collapses in a hammock lit only by the tiny spotlights reflecting off the silver, ivory, jade, polished-steel hilts and blades of the* dha *in their wall case inside the house.*

*Here there is nothing to watch except the ripples on the water from fish feeding just like they do back on the Chao Prya. From a distant speaker come the chords of a guitarist playing a song called "Cavatina." The song is from the soundtrack of* The Deer Hunter.

*While she is thinking of nights riding the river taxis in Bangkok, a handsome man in his early fifties sits down on a nearby deck chair to listen to the music. He looks more casual than the rest of the guests in his Hawaiian print shirt, baggy chinos, and boat shoes. He is huge. Maybe six feet four with the hard, broad shoulders of a younger man.*

*She guesses he works at keeping that body. He is wearing Blues Brothers sunglasses, and she can see the flash of emeralds, rubies, and sapphires from his rings as he moves his hands.*

*They call him the "Great One."*

*When "Cavatina" ends, he looks her way, takes off his sunglasses, smiles at her with piercing blue eyes and claps. Just twice.*

*He asks her if she knows the song. His voice surprises her. It is raw, husky, but sweet, too. She thinks he has Brando's voice, the voice from A* Streetcar Named Desire. *She loves that voice.*

*She sits smiling her silly grin, says she loves this song in* The Deer Hunter. *The next thing she knows, he is replaying the movie, talking about DeNiro, Meryl Streep, Christopher Walken ... and Vietnam.*

*He says he can never forget Saigon. She says she can never remember it.*

*The man squints at her. Her body wants to shrivel into a grain of rice. He says that she should have seen it before. She does not understand. He says something in Vietnamese. She knows that he is speaking Vietnamese because he sounds like Delta's opera tapes. But she has no clue what he is asking.*

*Then he asks her in English, "Aren't you Vietnamese?"*

*She shivers a little, wonders if this is an accusation. But the man is smiling.*

*She tells him her mother was Vietnamese. She is an American. This is a declaration. Five years in New York City!*

*For a long time, neither of them speaks.*

*Finally he points with a finger toward the swords and knives in the case. He asks her if she recognizes them. He tells her they are from Vietnam.* Montagnard dha. *He thinks they are beautiful. He saw them first when he was a Marine in the highlands north of Pleiku. For a thousand years the hill people used to give them away as dowry. They were still fighting communists with them in 1971. Now, thirty-five years later, they are only to look at, or open letters. He has a favorite little one with a dark jade handle to open his letters.*

"Weird guy, huh?" Michael can almost see the case of knives and swords sparkling silver in his own mind.

Tuki nods. "You have no idea! He owned it all. Shangri-La. The *dha*. Everything. And he was a Marine. I should have known, la. I should have sensed it. I have seen all the movies like *Platoon*. I know Marines ... my father was a Marine."

Michael shifts his weight to the edge of his seat, runs his fingers through his damp hair to keep it off his forehead. Little beads of sweat are popping up in his chest hair. "Did he come on to you?"

She sits up in her deck chair, turns to face her attorney beside her. Puts a hand on his knee. "He asked if he could take me to dinner after my next show. He rose from the couch, smiled that beautiful smile again, pressed his hands together like a Buddhist person in prayer, then bowed from the waist. His eyes drifted away to the *dha* on the wall, his collection, as if too much eye contact made him nervous or embarrassed."

"And you told him yes?"


*She is working a club called Silk Underground, where Ingrid's mother is tending bar—top of the Patpong circuit. It is the summer when she is turning twenty-one. Her first summer doing Janet Jackson; her first gig working alone without Brandy and Delta, who kind of half-retired to tend bar at a place on Suriwong Road four nights a week.*

*So she is alone. Top billing; a diva. Packing in the house, making so many* baht *in tips—maybe a thousand dollars a week U. S. She plows it all back into better and better music, costumes, wigs, street clothes, and shoes. Her life is her shows. Ingrid is long gone, disappeared with her sailor boy. Tuki has no one to show up, to share with. Sometimes she sings a love song. Thinks like maybe later, la, for that. She is entirely too busy. And where and how would she meet someone who is kind, not twisted? Who would love her forever?*

*While the sex tours from Japan and Singapore, and farangs in general, make up most of the business in the Patpong, the rich boys from Bangkok's penthouses and suburbs also come slumming to the Patpong.*

It is the retreat of choice for birthday celebrations, bachelor parties. Almost every night the wealthy young men of Bangkok show up after midnight to look at or rent what their girlfriends are not giving up. Every night Tuki is filling her bra and G-string with baht from a lot of young Thai horseflesh in tuxedos and suits.

These boys are more or less her age. Not a night goes by without flowers, love notes, outrageous offerings of thousands of dollars if she will perform at a private party or take a limo ride around the city after work. But she never gives in. First, the Johns are always drunk or high. Second, Brandy and Delta have pointed to a thousand examples of broken show-girls who end their lives turning tricks for peanuts on the street.

"Life no like you movies, la," says Delta one night when Tuki finds her crying after a date. "Men very dangerous."

## SIXTEEN

"Please don't hate me," she says.

"So you slept with him?"

She drops her fork with a splat in her crabmeat salad.

It is three o'clock. They have put on street clothes and left the Slip, at last, for lunch at an outdoor café on Commercial Street.

He does not know why he asks this question. He already knows the answer. The police report calls her the victim's estranged lover. Still, something in him feels the urge to nail her here. Maybe he is just flailing. He is frustrated, suddenly feeling a little mean. He has less than four weeks to sort out her story, prepare a defense. And get married. Maybe he just wants to get an honest, emotional reaction by which to judge other things she tells him. He still cannot help wondering if she did the crimes. In his mind, he is hearing the message from the Thai detective telling him that he may not know what he is dealing with here.

"Why do you try to make me feel shame?"

"I don't."

She spits air, like there is a bug on her lip.

"What kind of a lawyer are you? Beat on your clients? Make them feel small? Look down your big nose at me and my friends at the Slip when all I want is to show you a good time? Make you feel less strangled by life. Alby was a terrible mistake, la. You think I am proud of this? Is that what you want to hear? I am sorry. Very, very sorry I ever slept with an American."

He shrugs, takes a sip of his Corona. In his mind the silhouette of a woman beckons from a small boat on dark water.

She picks up her fork, points it at him. "I asked a question. Your turn to answer."

"What? Which question?"

She gets a sad look in her eyes. "Maybe you should go away. Let the crazy little *luk sod* tranny eat her lunch alone, okay?!"

He can almost feel her fork sink into his chest.

His forehead is starting to pour sweat again. He wants to tell her to just back off a little. Wants to go fishing, wants to spend about forty-eight hours in bed with Filipa. But he knows she is right. He is being a jerk, and this is getting the case nowhere. Except that now he knows that she is not afraid to admit her mistakes. She is explosive. And she will stand and defend herself when attacked. He is betting that she did not run from Bangkok or New York out of fear and cowardice. Something else is driving her.

"How do you say 'I am very sorry' in Thai?"

For a moment he wants to reach across the table and cover her long slender fingers with his. Instead, he picks up a book of matches and lights the black candle in the center of the table. He fingers the hot wax as it starts dripping down the side. Something to do.

There is an emotion swelling in her throat.

"In the beginning ... he seemed so sweet," she says. Big tears are rolling down her cheeks. A sad little smile of recognition grows across her lips.


*She sits facing Alby across a table for two in a private room in an East End Italian bistro. There is accordion music playing. If you count champagne, Tuki is breaking her no-alcohol rule.*

*Alby looks good. Ever since she saw the movie* The Great Gatsby *with Robert Redford when she was about thirteen, Tuki carries a torch for men with freshly scrubbed skin; slick, trim hair; pressed shirts; linen slacks; loafers; and smiles that go over the top with teeth. This is Alby Costelano tonight. She is staring into his blue eyes, wondering whether he could get down with a little safe you-know-what.*

*The* frutti del mar *comes and goes. But she does not even notice. They are talking nonstop. She is cataloguing every dimple in his smile, drinking in the smell of his cologne, picturing yards of holy flesh in that body.*

*After another hour goes by, she knows his story, she thinks. He has spent the last twenty years in P-town, buying and selling real estate, watching the price of property and his holdings double almost five times. He is rich. Now he owns Shangri-La, the Painted Lady, and thirty percent of the business property on Commercial Street. But he still puts in twelve hours a day, six days a week at his Commercial Street office, Pink Dolphin Reality, just a shout away from the Painted Lady.*

*He says he is addicted to the carnival. She thinks he means queens. He says things that make her think he first fell for the trannies in the bars and clubs of Vietnam, tried to go straight when he got home. Could not hack it.*

*The man does not laugh the "ha, ha, ha" of most men, but rather like waves rolling along the beach. And he makes her laugh, too, about their funny accents. He says he comes from Pittsburgh where they say things like "Aoh, moy gawd, Muriel, we ain't seen yoons guys dawn tawn inna coon's age. So where yoons bin at?"*

*She is staring into Alby's eyes and starting to wonder how her "la" would fit into a place like Pittsburgh ... when he changes the subject. He says she reminds him of someone.*

*Her left eyebrow arches. She thinks, please, do not spoil this. Like what else is a drag queen SUPPOSED to do if not remind you of ...*

*This is not good. Tonight she wants to be attractive as Tuki, not Janet or Whitney.*

*Alby reaches across the table, puts his big paw up under her hair, alongside her neck. His fingers whisper to her ear.*

*Her eyebrow arches again. She is beginning to smell stale* plaa, *stinky fish.*

*She lifts a hand from her lap and flashes a palm toward his face like, "Stop in the name of love!"*

*Maybe it is the champagne, but she does not even try to make her words tip toe. She tells him please, please, do not tell her she reminds him of some girl who broke his heart.*

*He slides his fingers from her neck to her lips, silences her. He says that he is trying to tell her that he thinks this might be the best night of his life. But if she wants, they can call it an evening.*

*She feels something churning inside her. Then she hears herself asking him if she can come home with him.*

*At the Glass House, Alby's private residence at Shangri-La, he puts Gladys Knight in the stereo. And they rewrite the* I Ching, *with the help of some of Kama Sutra's minty lip balm, sex oil, and Pollaner strawberry preserves. She thinks it is like riding the Uptown Express all night long—*

"Stop!" Michael jumps up, waves the bill and his credit card at the waitress. "I don't need to know about the sex."

# SEVENTEEN

When he gets back to Chatham, there is another message from the Thai detective on his machine.

"This is Varat Samset of the Royal Thai Police calling again, Mr. Decastro. I am very anxious that you return my call, very eager to speak with you about Tuki Aparecio. As you may remember from my first message, I have been looking for her for five years. And now, thanks to Interpol and the computer age, she has resurfaced for me because of certain murder and arson charges in America. She left unfinished business with our office here in Bangkok. But that is not my major concern at this moment. There is something else, something related. More important now. I have reason to believe that she may well be in immediate danger. There is more here than meets the eye. You are my only way of reaching her. This is urgent. Please call me at ..."

He grabs a paper plate, writes down the number on it, skips to the next message on his tape. He heads for the fridge and a can of Old Mil, wonders what time it is in Thailand, what day it is—yesterday or tomorrow. Then he hears Filipa's voice coming from the machine.

"Hey, it's me. I know I told you I'd be down tonight. But it is Monday. Seems like about half the staff blew off work today and I'm way jammed here. I've got to stay in the city tonight. I want to hear your voice. Wish you could give me a call, but I'm running around like a firefighter, and you know they make us turn off our cells in here. I'll try you later if I get a minute. There are some new wrinkles on the wedding front. Love you."

"I love you, too," he says to the machine. The tone of his voice is a mix of exasperation and relief. He has been so buried in the case all day, he totally forgot Filipa was supposed to come down for the night. Well, it is a good thing she's not going to show. He feels like he has just gone fifteen rounds with the cat lady. He would be rotten company. She would want to have sex, and after a day in

the Magic Queendom, he has overdosed on the human fascination
with carnal desire.

Since starting back to Chatham in the Jeep, he has been trying to
make sense of the police reports and everything else he knows about
his client. Then there are these calls from Thailand, putting huge
question mark over his investigation. Everything seems a muddled
mess. He still is not getting a clear sense of Tuki Aparecio. But he is
trying to put together the bits and pieces she has told him, especially
about her life in Bangkok. Sometimes when she talks about it, he can
almost smell the curry, the ginger, the sex, the tearing of flesh.

*Dusk in the Patpong. The in-between hour. The only time of the day
when the noise of the streets is muted, and you can hear chickens cack-
ling in their cages. Thai love songs echo through the halls of the cheap
hotel where chambermaids are still preparing the lala rooms for a night
of rendezvous. The combined scent of diced scallions, peppers, steaming
rice, roasting peanuts, frying fish, and ginger filter through the hot air
of the concrete building.*

*Since she does not eat until after the show, this is Tuki's time to gather
herself. So she is wearing just her underwear and a red silk robe, swinging
easily in her hammock, painting and drying her nails before a huge pole
fan in the little apartment above Silk Underground. Life is easy.*

*Then she hears shots downstairs. First two, loud and close together.
After a couple of seconds, a third. A bit muffled.*

*Brandy and Delta, who have been sleeping in their hammocks,
jump to their feet, their robes hanging open until they cinch them closed
with the belts.*

*"Get down. Hide!" They shout at Tuki, point to the clothes closet.
"No move!"*

*The door to their apartment squeaks open, then clicks shut. Her
mothers are gone. She can hear their bare feet padding down the hall,
down the stairs that lead backstage in the club. She is alone, curled in a
dark corner behind three dozen dresses hanging like a curtain between
her and the rest of the world.*

The odor of cheap cologne from the dresses is starting to make her dizzy when she hears the first of the screams. Then the bawling, like cats in the night. Keening in Thai and Vietnamese.

Suddenly the door to the apartment bursts open. She peeks through the dresses, sees Brandy grabbing an armful of towels.

"What ..."

"You no come. Stay here!" Brandy's voice sounds fierce, but her face is streaming tears as she runs back out the door.

Tuki cannot help herself. She has to know about these shots, this emergency that makes Brandy scream and cry. Slowly, she creeps out of the apartment, tiptoes down the hall, descends the back stairs. The concrete chills her feet. And all the while the sobs and the keening are growing louder. Now she hears sirens in the street. People are shouting.

She is backstage, pulls open the curtain until she can see the main room of Silk Underground where the bar, the tables, and the stage are bathed in faint violet light coming in through the door from the street, the red neon over the bar. The room is empty of patrons, but there is a crowd of queens and B-girls around the far end of the bar. Some are holding their heads, some shrieking and howling, wandering away from the huddle in a daze.

Suddenly, about six policemen come storming through the front door. The crowd scatters. Tuki sees a figure lying on the floor, leaking blood everywhere. Brandy and Delta are on their knees in this mess, pressing the towels to the figure's chest.

When she gets closer, she can see the face. White and ghastly. The eyes are rolled back in their sockets. It is Ingrid's mother, her blonde hair fanned out around her in a pool of blood. She is dead. Two holes in her chest where her heart used to beat. Not far from her lies a second body, a man. He looks Chinese. There is a pistol in his hand. A big purple dimple on his right temple. The left side of his head is a pulpy mass of hair and blood and brains.

Tuki feels her head starting to spin. She starts for the stage to sit down for a moment. But her knees are buckling.

The next thing she knows she is lying on the stage, Delta is pressing a wet towel on her cheeks, forehead.

*"You faint, la. But you okay."*

*She tries to rise up on an elbow. Delta pushes her shoulders back down against the stage.*

*"Not for you. No more look. This terrible sadness." Tears are running down her cheeks.*

*"I don't understand."*

*Delta turns her head and starts to cry. "Not your business."*


He gulps his beer, hardly tastes it because his mind is racing. If you believe the police reports, she is a cold-blooded killer, a psychopath, an arsonist, and a high-priced escort tied into a nasty nest of tranny prostitutes. But from the stories she is telling him about Bangkok, she seems hardly the type to trade sex for money. Or murder. She does not sound crazy. Maybe a little out of touch with reality, but not nuts. He sees her as loyal and loving, and nearly obsessed with performing. She seems to idolize her surrogate mothers. And she is attached to a homespun morality that she keeps reinforcing with a collection of Thai proverbs.

He thinks that she is a little sad, definitely in need of approval. Even her deceptions, the shoplifting, the sneaking out in drag as a teenager, seem remarkably innocent for someone who has grown up as she has. Hell, he did a lot worse back in high school in Nu Bej. He and his buddies boosted a beer truck once and threw a party at Horse Neck Beach for a cast of hundreds. But Tuki? She left flowers when she stole from the boutiques. True, she seems to have a tendency toward revenge when she is betrayed, but who doesn't?

He tosses down the last of the beer as if he is eighteen again and the police are chasing him down a dark road. He crunches the can in his fist to destroy the evidence.

"Everybody, back off," he feels like howling. Prostitution, murder, arson just do not make sense here. Not with the Tuki he knows. Not unless someone has been squeezing her.

Forget about a restaurant meal tonight. He has got to order out for a pizza again, sit here at his table, and read the cop reports.

He wonders how he can get his hands on the videotape that supposedly puts the stolen knife, this *dha,* that killed Big Al in her hand. He wants to see what the police and the D. A. already think they know, exactly why they charged her. And he wants to see what they have missed.

He needs to start putting together a list of suspects that does not include Tuki. Other people with motives, opportunities, means to kill Big Al and torch P-town. People who maybe have something against Tuki, too. People who would frame her. Maybe people from the Follies. Maybe from this escort service that she has talked so little about. Maybe business associates of Costelano. Or someone from Thailand. Maybe even some kind of international mob.

Time to dig in. Do the research, pal. No big deal. Just about six months worth of work in ... how long until the trial? Twenty-seven days.

# EIGHTEEN

He has polished off most of a pepperoni pizza, and still tastes the salt and grease, even after downing a bottle of water. Michael stares out the window at the fog glowing more yellow than ever in the lights of Chatham's Main Street. He can hear chords seeping from a piano bar up the street, a soft, female voice sings "As Time Goes By."

This Thai detective. What the hell's he mean he has reason to believe that she may well be in immediate danger?

Maybe the guy is jerking him around. There is something kind of sketchy here. Something about the way the detective talked, like he was reading a speech. But the phone number he left looks real. It has about twelve digits.

His instinct is to call Tuki, tell her about the second phone message and grill her about Thailand. So he does. But she has shut off her cell. She is probably at the Follies getting ready to go onstage. So now he punches in the number of the Thai dick. It seems to take forever before the phone rings. But it finally does. And before he is ready, there is a voice at the other end, speaking in Thai at first, then English.

"Hello. Hello. Who there?

He just listens.

"Speak ... please, speak." A cough. A grunt. A rough phrase in Thai. The voice sounds hollow, not menacing exactly, but more ragged, less easy with its English than the smooth one on the tape. He pictures an emaciated little ferret, chain-smoking in a windowless, concrete cubicle.

"Hello?"

This call seems all wrong. He clicks off. He needs to get control of what the cops already know before he goes wading into a Bangkok swamp. But he better get on the stick. The guy says she is in danger. Start with the escort service. What else did she tell him this afternoon?

The sun is warming her face as she wakes up in the hammock on the bedroom deck of the Glass House at Shangri-La. There is no noise except bird songs and the light rush of wind in the trees. The water on the inlet is a perfect topaz. Alby is nowhere in sight. But someone has put a knit blanket over her.

She hears a woman's voice saying that she likes to see a girl smiling to herself. The voice is Ruby's, the hostess. She is standing in the doorway between the bedroom and the deck in a sheer burgundy robe, holds a tray with orange juice, coffee, English muffins.

Tuki stretches her arms over her head, swallows a yawn.

Ruby says that everybody but Alby sleeps late around here. It is after ten.

Tuki yawns again, listens while Ruby tells her how Alby said not to disturb her. How she looks like an angel when she sleeps.

She smiles, takes the tray on her lap. Wonders if she can just stay gently swinging in this hammock, listening to the birds sing ... maybe forever.

Later Ruby sends her off with a cup of coffee for a morning shower in what she calls Bungalow Number Three. Alby is kind of particular about the bathroom here in the Glass House. Let it be.

Bungalow is not exactly what she would call the little building she finds among the trees near the inlet. Number Three is more like a miniature fisherman's house along the klongs of Thonburi—but not so rickety and not so poor looking.

It has a big picture window, a porch with a hammock near the water's edge, baskets of hanging ferns ... everything gray and woody. The shower is a cedar enclosure outdoors on one side, but it has one glass wall looking right back into the cottage. When she takes her shower, she can gaze inside at the studio apartment with potted palms, a giant turtle shell on the wall, a queen-size bed on a low frame, a tiny kitchen. Maybe the best part of all is that she can look right through the house and out the open picture window to watch a family of ducks paddling on the inlet.

Ruby meets her as she walks back toward the main house, the party place. She is still wearing the burgundy robe. She kisses Tuki on the cheek, asks her if she would like a little tour of Shangri-La.

After about thirty yards of walking, they come to another little bungalow, identical to Number Three, except that the fabric on the curtains and the bed are all pinks and greens instead of oranges and yellows. Before the walk is over, they have circled around the knob of a small hill, seen two more places just like her bungalow hidden in the forest on the hillside. She notices that these three bungalows are occupied. Women's shoes are scattered here and there, lots of clothes in the closets. Ruby says she stays in the bungalow nearest the party place. She calls it the Lodge. It is strictly for entertainment. For the first time since she has been here, Tuki realizes that Shangri-La is on a small island. Cars cross a little bridge over a lagoon to get here.

Ruby says that when Alby is here, he keeps off by himself in the Glass House. But he is hardly ever around to help with the day-to-day needs of the compound. That is Ruby's job. He is always at the office or flying off in the Lear to one place or another. He rarely shows up at Shangri-La, except on the weekends to throw parties. The long-term guests pretty much have the place to themselves.

There is a Jacuzzi looking out over the inlet. It bubbles away on one end of the deck at the Lodge. The spa is the size of one of those large wading pools for kids you see on TV. When Tuki sees it, there are two silhouettes that seem to wiggle like fish beneath the waves. Sheryl Crow is whining about leaving Las Vegas over the sound system.

Silver shoots her a plastic, eff-you smile.

Nikki gives a little wave.

Tuki smiles, cannot think of what to say. She cannot figure out what is going on here at Shangri-La. Why are these other queens here? In Alby's spa?

Nikki pulls herself up on the side of the Jacuzzi, groans, says that she has had enough of men in the last twenty-four hours to last her the whole summer. She is looking unusually girly in a purple one-piece. Little buds of breasts. She looks at Ruby standing there beside the spa and says she needs a night off. Nikki is not pleading, she is coaxing—or is it flirting?

Ruby reaches over with a wet hand and brushes the hair off Nikki's forehead. Calls Nikki "sweetheart." Says why doesn't she crash after her show? Nobody will disturb the little Russian tart.

Suddenly Tuki is starting to get a picture. Nikki, Silver, Ruby. They all live here.

Silver says, "For the moment, honey," and growls, like maybe she is thinking about a change. She has a margarita going for herself in an ice-filled beer mug. Takes a long drink, closes her eyes, turns her back on Tuki.

Nikki smiles again. "This is home, sweet home, padruga."

Tuki still does not get it. How can showgirls afford a plush place like this?

Nikki says Richie works a deal. Takes a hundred a week out of their salaries.

Tuki raises her eyebrows. That is peanuts. She thinks she smells rotten fish. She just does not know how rotten yet.

Ruby says that the Great One, Alby, likes the girls to be around when he throws parties for his friends.

Tuki feels something hard and heavy in her chest. Alby is a collector. Shangri-La is a tranny stable. Now she wonders what last night with him was really all about. And she is thinking that it is time to leave when Nikki catches her eye.

She says Shangri-La is not what Tuki may think. You do not have to date anybody if you do not want to. The queens are Alby's stars. He has other girls and boys for the dates.

"We are hoping you might like to join our sisterhood," says Ruby. "Say, the word, Number Three is yours for the summer, meals included."

Nikki gives a hopeful grin.

Tuki still smells rotten plaa, but her body is whispering shamelessly in her ear, "Take a little risk, la. You can walk anytime."

# NINETEEN

The screeching of gulls outside the window wakes him. It is morning. He is still in his clothes, at his worktable, his face planted against a yellow legal pad. He rubs his eyes and stares around him at the shambles of his attic as if he has never seen it before. He still has one foot in a dream about riding out a wicked storm on Georges in the *Rosa Lee*. When he raises his head, his eyes catch on a note that he must have scribbled on the legal pad before he fell asleep last night.

**WHAT WENT DOWN THE NIGHT OF THE MURDER?**

He staggers to the sink, spoons two tablespoons full of instant Folgers into a cup, adds water, locks it in the microwave. When it is hot, he settles at his table and finds the police report about events leading up to Alby's murder.

*Tuki gets to the Follies a little late. Silver is already onstage. Richie is running around croaking like a bullfrog, worrying whether she is ever going to show up, when Tuki comes through the door. His eyes shoot lasers. She gives him a look. She is in no mood to take any of his you-know-what.*

*"Just let me put on my makeup in peace and quiet, la!"*

*Nikki is in the dressing room adding the final touches to her Janis Joplin gear. She is in a panic to talk and sits down on the stool next to Tuki at the makeup mirror.*

*Tuki is just about to brush some static into her dreddy curls. Tonight, for the new show, she is going with her own wild-woman hair. Nikki takes the brush. A little look, an understanding, passes between the two. Then Nikki starts stroking Tuki's curls while she works on her eyeliner.*

*Nikki says that things have gone from bad to worse at Shangri-La.*

*Some kind of special knife or letter opener that Alby got in Vietnam is missing. His favorite thing. And Silver says she is missing two DVDs, her greatest music video gigs. The ones she uses for promotion.*

*Tuki sighs.*

*"Padruga," says Nikki, "Silver is telling Alby and everyone at Shangri-La that she saw you sneaking around the Glass House when it was getting dark this evening."*

*Alby and Silver were having an intimate moment when Silver claims that she spotted Tuki coming into the room, taking the DVDs from the TV stand, the knife from the desk. But the Great One did not see. And Silver did not try to stop the robber because they were in the middle of having sex. And it was good sex.*

*Tuki does not know what is cutting harder in her heart—news that Silver is accusing her of theft from the place where she has only been once in her life, or that the man who said he loved her just forty-eight hours ago is having sex with Silver.*

*She is way past crying. She thinks her head is splitting from the sound of her screaming heart. But when she opens her mouth, nothing at all comes out. Her body is suddenly shivering all over ... Nikki hugs her until they hear hoots and clapping for Silver's last number.*

*Nikki stands up and smoothes out her pink mini, gives her friend a big soft kiss on the lips. She says forget about the prick, Alby. Get out of town while there is still time for a clean escape. Then, like almost everybody else Tuki has ever loved, Nikki goes.*

*Tuki is weighing her options when Silver comes back into the dressing room in a platinum wig and a blue sequined evening dress.*

*"You are a lying rat," says Tuki.*

*"Come again?"*

*"You told everyone you saw me steal his—"*

*"Just stuff it, love, will you! Nobody is buying any more of your poor-little-miss-space-cadet bullshit. Your stupid little wannabee twat is toast, dearie."*

*The Ice Queen raises her chin, looks down her nose at Tuki, gives a real Sharon Stone, eff-you-for-ever-living smile. Then she reaches into her big sequin purse.*

"Here, darling, you might want this." Silver throws a pink dildo in Tuki's lap.

"Go sit on it … when the cops lock you up, babe!"

Tuki is beginning to taste blood. She has a rat-tail teasing comb in her hand, moving in, turning the tables on the Ice Queen.

"Oh, bugger off, you cheesy wench," says Silver. She is backing away. "You don't have the balls to—"

"You set me up, la!" She is closing in on Silver, holding the tail of the comb out in front of her. "You are jealous! So maybe you are the one who steals his dha. Maybe you take your own DVDs. Maybe you are saying you saw me do it because you are so—"

"In your dreams, darling. Please, spare us this little scene. Just cut the crap. Face the facts, bird. You've been caught for the lousy thief that you are. I saw you, the new security camera saw you. Now Alby has seen you. You slipped right into his room in that stupid blue bathrobe of yours. Then you took my DVDs and the knife. Got it, love? Your skinny little mulatto ass is grass. Caught in the act. And if you think Alby is going to stand between you and the cops, you are dreaming!"

Maybe she hears all this. Maybe she does not. But either way, Tuki's head is spinning from the stench of this mound of dead river carp that Silver is trying to shove her way. The truth about where she was when the dha and DVDs were stolen? She was taking one of her long walks along the Race Point beach with her friend Prem. She was not even within ten kilometers of Shangri-La.

So! So the Ice Queen is lying through her teeth about watching her steal … Alby seeing her … all of this new security camera trash.

"Ja long thii nii," This is where I get off.

"Speak English, you stupid gash. Face it, you had him. But you lost him, Tuki, because you're a greedy, jealous, vengeful, little low-class cunt who thinks jewelry and paint can make her what she ain't. Just like bloody Ruby!"

Smoke is filling Tuki's head. Now she is backing the witch out onto the balcony that hangs over the alley. And when she has her up against the railing, she spits in her face.

"That's it, you stinking piece of bung fodder. I promised Richie I'd *let you finish your show before I kicked your cunt all over Commercial Street. But that's it, bitch. You lose. Kiss your ass goodbye!"*

*The next thing she knows, Silver's hands are around her neck. Her eyes are starting to pop out like a couple of plums.*

*Her heart screams.*

*Then she slashes. Really slashes! She feels the pointy end of the aluminum rat-tail comb sink into Silver's left breast and rip toward her belly. She screams. Her hands fly off Tuki's neck. Blue sequins shoot everywhere. The top of the dress tears open and splits right down to the waist. Blood spreads across her torn white slip. And when Tuki pulls the comb away, it has a size-D falsie stuck on it.*

*"I'm fucking cut!" Silver stands in the middle of the dressing room, screaming, looking down at her chest. She hugs her shoulders as if that will stop her Miracle Bra, her right falsie, and all the rest of her lies from falling out.*

*Tuki stares at her with blank eyes.*

*Silver collapses into one of the folding chairs at the makeup mirror. As her slip and bra fall away, she can see that the tail of the comb made a long, red scratch across her chest. Blood is flowing from the top of the cut. The rest is just red and swollen like a claw mark.*

*Downstairs in the Follies, the crowd is cheering for Nikki's last number.*

*Tuki is thinking, "Buddha, be with me ..."*

Scribbled at the bottom of the report are a detective's notes:

*Aparecio has no witness to the alleged walk on beach when knife was stolen. The friend called Prem is nowhere to be found ... and may well not exist. Image on security tape is shadowy but does appear to be Aparecio. Conversations with Richard Guilnor, manager of Provincetown Follies, and victim's housekeeper (calling herself "Ruby"), confirm that Aparecio was involved in a heated love triangle with the victim and a transvestite called Silver Superstar. SEE SECOND INTERIEW WITH SUSPECT!*

Michael jumps up from his chair and stares out the window.

He squints over the tops of the roofs to bring Pleasant Bay and the Atlantic into focus. A dark blue long-liner is heading out across Chatham Bars on a trip to Georges.

"God, Tuki! How many ways can you paint us into a corner?"

## TWENTY

By the time that the long-liner disappears over the horizon to the east, he has decided that while the case is looking more dismal than ever, there is still a chance that Tuki may have been framed. Silver sounds like a world-class vampire who might do anything to keep her claws in Big Al Costelano. But what about this alleged friend Prem, her alibi for the beach walk? Is this person fiction or real? And why can't the cops find him/her?

He has to go back up to Provincetown and start talking to a whole pack of people. But first he needs to digest the rest of the bad news about the night of the murder. He read this stuff the day the judge handed him the case, but now it all seems like confetti in his mind. This time he is going to pay better attention, there may well be something important here in a second interview the cops had with Tuki. Something that can clear her.

*The lights in the dressing room after the show are off except for the glow of the bulbs around the makeup mirror.*

*She cracks open a Perrier that Richie sent up, sits on a chair in front of her mirror. She is wearing nothing but a Spider Woman teddy, G-string, and red satin robe that she bought in Chinatown.*

*Then she sees Alby push open the curtain, come through the door-way. He has a strange look on his face. Maybe the look of a man come to get even. He is smiling, his front teeth biting into his lower lip.*

*She stops breathing. The disco rocks downstairs, the bass line shakes the building with its pulse. No one will hear her if she screams.*

*She shouts for him to get out, looks around for a weapon, maybe a fire extinguisher, to scare him off.*

*But the fire extinguisher hangs on his side of the room.* So ngom khem nai mahasamut. *She may as well dive for a needle in ocean.*

He says he will make her a deal as he is walking toward her with his hard, killer face.

She thinks, "Yes, sure, la. My booty or my life." Her body is searching everywhere for some way to defend herself.

"Xin loi ..."

"Don't even start with that, la!" She shouts, because she knows from Delta and Brandy xin loi is how Vietnamese people always begin when they are sorry for something. She is not believing a word of an apology ... not while he is backing her into this corner. The man is eight feet away and closing. He has a stony look in his eyes.

He does not stop with the Vietnamese. And he is still coming and coming. She is just about feeling his breath and—

"Back off!" She lets him have it. She makes a flamethrower just like she has seen them do in the movies, releases a fog from her can of hairspray toward his face. Fires the sticky vapor with the lighter Silver left by her makeup kit.

POOF!!!

The man wheels backward, his hands pressed to his eyes. Smoke rises from his head. The air stinks of burnt hair.

Her mind staggers. What if I killed him?

Suddenly, she feels a softening in her chest. And as he trips and tumbles toward the floor, she catches him.

Now it is her turn to start babbling like the people in The Killing Fields. She says she is sorry in every language she can think of, all the while pressing a dry towel on his hair to crush out the last of the flames. She can hear him panting like a cat. If anyone wants a real reason to keep her locked up in jail, this is it. She tried to kill Alby. She did. An act of passion. An overwhelming desire. The Buddha must be very disappointed with her.

For long minutes they lie together in the shadows of the dressing room. He is on his back. She is tucked up on her knees with her head on his chest, listening to his heart. Telling it to beat. He says nothing. She cries and mumbles. She is sure any moment the police will come in to drag her away. She is more than just a robbery suspect now. Downstairs the DJ has slipped into old-school mode. Barry White, "You're My Everything."

*"You sure do cry a lot."*

*She is so glad to hear him speak, she kisses him all over his face, starts mumbling again that she is so sorry. She kisses his forehead and his eyes and his nose and his cheeks and his chin because ... because of lots of things. But mostly because the skin is still all there, not burned. Her flamethrower fired high and only got his hair.*

*Now he is sitting up.*

*"I want you to keep the* dha, *Tuki. Keep it as a souvenir of a truly great night when ... But it would really sort of help me get out of a jam if I could give Silver back her DVDs and—"*

*The hammer of his suspicion smacks her in the chest. Why did she ever care about this faithless eff?*

*She curses him in Thai, throws her robe around her shoulders, runs down the steps of the Painted Lady ... to the beach, to the fog. It is about midnight. And he is still alive.*

# TWENTY-ONE

Before he knows it, his fingers are punching in the numbers for a phone in Bangkok. It rings about eight times before someone picks up. The voice starts in with a machinegun barrage of Thai.

"Detective Samset, please. This is attorney Michael Decastro calling from the United States."

A grunt.

"You know what time it is in Bangkok, attorney?" The voice sounds ripped apart by a dream. "Middle of damn night."

He lifts the portable phone away from his ear. His finger is on the talk button. Part of him wants to hang up just like he did before, doesn't want to know anything more about Tuki Aparecio. He wants to quit the case again. It is too much, especially with his own wedding looming.

But now he has given away his identity. He swore an oath before the bar to do his duty for his clients. And there is something about his client that fascinates him. Everything about her and the world she lives in seems so alien, so decadent, so strangely familiar, ripe, terrifying to him. Beyond the makeup, the drag, the exotic settings, the lifestyle ... there is a vulnerability and innocence about Tuki that he has never seen before. She almost seems like someone out of a fairy tale.

"I ... I'm so, so sorry. I didn't realize the time. This was my first chance to return your call—"

"Don't bullshit me, Decastro. You think we do not have caller ID in Thailand? You called me yesterday and hung up. What's the matter? Afraid of what you do not know? That little dragon ho got you spooked or wrapped around her finger yet?"

"Look, I want to apologize for—"

"Save it, attorney. Before your case is over you will be on your knees begging before more people than Varat Samset. Call me tomorrow morning ... *my* time. I need my sleep."

"But what about the danger that you—"

"I have a name for you. Prem Kittikatchorn. Ask your client if he has made contact. And duck if you hear shooting. Good night."

He feels adrenaline jolting through his head. So the mystery alibi has a last name. Kittikatchorn.


He is marching along the beach beneath Highland Lighthouse, trying to keep pace with her. The sun is high. Hot. She is wearing a red bikini top and loose jeans rolled up almost to her knees. She's walking right at the edge of the tide line, letting the water rush around her ankles with each new wave breaking ashore. She told him that if he wanted to talk today, he must come along while she gets her exercise, cleans her soul. So here he is in a faded old Red Sox shirt and his jams, chasing the dragon lady around the very tip of Cape Cod.

"Hey, hey Tuki. Slow down, huh? You going to tell me who this Prem is or not?"

"It is none of your business, la."

"Hell it's not. Some detective calls me all the way from Bangkok to say you're in danger. Asks if this Prem has made contact yet. Tells me to duck if I hear shooting. Damn right it's my business."

"Watch your mouth."

"Jesus. Did you or did you not tell the police you were with this Prem? Walking, when the security camera supposedly caught you stealing Silver's DVDs and the murder weapon, the Vietnamese *dha*, from Costelano's bedroom?"

"I made a mistake. Forget Prem. He is gone now."

"So Prem is a guy?"

She lowers her eyes, looks at the surf crisping on the sand.

"He was here?"

"Yes."

"When?"

"What does it matter?"

"Because he's your alibi. Because he might hurt you! How's that?"

"Prem is a cowardly lion. He cannot hurt anybody ... except maybe ..."

"Stop, dammit, Tuki. Look at me!"

She takes four steps out into the water. A wave rushes through her legs, soaks the thighs of her jeans as she turns to face her attorney with a squinty-eyed, resentful look.

"I am looking at you now, Michael Decastro. What do you want me to see?"

He is thinking, screw this. He is tired of playing twenty questions. "Well?"

"Why are you protecting this Prem? We are down to the same old question we have been dealing with for three days aren't we? What happened in Bangkok? Why is it coming back to bite you now?"

He stares at her, waiting for an answer.

She is sucking on her bottom lip.

"All right, Tuki. Don't tell me. I'll get the story from that Thai detective when I call him tonight. He seems like a big fan of yours. Called you the dragon ho. In fact, I can't quite figure out why he cares to warn us that you are in danger."

Suddenly tears are rolling down her cheeks. She is wiping her eyes with her hands.

It is an instinct. He wades out to her and hugs her. He hugs her the way he hugs Filipa when she cries. He lets himself mold around her, the way his mother taught him.

After a long time she says she met Prem Kittikatchorn in the Patpong. It is a long story. But she can start it for him if it is important. *Khwan pha sak.* Sometimes you have to call a snake a snake.

*One night after a show, a chauffeur in a baby-blue suit knocks on the stage door that leads from the dressing room right into the street. He asks for Tuki, presents her with a dozen flaming tulips and a note written in big smooth looping English words.*

Dear Miss Aparecio:

I would be most deeply honored if you would join me for dinner at the barbecue on the terrace of the Oriental Hotel tomorrow evening. I have no illusions about your gender. But please do not think of me as one of those foul men who hoot and whistle at you or make you indecent proposals. Mine is not a hasty or lewd offer. Since I first heard you sing two weeks ago, I have thought of little else but the sound of your song. If your mind is as clear as your voice, and your heart as rich as your music, as I think they are, then you will know with what deep sincerity and hope I write these words.

If you are agreeable to my proposal, please tell Pon where and when we can collect you tomorrow for dinner.

Most Sincerely,

Prem Kittikatchorn

*The Oriental. Many times she has heard that this hotel is the most glamorous hotel in all the world. And most of her life she has passed by the riverside deck of the Oriental on her way to the water taxi landing, dreamed of eating cold crab and grilled steak among all of those rich and beautiful people. But she is not accepting ... even though she feels the truth and sincerity in this man's offer.*

*She tells the chauffeur in Thai, who is standing at attention all the time she is reading—and re-reading—Prem's note, that she is very honored by the gentleman's request. But she does not even know whether the fellow writing this letter is a prince or a frog. And he should understand that she must be introduced before she could consider such a request.*

*He bows and strides back to the dark blue Mercedes limo. Pon opens the back door of the limo and says a few words to someone inside. Then she sees a tall, thin man in a cream-colored suit step out of the car. He is in his early twenties, with fine features, black hair slicked back from his forehead. His eyes twinkle in the streetlights even from this distance. As he walks slowly up the street toward her, she hears the click of his shoes on the pavement and sees a sad little smile on his face ... like the look of a sick child coming to take his medicine against his will.*

# TWENTY-TWO

*Everything seems to be happening in a great rush—but the world is in slow motion at the same time. It is a Monday, the quietest night in the Patpong. And even quieter tonight because Bangkok is in the lull of early December, a couple of days after all the craziness of the King's birthday celebration when the Patpong was filled with crowds. This Monday is the calm after the storm, one of the only nights when a showgirl can get some time off. It is the dry season. For a change, the air feels almost fresh in Bangkok. The sun stays up until nearly nine at night. Tuk-tuks drone through the streets.*

*He is coming at eight because she tells him she wants to watch the sun set over the river as they eat on the terrace at the Oriental. It is seven forty-five and she is wandering around the little fourth-floor apartment in a silk slip.*

*"You very crazy crazy girl, la!" says Brandy. "Dinner at Oriental!"*

*She shakes her head like this is something impossible for a Patpong queen.*

*"Help me with my hair."*

*"Oh, now she such big shot she give us orders, too!" says Delta rolling her eyes. "She think she got a rich boy on kite string."*

*"Pa- leeeease!"*

*Tuki is not much more than a kid. This is her first real date. Dinner with a man who looks like a tall, thin lion.*

*"This no good!" says Delta. "This boy just want take advantage."*

*"I think we go, too. Chaperones, la!"*

*Oh, dear Buddha, she thinks, why did I ever tell my mothers about this date. I could have just said I was taking a night off to go to the movies.*

*"You not ready for this! You just baby." Brandy grabs her comb and shakes it in Tuki's face.*

*She grabs her own comb and shakes it right back at her. Then* she unloads. How stupid do they think she is? Do they think she can live here in the most famous meat market in the world for just about all her life and still be just a baby? Do they think she can strip to a G-string six nights a week in front of crowds of drooling men and not know what drives them wild, what crazy and terrible things they can do when they are following orders from the hard little general between their legs?

Do her mothers think she has had her eyes closed when the live sex acts were onstage in some of the sleazier clubs where they used to work? Does she not see when the bar queens go down on someone in the dark corners of a club? Does she never hear the squeals of the hoes putting out in the lala rooms down the hall from her dressing room? Do Brandy and Delta think she really believes them when they come home from "dates" bruised or bloody or crying, saying they got mugged by someone on the streets? Does she not hear the cries of the young girls and little queens who have been "bonded" to the Patpong pimps? Is she not there when a dozen queens and whores they know whither away and die from AIDS? Was it some other Tuki who saw the body of Ingrid's mother seeping blood all over the barroom floor?

"I swim in this water, la!"

"You know only pictures," says Delta.

"You not know how a man can feel in your heart or in your body." Brandy shakes her comb. So you know nothing at all. Men like pung chao—like heroin, la. They always make feel good at first—"

"Trust me," says Tuki.

"What else we do? We know you going? Girls always go."

"Right. Khi mai ma hom. New shit smells sweet to the dog."

Brandy arches her eyebrow and gives a sly smile like Eddie Murphy in drag.

"Where we get such crazy girl?!"

"Courtesy of one sexy little Saigon bar ho." Tuki smiles. She pictures her mother, and suddenly she knows exactly what she is going to put on for this date.

She makes Prem wait down on the street in the limo for fifteen minutes before she steps out into the street wearing a long gold *shantung silk sheath with a Nehru collar. Pumps to match. Hair up off her neck in a French roll.*

*Pon stands waiting in his powder-blue livery alongside the Benz. When he opens the back door she hears Lionel Richie singing "Stuck on You" over the sound system. There in the shadows of the car is her tall, thin lion in a tan suit and denim button-down shirt open at the neck. His hand shakes as he reaches out to grab hers. For a second, she thinks he is going to kiss her hand like a prince in an old movie. But when she catches his eyes to give him permission, he quickly drops his gaze and guides her onto the seat beside him.*

*"I ... I must be dreaming." He stutters in very royal-sounding English as if he is talking to himself. "You look so lovely. Your presence is a great honor," he adds in Thai.*

*There is a little sweat on his forehead. So she is already thinking that this man is more or less at her mercy. Even so, she is blushing and staring at her knees.*

*"You really like Lionel Richie, la?"*

*"All night long," he says, echoing the title of one of Lionel's classics. Now she can really see those dark eyes as he smiles.*

*He offers her a glass of the white French wine he is drinking, but she sticks with Perrier. Prem is telling her that he has been totally addicted to Lionel since the days when his father sent him to a military high school in America to shape up, learn English, and be a man. He used to make his own mixes of Lionel's songs instead of doing his homework.*

*He says except for all the money and nice things he has, his life is hell. He is the only son among older daughters. The child of a man who owns a company that makes sleeping pills and ships them all over the world. A man who used to be high up in the Thai Navy. A man who calls his only son an art fag. His mother, he says, is easier. She collects. She is on the board of Bangkok's museums, one in New York, too. Prem went to college there. He studied filmmaking. He says his father cannot understand why he spent his time in college working on music videos with a whole zoo full of Greenwich Village fairies.*

*But Prem does not care. One of these days he is going to get his trust fund, be independent. Then he is going to tell his father where he* can go, start making music videos and other films in Bangkok. Like, goodbye, Father. But first, after all of those years in school and all the stinking plaa he has put up with from his father, he is going to suck up a little of the good life. He thinks he deserves to give himself a little vacation at Daddy's expense. And it is starting tonight.

"Ya ching suk kon ham," *Tuki mumbles. Early ripe, early rotten.*

*He gives a sad little smile like maybe he agrees. But then he laughs, raises his glass of wine in a toast, and says, "To the good life!"*

*It is the first time she ever hears this expression. Thinks, give Tuki some of that!*

## TWENTY-THREE

"So now he's here?" He thinks he has asked this question before but got no answer from her.

"He came. He is gone."

"When?"

"Two weeks ago, maybe. I don't know, la."

"But before the fire, obviously. You were walking with him early on the night when—"

"Three days before the fire. I thought I saw him out there in the audience. I told myself it cannot be. How did he find me here after all of these years? I wanted to die."

"I don't understand."

She looks around her. They are at lunch in a fancy West End restaurant called the Red Inn. After the beach, they changed into dry, clean clothes back at his Jeep. Tuki adjusts the new pink jersey shirt she's wearing. She can still feel the salt left from the waves scratching at her body. Michael is back in his white shirt and gray suit, ever the young attorney at law.

"I think he has come to settle some old business."

"What happened?"

"Not important. That is very old news. Just something, la. Okay?"

He grits his teeth. She is doing it again. Holding back. Like his cousin Alicia did after the night he ran into her at a high school keg party with a ring of love bites around her neck.

"Did you see him after the show?"

She shakes her head no.

"The next day. Ruby came to me in the morning saying my boyfriend from Bangkok was in town. Alby had seen him. It seemed impossible to me that he had found me, that he had come all this way for me. I thought maybe Alby was lying to Ruby ... or she had things mixed up. It could not be true. Prem could not be here ..."

*She feels scared. She does not want to be alone. So right after her morning rehearsal, she heads to the Slip for sunlight, breezes, and lots of company. She has been there for maybe an hour when she hears a soft, shaky voice saying her name. She opens her eyes, sees a silhouette standing over her in a white bathing suit. She squints, stares to see him against the bright sunlight. It is him, her one and only cowardly lion. Live in the flesh, after more than five years.*

*"Do you mind if I sit down," he asks like they are strangers. He nods at a vacant chaise next to her, "Or are you with someone?"*

*"Without someone," she smiles. Then she remembers Alby. "At the moment!"*

*He says maybe he should just leave her in peace.*

*Yes, please just do that, she thinks, because she has been on one crazy ride with men in general, and him in particular.*

*She stares out at the bay where the water is a deep blue.*

*He says he is sorry. He has come a long way. He just wants to see how she is getting along.*

*"Now you see," she says in this totally neutral voice. Then she lies back in her chaise and closes her eyes. She can feel his eyes on her.*

*He says that he has started working again. He thinks they should talk about a movie project he has in mind that would involve her. He wants to make a serious film about the queens in the Patpong. He wants her to come back to Bangkok to do it.*

*"I will make you a deal," she hears her voice saying, and is already regretting her words for about a thousand reasons. "Maybe you understand why I am still feeling more than a little hurt, and I will try forgetting about how you just stopped calling me. I will try not remembering how you, your* pung chao, *and your nonsense about always and forever danced on my heart and rubbed my soul in the mud. And ... and ... then the River House—"*

*"Forget about the house. It is not important," he says. "Look, Tuki. I have been a fool. My father made me stop. My mother said he would disown me, turn me out on the streets. I still loved you. I always—"*

"No," she almost shouts, "you cannot do this!"

Then she closes her eyes and covers her ears and counts to about fifty in Vietnamese, which is not easy for her. When she opens her eyes, her mind is telling the rest of her that they have no past with this man. They have no interest in this coward. What they think they remember is just a sad movie with people who look like them.

"I never knew you," she says. "Okay? I have a new life now, la. An important boyfriend and boss. He will send you back to Thailand in a body bag if he finds you here."

He says he knows. He rubs his ribs as if they are sore.

For a second he looks like he is going to cry, but he does not. The more she thinks about the film project he is describing, the more she thinks exploitation. And cheating heart, too. Now that the blush is off his marriage, rich boy, big-shot film director wants to walk on the wild side again. He is thinking a film project is maybe just the bait he needs to hook into her heart again.

"So, where are the wife and kids?" she asks. She think this shot to the chest will send him running ... and she will soon be chilling in solitude once again, free of any illusions about a film he will never really make.

He says they have rented a place on the beach at Phuket. His marriage is a big mess. He walked out last month.

"That's not my problem!"

The man looks beaten. But he is not standing up and walking away from her tongue. So maybe he really is not here for revenge. Maybe it is not a mistake to give a care again, she thinks. Especially because she suddenly gets this strong sense of pain from him as she drowns in his black eyes.

"She does not know about you? She thinks you are straight?"

He shakes his head, right. And she knows he is trying to tell her marriage and kids have not settled his restless heart. He feels locked in a golden closet, afraid of what will happen if he tries to break out again.

"Oh, la," she sighs. "You need a big shot of courage."

He gives her a sad smile. She cannot help herself. She just slides over onto his chaise and hugs him. Fifteen minutes go by before he comes *out of his daze, shakes his head, asks, "Will you come back to me?" He sounds so sad, so sincere. She does not yet know he is already stirring up a whole pot of trouble with Alby.*

"Do the police know about all of this?" asks Michael.

"No. It is no matter now. Leave him out of this. You find the real killer. Prem is gone. This time maybe forever."

# TWENTY-FOUR

*She should remember every detail of her first dinner on the river terrace at the Oriental, but she does not. All she recalls is the heaviness of the water glasses, more forks than she can use, the waiters in white jackets, tables full of farangs glittering with real diamonds, the sounds of a string quartet, the smell of grilled shrimp, a sunset swirling with violet in a sea of crushed roses. Mostly what she remembers are Prem's big dark eyes taking in every inch of her, like she is the rarest angel in all of Bangkok. She thinks about the lime scent of his cologne and how she might take a bite of that long, hard neck and feast on his golden skin.*

*He says that until he sees her at the Underground, he has been lonely since he has come home to Bangkok. He has spent the last ten years in America and Europe. He misses New York. The long nights, the Village, the clubs, the outrageous queens. The laughter of gay couples on Christopher Street. The crazy bums in Washington Square. And other things, like the subway musicians and the street-front restaurants of Little Italy, Chinatown. He finds himself coming to the Patpong to look for the things he misses in New York. He does not mention the drugs. Not yet.*

*The next thing she knows, dinner is over. Prem is holding her hand like it is a jewel, begging her to not let the night end here. He is asking her to go for a ride with him up the river and look at the lights of the city.*

*She loves the river, so they hire a water taxi and ride for hours. They go so far up the river they go beyond the Krungthon Bridge. Then they come back down to the Royal barge sheds where the boatman stops and shines a light so they can see the golden dragon heads on the King's barges. They detour through all of the klongs in Thonburi, watch the charcoal fires going out, and the windows turning black in the stilt houses built out over the water. All this*

*time Prem is asking her how such an exotic flower as Tuki Aparecio
came to be in his city.*

*She wants to lie. She thinks he wants her to be something more
than a common little Patpong* luk sod. *She is still scared that he only
loves her illusion, that he is too straight for anything but dinner with
a girl like her. She wants to make up a story about being the child of
wealthy Vietnamese movie stars who the communists murdered. She
wants to say Tuki is the survivor of the Killing Fields, the adopted foster
child of a jade merchant ... who tried to rape her when she was thirteen,
so she ran away to the Patpong to do what is in her blood—sing and
dance and ...*

*But she cannot lie, and she cannot admit the truth. So what she
does is nuzzle her head deeper into the shoulder of his suit jacket. She
says, "Kiss me."*

*He hesitates. Then he pulls his head back and looks at her with
those black eyes that are soft and full of a thousand questions.*

*She feels a rush of panic stiffen his body, and now she is wishing
that she had listened to Brandy and Delta and never come out with
this man. She closes her eyes and braces herself for whatever is coming ...
maybe a defeated little sigh or a look of disgust or the sting when he hits
her, tells her to swim home with the rest of the river rats.*

*But then she feels his breath on her cheek and his thin lips brush
against hers.*

*Does she remember her first real kiss? Does she remember the
lightning bolt of electricity that stings her lips and tongue, races to
the tips of her fingers and toes, and finally settles into a low buzzing
between her legs? Does she remember thinking that she is suddenly
born again, and the past is nothing more than a handful of dry rice
scattering before the winds of a typhoon? She remembers every detail.
She still remembers how it felt to have the most beautiful young lion in
the world glued to her lips ... in her twenty-first year ... on that river in
the city of angels. The colored spotlights blazing on the towering prang
of the Wat Arun, the Temple of the Dawn. With Lionel Richie singing
"All Night Long" in her head.*

*And she knows how it feels to discover that by stepping into that river taxi with a young lion, she has cut herself free from her family. Whatever happens now—whether she is wounded or killed or becomes a movie star—it is only her business. No one else will know what she knows now. After this kiss she wants to cry and sing!*

# TWENTY-FIVE

He is down at the fish pier in Chatham watching the long-line boys and the lobstermen unloading their catches at suppertime. He knows how hard their life is, knows the sorrow, shame, frustration of coming home with an empty hold, a busted trip. But he misses it, wonders where his father and Tio Tommy are right now in the *Rosa Lee*.

It has to be better than this mess he is in. He started today with high hopes that he might make some progress toward unraveling his client's secrets, finding some alternate suspects, picturing his defense strategy. But now he is more confused than ever. This ex-boyfriend, this Prem Kittikatchorn, sounds like just the kind of obsessed son of a bitch who might do anything—like burn and murder—to make her his again. A stalker. Why is she still defending him? Is she still carrying a torch for the guy? And what's with the passing allusions to heroin? Is there some kind of narcotics trade going on here? Another thing. This lying by omission is virtually pathological.

So he is thinking that he has to start talking to people other than his client. He is starting to psych himself up to call Varat Samset tonight, when he feels an arm curl around his back.

"Hey, sailor. Looking for a good time?"

It is Filipa. He feels her soft, large breasts slide against his rib cage as she pulls him against her. He loves the way she feels. He cups the back of her head in his hand, draws her lips to his, probes for her tongue.

"Wow! You want to go for it right here, big boy?"

"I'm thinking the beach." He is already feeling out of breath, kissing her again. One hand on her butt cheek. He can tell she is not wearing any panties. The fishermen are starting to notice the show, watching when she breaks the lip lock.

"Take me to bed, or lose me forever." It is Meg Ryan's line from *Top Gun* that he has always loved.

"You don't have to ask twice." He is thinking that there is nothing better than frisky sex to pull him out of his funk. Screw the case. Screw the dragon ho. Screw the stalker. Screw the call to Bangkok.

They clamber down a trail to a narrow beach in front of the swank cottages of Chatham Bars Inn. It is still hot. The mid-eighties. The water looks like a field of golden leaves in the evening sun. He peels off his jacket and shirt, throws them on top of a thicket of beach plums. She clamps him in a bear hug, feels for him with her right hand. Sweat is soaking through the back of her green cotton shift. He drops to the sand and pulls her on top of him. Ten seconds and he is in her. She is riding high. Her eyes close. Head tilts back, rolling on her neck to the rhythm of their lust.

"Jesus Lord, forgive me," she chants. "Holy Mary Mother of God, I love this!"

He closes his eyes, too. Thinks he can do this until the sun sets, pulls her hand to his mouth and sucks her fingers one by one.

"G-g-g-goddamn it. H-h-h-have you no shame?!" A man's voice rips him from a dream of dolphins swimming belly to belly.

He feels Filipa freeze.

His eyes pop open.

"What?"

A fat, balding fisherman is shouting at them from up on the fish pier.

"T-t-t-take it indoors, will ya?!"

Filipa rises up on her knees: "Eat your heart out!"

She lowers herself back onto her man. Bends down over him until her hair covers his face, blots out the sun.


*She does not give up this balance. She does not take her lover beyond a thousand new kisses, nine hundred moans, until five more dinners at the Oriental go by ... with five more rides on the river in the dark.*

*Tonight, another Monday, everything happens very fast. The water taxi turns down one of the* klongs *in Thonburi near the Royal barge sheds, and stops at a house that looks like a small temple, peaked* roofs of grey teak with a large deck on stilts out over the klong. There are red and green dragons carved into the woodwork like they live here.

"Welcome to the River House," he says.

He takes her hand and leads her out of the boat. She has to carry her pumps in her other hand so she can climb the steps up to the deck. She hears the growl of the water taxi's engine. Then it is gone. All she can hear are the songs of tree frogs and the hush of the currents around the stilts, along the banks. This is his family's oldest house. His great grandfather built it to catch the breezes off the river and get away from the cholera raging in town during the wet season, back in the days when Thonburi was little more than a jungle.

He says he loves the view of the Royal Palace and the wats from here, glowing like the Emerald City across the water. Then he opens about ten screen doors that expose the whole house's face to the klong and the river beyond. There are cushions like a big bed at one end of the deck way out over the klong. She knows she can make love here. And she will. She just needs a little help because this is her first time.

She stretches out on the cushions and waits while he brings the ritual wine and lights a fire, like an offering to the Buddha, in the charcoal brazier. In the flickering flames she undresses him, eats his soft flesh. It trembles to her lips. There is absolutely no talking. And this is how it has to be because she is surprised beyond words at her own boldness.

When he is a burning torch, he struggles with her dress. She hears something tear. They both laugh. She takes off her bra so he can taste the new fullness of her breasts fresh from Dow-Corning and the reconstructive surgical offices of Doctor Maa.

While her eyes are closed, he peels away the rest of her clothes. His hands skate over her skin with smooth, warm oil while she lies flat on her belly, feeling the oil spreading over the backs of her thighs. Then she opens her eyes to see flames of light shooting off the river as he curls around her back and makes love to her until he locks her in the pain. And then they melt together in the pleasure.

He says that he loves her, he will always love her, cherish her, protect her, buy her pretty things.

Over fish and chips at the bar in the Chatham Squire, Filipa wants to talk about where they are going to live after the wedding.

"I'm thinking the North End." She is talking about Boston. "Don't you just love it? It's like Italy. Ethnic. Mediterranean like us, right?"

He courted her in the restaurants along Hanover Street, proposed to her one night in a bistro facing North Square. The North End definitely has romance, and the harbor is right there when you need a boat fix. She would be close to Cambridge and her internship. Perfect, right?

"How would I get to work, Fil? It's sixty miles back down to the Cape and the traffic can be—"

"You'll have the reverse commute. It won't take you more than an hour, hour and a half tops. I'm making the drive now. All the way out here to Chatham. Do you hear me complaining?"

"Yeah ..."

"Well, come on, Michael, I'm here aren't I? I didn't hear you protesting on the beach an hour ago."

He cannot believe how fast she has turned on him. This wedding is starting to wig her out. Or is it him? What can he say? Driving two hours after work a couple of times a week to make love is a little different than schlepping off at rush hour five mornings a week. Starting off in snarled city traffic.

"Hey, maybe we don't need to talk about ..."

She bites her lower lip, looks like she is about to cry. "Do you realize that we will be married in less than a month? And we don't have a place to live? Do think we're going to shack up in that attic or with my crazy roommate? Don't you know that I get a call almost every day from my mother? People want to know whether we are going for a house or an apartment, big or small. It matters. They have to buy gifts to fit."

The bartender hears the rising tone in her voice, catches Michael's eye, and shakes his finger, a warning: Women, man, handle with care.

"Hey, hey, Fil ... I know we can work this out. I just need a few more days to get my head around this case of mine. Then we can call some realtors and—"

"And what, Michael?" Her voice suddenly sounds shrill. "Tell them you've been so busy hanging out in Provincetown with the drag queens that you haven't had time to figure out where you're going to start a home with your new wife? Is that it? Is that how you want to start our life together?"

Jesus, she can be fierce.

"Can we please not get into this. It's my first solo murder case. I'm a little overwhelmed. My client, she—"

"She?! What the hell are you talking about 'she'? Michael, your client has a dick. Have you forgotten? You know what they call someone like your client in Portugal and Spain? A *travesti*. Travesty. A freak. And yours happens to be an arsonist, a murderer, and a whore to boot."

Her voice is louder. People at the bar are looking at them now.

He feels something burning behind his eyes, like a faded brown photograph of a boy in a man's suit, with his dark, curly hair tied back in a ponytail. He takes a long gulp from his beer mug and hears the whine of jets. Suddenly, he wants to shout, My god, we are talking about a human being here. A life is at stake.

But what he says is, "Maybe I should just shoot myself!"

She looks at him as if she has never seen this strange side of him before. "Look. I'm sorry. I just want to be with you. Forget about your case for a while. Can you do that?"

## TWENTY-SIX

For two days they shop for apartments in Boston's North End and make love. He thinks Filipa is right. He needs to get off the Cape and just plain forget about work for a while. They rent a cozy one-bedroom walk-up, right down the street from Paul Revere's house. It seems like an oasis away from the carnival of Provincetown, the loneliness of Chatham. Even though they won't be moving in until September, just knowing the apartment is there lightens his mood.

But now it is Friday. The week has rushed by, and he feels the case nagging at him. The trial starts in a little more than three weeks and he still doesn't have a suspect list. On the drive back down to the Cape from Boston, he calls Tuki to see if she is okay. But he gets her voice mail.

He wants to talk to the Thai detective about the stalker, Prem Whoever, but once again the time is wrong. Afternoon. The best he can do to break through Tuki's veil of mystery is to head for P-town, track down some of her acquaintances, hope somebody feels like talking straight.

A friendly cop at the desk in the P-town station tells him to check out a bar called the Last Tango on Commercial Street. Ask for Chivas. She pals around with Tuki a bit.

Inside, the Tango looks like a dark little cave. His eyes are blinking as he tries to adjust them from the bright sun of the street, and he is staring at the outline of what might be a creature from *Star Wars* standing behind the bar. Otherwise the place is empty.

"Take a good look, honey," she spits. "I don't bite!"

Now the figure is coming into focus. She is posing for him with a hand cocked behind her head like a forties pin up girl. A plump, red headed, cartoon version of Bette Midler. Complete with river-green eye shadow, lashes like Betty Boop, rouge all over the cheeks, flame lipstick. A pink halter top is holding up breasts like melons. Below the waist, billowing green pantaloons. By the looks of the wrinkles around her mouth, she must be in her mid-sixties. The drag queen from hell.

"Hey, good lookin'. Is that a rocket in your pocket or are you just happy to see me?" It's a tired old Mae West line. He knows this. But it kind of catches him off guard, and he laughs.

She pulls a bottle of scotch out of the well, sets it on the bar with two shot glasses.

"Tell me your troubles, partner."

He laughs again. The scene is so absurd. And it is like she is reading his mind. Something soft in her eyes catches him, and he sits down.

By the time they finish their shots, he has barely said a word. But he feels like he has known her half his life. Her name is Chivas Regal, and she has been a queen in P-town since the fifties. She starred in the Follies back in the days of legend when the police raided the place about once every two weeks, arresting her for female impersonation.

"In my day I did Marilyn Monroe and Liz Taylor. Lip-synched to 78 rpm records and reel-to-reel tapes," she says in a voice that sounds like Lucky Strikes. "But I was best at Ginger Rogers. Honey, Ginger could have taken lessons from me in how to turn up the body heat in an audience. And those were the days before silicone, hormone shots, and sex changes. God, we didn't even have decent wigs. We made tits out of old socks. But we had fun. We packed them in ... and there was never a shortage of creamy young boys like you.

"Then I met Harry, and our lives took a turn for the moon. At first he fished on the day boats sailing for cod and flounder, but eventually he got a job tending bar in a C Street dive. From time to time, I came in and did a routine for the crowd. My drag show became a regular thing during the more liberal sixties and seventies. The money was okay, but it was time to look for a new career because I was not getting any younger. Harry and I took out a loan, bought the dive, named it the Last Tango. We started our own little drag club with me acting as hostess. Mondays and Tuesdays were amateur nights, which were a big hit because there was no cover and you never knew when a girl was going to trip in her heels or lose a falsie or a wig.

"These days we get all kinds," she smiles. "Vampires, Joan of Arc types with nothing but a floor-length wig to cover their birthday suits, the Queen of England, as well as Natassia Kinski wannabees with boa constrictors that have a tendency to get loose in the house. Recently, we have been getting a queen with a little goatee doing Hillary Clinton in a gold lamé bathing suit. And a seventy-year-old retired Air Force colonel from Truro who comes in once a month dressed as Tootsie and offers all takers a free ride.

"But this may be my last season. Life at the Tango has not been the same since the day two years ago when Harry died of lung cancer. I am looking for someone to manage the club full time, with an option to buy.

"Then, dearie, I can move away from this windswept little sand spit and head on down to Rio, as in de Janeiro, and *fiesta forever*!"

With this remark she stands, does a little rumba across the room with a pet Persian bobbing in her arms like a stuffed fox. She winks at him, "You can take an old queen out of the drag, but you cannot take the drag out of an old queen."

She is definitely not sulking. Neither is he. What does he really have to complain about? How does a slightly twitchy fiancée and a murder case out of the tabloids compare to what Chivas has been through? And she is still dancing. He can see why Tuki might be drawn to this person.

"So you want to lock the door and get down and dirty? Or you want to tell me how you had the good fortune to become Tuki's lawyer?"

He is floored. "How did you know ..."

She taps the side of her head with an index finger. "Eyes like an eagle, mind like a steel trap, heart of a fairy godmother. Just like you, Tuki came to me when she was at her wit's end and needed to talk. You want to know if I think she did it?"

He nods.

"Hell no! It's a total put-up job. That girl ..." Something seems to catch in her throat. "That girl's one in a million. Heart of gold. Absolute soft gold. You hear me, Mr. Attorney?"

"It's Michael."

"Okay, Michael. You came to the right place if you want the straight dope. You think she's lying to you? Trust me. It is not that she wants to mislead you. She's just trying to protect her heart. The child has not had the easiest life, you know. You have to help her."

"How? Almost everything she tells me seems to have a backstory that she only lets out by accident, by offhand remarks. You know what I mean?"

"Like her relationship with that motherfuckin' Big Al?"

The force of these words almost knocks him off his stool. He really wants to talk about the stalker Prem, and Bangkok. But okay, start with the victim.

Chivas pours them both another glass of scotch.

"I suppose she's let you think Alby adored her. Treated her like royalty right up 'til all the bad shit about Silver and the stolen DVDs, the weird Vietnamese knife? And everything else that went down in the day or two before the fire, right?"

He nods. "Well, sort of. I can tell there is something off there. Something I don't know."

"You bet your bippy. I swear to you on a collection of my favorite show tunes she didn't kill him. But who could blame her if she did? Big Al Costelano was the worst of the bottom feeders in this burg. Good riddance to bad garbage, I say. That bastard tried to make a whore out of her. Did you know that?"

"The police reports mention the escort service."

Chivas jumps off her barstool with the slap of her pumps on the hardwood.

"Fuck the police! Pardon my French, dear. They have no idea what Alby did to her, how the Sisterhood worked. I bet you don't know a thing about her trip to Montreal, do you? Ever heard of the Mile-High Club?"

*Every night she sees her lion's face mooning at her through the spotlights and smoke at the Underground, looking like someone just ripped out his heart. And every time she sees those high cheeks and sad eyes, she feels tiny little fish swimming through her veins. More than once during the shows, she catches him looking at her, feels the fish scatter, misses beats, and—twice—a whole verse in her songs.*

*The crowd groans.*

*"We got big trouble, la," says Delta in the dressing room after this happens about three nights in a row. "She make lala with rich boy. He screw every song right out her mind. What we do now?"*

*"She big girl; all grown up," says Brandy, like Tuki is not in the room to talk to ... just for spitting on. "No more little princess. No song, no dance. Just cheap bar ho. Better get her good pimp and little lala room to do her business. Rich boy be gone like Saigon days when she no fresh."*

*She feels a storm exploding in her throat. "You have no idea!" she shouts. "He adores ..."*

*Then, before those nosy, old queens can see her tears, she is out the stage door into the alley, still dressed like Tina Turner in a silver mini and knee boots.*

# TWENTY-SEVEN

*The summer is in full heat this Tuesday after July Fourth weekend. Tuki is just starting to rake in some serious money at the Follies.*

*She is chilling in her little bungalow in Truro, partying a bit with the gang that Alby and Ruby invite to Shangri-La on the weekends, having an occasional night of dinner and sex with the Great One. No pressure, no commitment. Just amazing dates. She has not yet figured out that she is Alby's side dish. That Silver lives in the Glass House with him most of the time. That he has invested well over a quarter of a million in promoting Silver's TV and film career in New York. He owns the Chelsea loft she lives in during the winter. And a lot of the money that pays the big bills comes from the Sisterhood, extortion, and a collection of other shady deals.*

*Tonight she is expecting another romantic date after the show with Alby. Maybe something like the last one when he took her out overnight to watch whales on the motor yacht of a record producer from Long Island.*

*The limo shows up for her at ten forty-five, after the other girls have gone from the Follies for the night. Which is cool. She is a little embarrassed about what she has gotten herself into with the Big Guy. And she is a little nervous because she does not want Nikki to see her borrowing a hot-date suit she finds among Nikki's costumes at the Follies. Black, lace-trim crepe. A total mixed message to blow Alby's mind with a power jacket over a slip dress. She goes with tiny gold hoops in the ears, a subtle touch of white shadow, liner. Cinnamon on the lips and nails. Her hair is pulled back in a simple silver barrette. Then she takes a deep breath and grabs four condoms from Nikki's makeup bag.*

*The black limo driver named Justin gives her a twice over, whistles, and says, "Go, girl."*

*So when he opens the door, her body is all perky, tingly feeling. She sees a dark figure waiting inside with a dozen black roses in his hand.*

*But the flower boy is not Alby. He is a guy from Long Island. Alby's friend. A guy who everyone calls Joey. He is telling her that something came up at the very last minute. Alby had to leave for Boston.*

*"He wanted to tell you himself how sorry he is ... but you were on the stage when he had to leave. He did not want you to be disappointed, so he asked me to show you a very special evening."*

*She has been set up. She knows it. The Sisterhood is finally sinking its claws into her. She feels a fool, a soh phehnii—a complete ho. All she wants to do is cry because who else can she blame but herself?*

*She knows what Alby expects. Here comes payback time. An escort job. She played, now she pays. But this tubby little record producer does not worry her. She has seen him in action on the yacht. He just wants to show off his money, have a pretty face laugh at his jokes and smile into his eyes.*

*She takes a deep breath, then busts a smile, and says the night is young. She feels like dancing. No emotion here. She is a grown-up girl. Tonight is strictly business. Like maybe it is time for the Great One to get a new perspective on who's zooming who?*

*He was thinking Montreal, he says. The jet is ready to go.*

*She tries to act unimpressed, says she is very hungry. Can they pick up dinner to go? Chilled lobster tails.*

*So that is how it is. Justin makes a phone call, they stop by the Lobster Pot, then head off to the airport with seafood takeout.*

*She knows that she is out of her league here. The only airplane she has been on before tonight was the China Airlines 747 that took her from Bangkok to New York more than five years ago. So she is surprised by the little rocket that they climb aboard at the airport. The plane is so small you have to bend over to walk around. And there is nowhere to go anyway. They sit on a couch at the back of the cabin. Everything you need—a fridge, a table, a microwave, CD player, and TV/DVD player—surrounds them. It is like they are in just another limo with the pilot in his own place up front.*

*After the pilot closes and locks the cabin door, Joey asks her if she is afraid of flying.*

*She rolls here eyes. Like dream on. She flies every night onstage.*

*The next thing she knows, she is strapped in just to the right of the pilot with her own set of controls, earphones, and a mike on her head like Janet Jackson in one of her dance numbers. The cockpit is dark and glowing with little green dials, and they are rolling out to the runway. She sees the runway lights line up in front of the plane. The pilot asks if she is ready. A second later she is pinned pack in her seat staring at the stars.*

*When things calm down, she goes back to the couch. They feast at a little table all laid out with linen and silver and crystal goblets. Perrier and a pitcher of daiquiris sit in the center. The lights are dialed down low and Natalie Cole is on the stereo, singing about love on her mind.*

*She decides that under the circumstances, a little alcohol may not hurt, so—ever so cautiously—she sips two or three rum and lime concoctions while working her way through the lobster tail and asparagus tips. Now, Joey is starting to look a little studly with his dinner jacket thrown aside, bow tie hanging lose around his collar, and some funky, red suspenders curving around his belly. It crosses her mind that maybe she should give the folks back in P-town something to talk about.*

*He must be thinking the same thing, because they are only a few minutes into watching a Tina Turner video before his tongue is in her mouth. His hands are all over her breasts, and he is whispering about something called the Mile-High Club.*

*She tells him to shut up and kiss her. Joey comes through in spades with a serpent's tongue and musky cologne.*

*Things are moving along nicely until a little bell goes off somewhere in the cabin.*

*"What is that?"*

*"Nothing to worry about, love," he whispers. "Just the signal that we will be landing in Montreal in about twenty minutes."*

*They get down to more face.*

*But suddenly, without any warning, he just unzips his fly, pulls out his big red* chaang. *Pushes her head toward his lap.*

*What makes him think she wants any part of this scene? Not her hands, nor her mouth, have ventured anywhere close to his private parts. This ride in the dark is only about giving her body a little lobster, her weekly quota of face, and maybe causing a little envy with Alby.*

*"Do me," she hears his voice say. And it seems far away.*

*She is not believing this.*

*"I'm fucking bursting. Do me."*

Oral sex is the stock in trade of drag queens for some pretty obvious reasons. Heading south on a guy is hardly a new adventure. But at the moment the whole concept makes her sick to her stomach.

She tries to pull away. But she cannot move.

His pudgy hands pinch her neck and shoulder. He presses her face toward his lap, holds her eye to eye with the elephant.

"Do me, bitch."

"Please, no!"

She tries to jab her left elbow into his ribs. He grunts, lets go. For a second her head is up and free. She catches a glimpse of moonshine on the clouds through the window.

But an instant later he has her in a headlock, ramming her face toward his open pants again.

"Do me, for fuck's sake. Give me a million-dollar blow job to re-member."

Now she is calling herself ten ways a stupid little Patpong street sweeper because she drank his drinks and ignored the no-deep-kissing rule and generally let him think the wrong thing. But you know what? She did not ask for this. And no means "N-O."

Something is catching fire behind her eyes, and the next thing she knows, she is imagining herself saying, "Here is your million-dollar blow job, la—" right before she bites him and he screams for the love of Buddha.

But just as she is picturing blood spurting out of him like a fire in his crotch, she feels his breath against her ear.

"Don't let this get ugly. You know I really like you. Be a good girl now. Do me like you do Alby ... or I'll crush you like a bug. Just think of this as a business obligation. Something we do to please the boss. And since you joined the Sisterhood, that boss would be me. Because Alby owes me a bundle. So I give the goddamn orders now. Hear?!"

There is a click as he racks a pistol. When she opens her eyes, she is looking at his prick and a 9mm side-by-side in his hand ... so close they both are out of focus.

"I'm sure you know what to do next," he says. "And when you finish, we are going dancing in Montreal to celebrate our initiation into the Mile-High Club."

# TWENTY-EIGHT

He feels angry and shaky when he gets home. It is after dark in Chatham. There is a rotten taste in his mouth that he blames on the shots of scotch at the Tango. Now he rings Varat Samset with a mission fixed in his mind. While Samset fires out a barrage of Thai on the other end of the line, Michael is promising himself that he is going to get to the bottom of this case sooner rather than later. And he is not going to take any more shit from anybody. Tuki? God! A flower in the wasteland. She is surrounded by monsters.

"So you finally called back, counselor!" Samset is stealing the power already. "Feeling a little lost in a swamp with that *luk sod* shemale client of yours, are you?"

Michael cannot lie. He could use a little help here.

"Anybody start shooting, yet?"

"Jesus, no. You're kidding, right?"

The voice from Bangkok grunts. "I don't have time to make a joke, Mr. Decastro. I think you are dealing with a very explosive situation. Can you not see your client is very fragile? Very angry?"

"Not really. She seems a little giddy, a little in denial about her legal problems sometimes. Secretive. But she smiles a lot and—"

Another grunt. "You do not understand our culture in Southeast Asia, counselor. The more people in Thailand smile and make light of things, the more nervous we are. You understand that? A smile for us is not like a smile for you Americans. A smile is not always happy or content or delighted. Many times we smile when things are tearing us apart."

*Damn.* And he thought the Portuguese had cultural peculiarities. Like their fascination with *saudade,* that paralyzing form of nostalgia and regret that seeps from his grandmother's *fado* music.

"So what is tearing my client apart besides the possibility of spending the rest of her life behind bars for arson and murder?"

"Guilt and shame. We do not do well with these emotions."

"I don't understand."

"She obviously hasn't told you why she left Thailand."

"I'm reading between the lines. Something went wrong between her and this Prem guy?"

"That's putting it mildly, my American friend. He had a very sick and abusive relationship with your client. Then he dumped her. She raised what you call holy hell. Caused great embarrassment to a very important family in our country. Lot of problems for my office."

He is starting to get the picture. "Prem's family. She caused some kind of scandal. They put the screws on you to cover it up, is that what happened?"

"You are saying this, not me."

"What exactly did she do?"

"That's not for me to say. We do not make our suspicions public. Maybe you better ask Tuki. Your client left the country before we could find her, talk."

"So this Prem guy has come here to get even? After all these years?"

"That's what we think."

"He is stalking her because he's still in love with her, obsessed?"

"That too. It is a dangerous combination isn't it? Love, obsession, anger, shame?"

This does not sound like the gentle, sad, cowardly lion Tuki has been talking about. "How do you know he's dangerous?"

Samset grunts again. Seems to wish this American would just trust him.

"What aren't you telling me, detective?"

Another grunt.

"I am not at liberty to speak. Just accept what I am saying. We believe Kittikatchorn is in a dangerous way. Does everything have to be spelled out for you Americans? Just get your client back behind bars where she belongs before all hell breaks loose."

"Why? Are you trying to prevent another scandal? Are you feeling the heat from his family?" He does not say, "The ex-admiral, the pharmaceutical czar."

"I am trying to prevent more deaths."

"What?"

"Off the record. I am speaking off the record now, Mr. Decastro. You understand me?"

"Go ahead. Trust me."

"Prem Kittikatchorn's wife and children have been missing for a month. We think they are dead. We think he killed them and now he is coming after your client. And anybody who gets in his way. Okay, counselor? He left a note. For his mother. About his love for the *luk sod*, his hate for her, hate for himself. For the shame he has brought on himself and his family. His anger for being rejected for what he is, a man who loves the shemales. Does this get your attention?"

Michael feels his stomach drop. "*Cristo Salvador*!"

"Beg your pardon?"

"Nothing. What do I do?"

"I told you. Get your client back in jail where she belongs. Call me if you see Kittikatchorn. Duck if someone starts shooting. I would say you are in the line of fi—"

"I can't do that. I've got an obligation to ..."

A sigh from Bangkok. "Then you are on your own. I have done my job. It is your neck, after all."

He does not remember who hangs up first.

*Prem is waiting outside the club in his limo ... just as he has been every night. Just to see her one more time. He cannot get the smell of her perfume out of his nostrils. His eyes say he is helpless. He loves her. He will be her devoted admirer and protector. Forever.*

*When he sees her tears, he is out of the car, holding her. His long arms wrap around her like a soldier shielding her.*

*"What happened?"*

*She cannot answer. She does not know how to explain. She just cries.*

*Finally, she says she thinks maybe she needs to find a place to stay for a while. Brandy and Delta have told her that she is on her own if she persists with this liaison.*

*Not a problem, he says. But how about they start with a late dinner at the Oriental?*

*"I cannot wear these clothes."*

*"I know a little dress shop."*

*She kisses him on the mouth. Very long and very hard. She is telling him that maybe, yes, at this moment, she is falling in love with him.*

*This is the night she gets her first real string of pearls. This is also the night they make love to songs from the Beach Boys, drink his bottle of rice whiskey ... and move her into the River House. Prem speaks softly to her in Thai. He calls her his butterfly, his little Daughter of the Dark. She tells him of the silver beauty of his skin in the moonlight. And she calls him her River Lion, before he falls asleep in the big hammock with his head on her right breast.*

# TWENTY-NINE

It is almost midnight when she leaves the Follies. Another Friday of Mardi Gras in the Magic Queendom. Commercial Street is packed. But here in the alley, no one is around. It is another world, reeking of charred wood, cat piss, and beer puke. She is feeling, more than hearing, the heavy thump of bass speakers pulsing from the clubs when he steps out of the shadows.

"I just talked to Varat Samset."

She jumps, is not expecting to see him. "Who?"

"The detective from Bangkok. He says you're in danger. He says your old friend Prem has come here to kill you."

"What does he know? He is just trying to cover himself. He's feeling pressure in Bangkok from Prem's family—bring him home, keep him away from me. That is what they want. They are very powerful. They pull strings in Thailand, police jump. He is trying to scare you to do his dirty work, that is all!"

She is walking in quick strides from the stage door in the alley toward Commercial Street, where the yellow crime tape seals off the blocks of town leveled by the fire. She's looking up the street hoping for a sign of the cab she has already called to take her back to Shangri-La. There is a tight grin pasted on her mouth. He feels like a dog nipping at her heels.

"Come on, Tuki. I drove the whole way up here to make sure you were okay. The least you could do is stop and look at me."

She freezes, wheels, stares into his eyes. "You are a sweet man, Michael. An absolute prince. But sometimes you have no idea what you are dealing with."

He blushes a little. "That's what Samset said."

"So you see. This is the truth. You do not know—"

Something snaps in him. "I know his wife and children are missing. I know the police think he killed them. I know he left something like a suicide note. Do you know this?" So much for Samset's off-the-record confession.

Her faces grows pale. It cannot hold the smile that she has been trying to keep on her lips.

"Oh, la! This cannot be true. He has problems. But he is a very gentle man. And he has a big warm heart. Prem would not hurt a flea."

"Samset talked about your relationship."

Her eyes flash. "He knows nothing!"

Michael purses his lips, stares at his loafers. "He called it abusive."

She turns away. Bites her lip as she stares out into the debris field from the fire. A pair of front loaders have it heaped in a huge pile of wood and stone and pipes.

He knows she is having a memory.

A taxi honks. It is on a side street across the way.

She wades into the crowd on the street, heading for the cab.

He shouts her name.

She stops, looks back. "Come on ... I will tell you the real story."

It is only after the cab has made a U-turn and is winding its way along the back roads to Shangri-La that he remembers he has left his Jeep in P-town.

*She is not yet twenty-two when she moves in with him. He is twenty-five. But even though they share the same hammock in the dark corner of the River House, even though they bathe each other every night from the large urn of cool water in the bathroom, they almost never talk of their past or a future beyond the coming weekend. He wants to. He wants to tell her about all of the places he is going to take her—especially New York and San Francisco and Provincetown—where they can live like free people without what he calls his father's gestapos prying into their business, shaking a finger of shame and disappointment in his face. But she tells him it is bad luck to make such distant plans. She knows such things. She has watched movies like* Dirty Dancing.

*So they make peace. She finds her song and dance again. Brandy and Delta begin making jokes with her at work, treating her like a real* person, not their personal China doll. When she wakes up around noon from her late sleeps back at the River House, he is always gone. Family obligations, he tells her. They almost never see each other in the daylight, only in the dark.

After a while, he stops coming to her shows. This makes it easier for her to get her groove back. He says he cannot stand watching the desire cross the faces of other men when she sings and dances, cannot stand smelling their weeping sperm. He prefers to wait outside in the limo with Pon. Every night he is there to take her to a late dinner or shopping at little places that open specially for them. Then back to the landing at the Oriental and a water taxi. A water taxi to take them up stream through the rafts of water hyacinths, up stream on the black river to love.

# THIRTY

She has had enough, cannot talk about Bangkok a second longer. He knows there's more to this story. He has not heard anything to rule out Prem Kittikatchorn as a suspect. The guy sounds like a whack job, but to hell with him now. Tuki is crying so hard that she cannot pay the cabbie when they reach Shangri-La. There is a party raging in the Lodge. She is clearly in no shape to meet people. He wants to get her off to bed. Then he can figure out how he is going to get back to P-town to collect his Jeep. He has to get home to Chatham sometime soon. Filipa is coming down in the morning to spend the weekend.

But he cannot just leave her standing in the parking lot, cannot just hand her over to one of the bouncers. She is crying so hard she cannot even walk on her own. So he wraps an arm around her, guides her down a side path to her bungalow.

As soon as they get to her place, she collapses on the bed and buries her head in a pillow. Sobs are still coming. The room is in shadows. Only the porch light is on. And he does not see any reason to change this. He just wants to let her fall asleep. Samset may have a point about her being fragile. Even Filipa, who has a Portuguese woman's well-developed sense of drama, could not cry this long or this hard.

He wonders what his father would do. Part of him wants to stay with Tuki, just to watch over her, make sure she does not try to hurt herself. The other part screams for him to get the hell out of here. Blow her off and bum a ride back to P-town with someone from the party or one of the bouncers. He cannot decide. But first he has to calm her down.

Maybe a stiff drink will do the trick. A survey of the fridge and cabinets only turns up a dusty bottle of B&B that looks like someone left it here years ago. He pours them both about three ounces, takes the drinks over to the bed, sits beside her.

"Try this."

She rises up on one elbow, wipes the tears from her cheeks. Her big black eyes stare at him strangely as she reaches out for the glass. The light from outside makes the sun streaks in her hair look silver. "What is this?"

"Some monks in Italy or Spain or somewhere make this. It is a five-hundred-year-old recipe to soothe the heart."

She sips, squints like someone who has never felt the fire of brandy in her throat before. Takes another sip, a big one, just to make sure she did not imagine that sweet heat.

"Careful. It's pretty strong."

She sets the glass on the bed, rubs her eyes.

"Tonight, I need strong, la!"

"Look, I'm sorry. I was bullying you."

She rolls her eyes as if to remember, waves a hand to dismiss the subject.

"I mean it, Tuki. I feel lousy about making you so upset." He wonders why he is always apologizing to her.

She drops her head back on the pillow. "My head feels ready to explode."

He takes a long drink of the B&B, says nothing, listens to the songs of the crickets and the night birds, stares at that amazing mane of braids and curls covering her face. First with his right hand, then with his left he reaches under her hair and rubs his fingers up the back of her neck, along the sides of her head to her temples. It is what his mother used to do for him when he had the flu as a kid. Rub the knots out of his thick, dark, curly hair.

She gives a little groan.


*The nights are almost always the same; always as if they are in a movie like* The Blue Lagoon *or* The Emerald Forest. *He undresses her in the starshine until all she wears is her gaff, and he bathes her with the cool water from the urn. It runs off her body in little streams and drips through the big cracks in the teak floor. You can hear it splashing softly below in the river as he tells her how crazy he is for her ... how beautiful she is ... how he will always love her like this. He says that when the money from his trust fund comes through they can go away from this city, live together like real lovers, not like creatures of the night, river rats.*

*He talks and talks and talks until his words are like the song of a distant flute, and her mind wonders why he always wants her gaff on during these baths, why he never takes it off until the final act ... and sometimes not even then. She thinks he does not like her the way she is, she tells him. She tells him he wishes she were a woman like his mother, like his sisters.*

*He says never. Women like that are all the same. They just want you to suck all of the loneliness from their breasts, fill the space between their legs, and help them make the babies who will do the same thing. They do not understand what a man needs and wants. They do not understand that a man needs to feel dangerous, that he always feels like a wild animal—a cat in the night. Needs to feel like this. That for every day he does not walk on the razor's edge he dies a little. Women like his mother or his sisters or all of the girls they have tried to fix him up with—even tried to marry him to—cannot help him walk on the razor's edge. Danger is not in their nature, he says.*

# THIRTY-ONE

He is still massaging her. His hands are under her loose jersey, kneading her shoulders with his thumbs and fingers, when he hears a knock and jumps. There is a woman at the door. Then she is in the door, calling Tuki's name before he can even get his hands out of those dark curls. She is the queen called Nikki. And she is crying. Jesus, it must be the season. The light from the porch catches her square in the face. The left side is swollen. She is bleeding at the lip. Her green slip dress is wrinkled, stained with blood.

"Oh," she says when she sees Michael.

Tuki pops up, tears all gone.

"Nikki ... oh, la!" She does not bother to introduce him. It is like he is not even in the room. She jumps to her feet and sweeps her friend into a big hug.

Nikki gives a sob.

"I hope you killed him, la." Her voice is growling. "Because if you did not, I am going to!"

The two queens hold each other in a tight embrace. He is thinking this is his moment to split, snag a ride back to P-town, then the Russian opens her eyes and shoots him a tormented look.

"Who's he?"

"Michael, my lawyer."

Now he is on his feet, too.

"I was just leaving."

Tuki gives him a little shake of her head. No, don't leave. She says, "Give her some of the monks' secret."

He goes for a glass and the B&B.

"Where is the John who did—"

Another sob. "You don't understand, *padruga*."

One night, they are just lying there in the hammock together while he drinks his rice whiskey and rambles on and on. This is the night he tells her all about how he discovered trannies in high school. He says most of the guys in his American military school were a bunch of racist white boys. The few minority kids all stuck together for protection. He made a friend named Robert, a black kid on scholarship from Memphis. After their first year, they chose to be roommates. Robert was a football star, an amazing runner, ball handler. The whole school respected him. They stayed out of his face when he came on with the eff-you-white-boys attitude. So for three years until they graduated, no one bothered Robert or his sidekick Prem. In their room, in their free time, they had a separate and private life apart from all the young storm troopers.

After one vacation, Robert came back from Memphis with some wigs and dresses he said that he had stolen from his sister. At first he dressed up for fun, danced around the dormitory in drag singing along with Roberta Flack tunes and flirting with the other boys. But after a while, Robert started to change. After lights out in the dormitory, Robert began to wear bras, stockings, garter belts. His voice changed. He said he was Bobbi. Prem liked it.

They flirted in the dark for months. Then they did more. Then they did everything. They liked the idea that at any minute one of the boys or the hall master might catch them. Sometimes Bobbi came out of the closet, and they sneaked around the dark school. Had sex in places like the library and the chapel. Once they even stole into their hall master's apartment and did it on his bed, leaving skid marks to prove it. Then one vacation Prem's mother let him and Robert use the family apartment in New York by themselves. Prem and Bobbi discovered Christopher Street—Silicone Alley—and all the tranny clubs in the Village. They split up, picked new partners.

"We screwed our brains out," sighs Prem against her neck. "I think my parents knew it. But all through college they kept trying to throw these rich Chinese-American chicks at me. I played along. I cannot handle my father's anger. I was actually engaged once. But in my heart, I never came back to the straight—"

"*Screw MY brains out,*" she says because she has heard more than enough. She definitely does not want to know even one more thing about his other loves ... especially rich Chinese-American girls.

Then she takes his hands and draws him outside to the stairs leading down to the klong, where they make love in front of Buddha and the world with a fury that stops their hearts.

# THIRTY-TWO

She gets Nikki to lie down on the bed, and she cleans her face with warm water and soap. "Who hit you? Your date?"

"No." Nikki mumbles as Michael gives her a glass of B&B and some ice wrapped in a towel to bring down the swelling around her eye. "Duke didn't beat me."

"Duke? What are you talking about, la?"

"Duke. I was with Duke tonight. I have a thing for Duke, *padruga*! I don't know. He is so sweet and kind ... and maybe I am in love. How in hell would I know? How in hell do girls like us ever know where the sex stops and real love ... But he didn't hurt me, okay? Not Duke."

"Duke?" Tuki asks again.

He is trying to remember who Duke is, has heard Tuki talk about him, knows he has seen him. The guy has something to do with the Follies.

"How long has this been going on?"

"Seriously? Since July Fourth weekend, since you and Alby—"

Tuki's hand is up with the stop sign.

"Richie doesn't know?"

Michael is starting to make the connections. Richie runs the club. Duke is his main man, a bartender. Mr. Clean.

She nods.

"So Richie hit you and—"

"No, he cannot stand up to Duke. He just called in the KGB to do his dirty work."

"Like Immigration? For real, la?"

She nods again.

Tuki's breath just plain stops for a while. She stares out the picture window of her bungalow into the dark.

"About six of them. They found us in bed together in Duke's

room at the Follies about an hour ago. Like we were ... you know. Duke reached for his gun on the nightstand. Some guy hit him with a chair before he could even stand up. Knocked him cold for a second. I grabbed one of my heels, tried to poke out his eyes. Then another guy started on me with an open hand. But Duke got to his pistol, took aim, told them all to get the fuck out."

"Jesus!" Michael cannot believe what he is hearing.

"Really? This is not another bad date that Ruby made for you?" Tuki is still in disbelief, too.

"I got to pack. Duke's waiting for me up in the car. Those bastards will be here next. I know it."

She says Duke told her tonight that he loves her. He is going to stick by her. No matter what. Forever. He used to work some clubs in San Francisco. As soon as Nikki and Duke salvage what they can from here, the wagon train heads west.

"Maybe we all should go," says Michael. He is actually half serious. He has this terrible feeling that he has sunken so far into this pool of crime and drag that he may never get out. Filipa and the wedding seem like someone else's life. What is happening to him?

*Sometimes she tastes the tears on his face, knows they cannot go on like this forever no matter what he says. Then she cries, too.*

*She tells him they see too much of each other. They have been together more than a year. Maybe there is nothing new about these nights. Maybe he is getting tired of her. Maybe they would be happier when they make love if she did not live here, if she had her own apartment in the city.*

*He says he cannot stand this idea. But he does not beg her to stay, as she wants him to. Instead, he talks about his own crying. More problems with his father. Then he says he is deathly afraid that she will meet another man. He could not live with it.*

*Men, she says, are a dime a dozen. But a River Lion is a treasure to death. She makes love to him until the sun rises over the wats across the river. They look like strange, dark pyramids. When his long, thin body can no longer move, and his eyes are like glass, she dresses. Then she hails a boatman on the* klong *and pays him twenty* baht *for a ride across the river to Banglamphu. She is going to find an apartment. She does not know about the* pung chao *yet, but she knows he is into something bad.*

# THIRTY-THREE

Last night still feels like a nightmare to him when Filipa pounces into his bed at noon on Saturday. Really. He feels like total shit. It was not until after sunrise that he found his way back to Chatham.

And his sleep has been riddled with images of standing before a tribunal of uniformed men. They want to know how long he has been helping a bunch of foreign flits and hookers avoid deportation. That is the Sisterhood's game. He sees it now. All these queens like Tuki, Nikki, and Silver, are from overseas, illegals. After Alby Costelano set them up with jobs and a place to stay at Shangri-La, he and his stooges like Richie kept the harem in line by threatening to turn them in to the INS if they did not put out for the customers. Sweet. There's motive for you. The suspect pool has just gotten larger.

When he feels Filipa's tongue in his ear he is wondering about the hostess, Ruby. He wants to talk to her. What is her role in all of this? Is she foreign and illegal, too? Under Alby's thumb? It's beginning to look like a lot of folks might have wanted the Great One dead.

"Rise and shine, sleepyhead." She nuzzles his neck. "And brush your teeth. You reek of booze. Where were you last night?"

"Shut up and kiss me!"

He rolls her off the bed and onto the floor. Pins her wrists to the hardwood, devours her face with his lips and teeth. She struggles for a while. Finally yields. Then he takes the rest of her. God, how he loves this zest intimacy, the way it beats back the rest of the world.

When they finally collapse onto each other, raw and hot and out of breath, he hears a Jimmy Buffett tune about changes in latitude seeping up through the floor from the liquor store downstairs. He smells fresh fish. Pictures the pale blue of Pleasant Bay, the indigo of the Atlantic beyond, a figure waving to him from a small boat.

"I'm thinking about buying a boat, Fil. Just for noodling around, maybe a little fishing. There's a seventeen-footer and a trailer for sale down on Ryder Lane. If I got it today we could take a picnic to the outer bar or Monomoy Island. What do you say?"

"What's wrong, Michael?"


*Weeks pass, and she does not see him. She lives in Banglamphu with another showgirl named Mercy. She wants him to find her, beg her to come back. She wants him to tell his father and mother that he loves her no matter what they think, that they are going to stop living their life together like creatures of the night river ... that they are going to be O-U-T with their love. She wants him to tell her that he is going to start making his videos, that he is going to stand on his own—without Pon, the limo, the River House. They do not matter. Only Prem and Tuki matter.*

*But he does not come; he does not find her. Something is wrong. This is not just a pride thing. She knows because all her pride runs away down her cheeks when she sings her sad songs at the Underground— gone with the dust on the floor, the smoke in the air. She just wants to see him, to smell his skin. He does not have anyone he can even talk to besides her. Something is terribly wrong. Maybe there is another girl!*

*The night she thinks this, she cannot help herself. Right after the show, she goes to the Oriental landing and takes a water taxi to the River House in Thonburi. She sees the low flames of candles burning like a funeral inside the house. There are no shadows of lovers on the walls. Only long, distorted shapes like monsters with a dozen legs. Lionel Richie is playing low on the sound system as she crosses the deck to the open door.*

*From the doorway she can see him curled up in the big hammock. Passed out. Naked. A syringe sits between the fingers of his right hand. The hand lies cupped palm up just above the black bush of his pubic hair. She moves closer, walking on tiptoes. She moves like she must not disturb the dead. She can see the spoon on the floor, a strap of surgical tube, a bloody glass of water. Even when she bends over him, sniffing, looking at every curve of his body from inches away, he does not move.*

*Pung chao, she thinks. Heroin. But how bad can it be? She thinks that she knows this body right down to the pits of his arms. She has never seen needle tracks. So, really, how bad can this be? Where has he taken his poison?*

*His hand with the syringe moves a little and the syringe rolls out of his fingers into his bush. Without thinking, she reaches to grab the needle before it hurts him. Then she sees the marks. Down there under the luxury of hair are the dark purple lines of needle tracks going into the veins at the root of his sex. Dozens of holes. Maybe more. The skin is hard and swollen to the touch like the holes have been used again and again.*

*He stirs to her touch, and smiles a little smile in his chemical dream.*

*How could she have not known about this? How could she not have seen? It is like the movie* M Butterfly. *After all those years with Butterfly, how could the French diplomat not know his lover had a penis? Well, here is the sad truth. Lovers see what they want to see, need to see. And mostly they keep their eyes closed, mostly they make their love in the dark. They are just thankful for a little pleasure and company. Why is she any different?*

*"Butterfly ... daughter?" he asks suddenly.*

*His eyes open. He spreads his arms for an embrace.*

*I am not your effing daughter, screams her mind.*

*But her heart says, My poor, poor River Lion.*

# THIRTY-FOUR

"Why do you want this boat? Are you trying to run away from something? Is it me? The wedding?"

He nuzzles her neck. "No. I love you. I'm going to marry you. It will be the best wedding Nu Bej has ever seen." He hears himself say these words, but part of him wonders whether he is lying to her, to himself. It is a scary thought.

"I don't know if I believe you anymore. You think I can't tell something's going on with you. You're a different person every time I see you. More and more distracted. And kind of manic."

He kisses her cheek. "I'm sorry. I don't mean to be."

She strokes his head. "I know. But you are. It's this case isn't it? It's taking you away from me. Tuki is taking you away from me."

This is the first time Filipa has ever called his client by her name. He does not know what that means, except that something has changed. Things have gotten personal.

He rubs her thigh with his hand.

"Please. Can we talk about this later? I don't want to drag my client into our bed."

Filipa reaches, finds his hands, tightens her fingers around his. "I'd kill the bitch first. I swear!" she says. Then she kisses him so hard he thinks his lips are bleeding.

He looks over her shoulder, out the window at the blue sky. He hears the gulls taunting him, knows that there will be no boat buying today. But Jesus, wouldn't it be fun to get that boat? They could be alone on the outer bar on the far side of Pleasant Bay in an hour. Take their clothes off, dive in the surf, dry off in the sun on the beach, go for a long walk. Then. Then they could talk about the case and Tuki and all the crazy things in her life, too. All the insane things she sees go down in the clinic. And they could deal with the wedding plans. Just plain deal with all the other stuff they need to get off their chests. He is a planner. Maybe they could come up with a loose plan to help them get through the days and weeks to come, then—

She jumps to her feet, pulls on her panties.

"I can't do this anymore, Michael. I just can't! How long have you known me? Five years since we met in Cambridge at the Plough and the Stars when you were starting law school. Isn't that long enough for you to know I'm the kind of girl who needs real intimacy, not just mad sex? Really, you are not here, except in body. Where are you?"

He thinks about last night. The stories about Prem and his *pung chao*. Shooting up in his ... damn! Nikki coming in beaten up, claiming she had been attacked by the INS. Tuki's immigration status. Christ, *there* is a new wrinkle to the case. When the court finds out she is an illegal, they may well send her straight back to Thailand, where it seems she has charges pending, too.

Meanwhile, this shadowy figure Prem is lurking in the wings somewhere, with an alleged death wish for himself and Tuki and anyone who gets in his way.

So why is he bothering with any of this? Why does his gut still tell him Tuki is the pawn here, that she is innocent? Why did he spend the better part of the night in the same bed with a drag queen? Nothing happened. But, still, Filipa would just freak. His father and Tio Tommy would probably disown him.

"I just want to get out on the water, go fishing."

"How much is this boat?"

He thinks he hears some sympathy in her voice. She is standing in front of the window, naked except for her panties, fiddling with the bra in her hand.

"I don't know. I think I can get it for about thirty-five hundred."

She shakes her head, cannot believe he is considering spending that kind of money for a boat when they could use every penny they have saved to get started on their life together in the North End. "What are you really thinking about, Michael?"

"Vietnam," he says before he even has a second to reflect. It is the weirdest thing. Suddenly, he realizes there is a tape playing in the back of his head, so faint he does not see it unless he really looks. It is something like a scene he saw once in *The Deer Hunter*, a scene shot in a dark Saigon Bar. "Midnight Train to Georgia" plays on the jukebox. A B-girl is dancing on the bar. Her hips pumping to the rhythm. A soldier sits at the bar watching, nursing a Budweiser. The GI's face is lost in shadows. But something about him seems familiar, almost ...

"Michael?"

"What?" He stares at her. Coming out of the Twilight Zone.

She flips her sports bra over her head and torso, adjusts it around her breasts, stretches out the back strap to get the kinks out.

"What?" he says again.

She grits her teeth. "I need to go running."

# THIRTY-FIVE

Monday before noon he is heading back to Provincetown. He cannot believe it, but he has started driving with one eye on the rearview mirror in the Jeep. He is not sure what he is looking for. Maybe an Asian guy with murder in his eyes.

He is standing in the hot sun outside the entrance to the Lodge at Shangri-La when Ruby shows up in a golden silk robe looking a little like an alley cat with makeup smeared all over her cheeks and her hair going twenty directions.

She swings open the door and ushers him inside with a sweep of her hand. He tries to introduce himself, but she has turned away and starts to groan.

"Rough night," she sighs. He follows her into the kitchen, watches her pour a big glass of tomato juice with a shot of vodka, before squeezing in the juice from half a lemon.

He just nods and smiles like he knows the feeling.

"Want to kick start your day?"

He thinks about the jumbo latte he scored in Orleans for the drive up. Feels his eyes already starting to pop out of their sockets, his teeth on edge.

"I'm good, thanks."

They sit down at a table out on the deck. Her head is bent, but she is staring at him like a person peering over the top of her glasses.

"She looked so cute in her tennis dress a half an hour ago when she left for her walk ... like a China doll."

"Who?" he asks, thinking he is in for the saga of how she came to be hung over.

"Tuki."

He closes his eyes and purses his lips. What's this viper thinking?

"Don't play coy, buster," she teases. "I saw you leave Saturday morning. So ... are you smitten?"

"She's my client." He knows his words sound defensive and hollow the minute they leave his mouth.

She takes a long sip of the Bloody Mary. "What ever you say, counselor. But you came here to talk about her didn't you? I can see it in your eyes. You're on a mission. You want to rescue her from the Blue Meanies."

He hears an accent in her voice. Irish maybe.

"I just want to talk. I want to understand the situation around Shangri-La in the days leading up to the fire and Mr. Costelano's death."

"It's all in the police reports."

"Somehow I don't think so."

"Why? They interviewed all of us for hours. They got what they were looking for. Hey, I feel sorry for Tuki. She doesn't deserve this mess. And Alby shit on her. He was a pig. But, bloody hell, they've got her on the security tape, stealing the murder weapon. By her own admission she tried to set the man on fire the same night he died and P-town went up in smoke."

He is getting the sinking feeling he used to have aboard the *Rosa Lee* when they were hauling back and he could just tell by the way the net was coming in that it was empty except for some trash fish.

"They barely mention the presence of Tuki's ex-boyfriend from Thailand. There's nothing in the report about blackmail. There's nothing saying that everyone here is an illegal, that Costelano kept you all in his harem by threatening to turn you in to Immigration."

Her head jerks up. Her eyes sting him.

"You're speculating, love."

"What are you trying to hide? Who are you trying to protect, Ruby? Not Costelano. He's dead. So who? Come on. Cut Tuki a break. Give me something to work with."

She stands up.

"Leave me out of this. You're welcome to wait for your girlfriend down at her bungalow. But we're through here, counselor. G'day!"

He is feeling stupid as he watches her sashay off the deck, wondering whether she's a tranny or a female, when a question grips him.

"So why did you leave Dublin, Ruby?"

She stops, looks at him over her shoulder, then tosses a thick strand of her yellow hair out of her eyes.

"It was Melbourne, love, if you want to know. And there were too many bloody lawyers."

*She does not go to work or leave his side for a week. For the first three days after she throws his bag of* pung chao *in the* klong, *the screaming and the crying are terrible. She buys rice and vegetables, lots of durian and star fruit from the vendors who go up and down the* klong *in their boats. She makes stir fries, tries to force him to eat and drink the fruit juices. Nothing seems to work. He refuses almost everything she offers him. She is just twenty-three, but she is so tired she feels one hundred and eighty.*

*"Let me die," he says in Thai.*

*Then one day a water taxi comes to the landing. Brandy and Delta get out, wearing the saffron robes of monks.*

*"This bad," says Brandy.*

*"How long he like this?" asks Delta.*

*"Five or six days," she says. She has no clue any more.*

*"He dying, la," they say ... and both look at her with empty eyes.*

*"You got choice. You want him clean or live? No both."*

*Typical. Her mothers always see life as a simple choice. Maybe, at this moment, they are right.*

*They say he is too sick, too strung out on* pung chao. *He cannot quit his habit like this—cold lizard. No way. He needs a doctor, a hospital, to slowly eat into his dependence. Then maybe he gets clean. Now this poor little rich boy needs heroin to live. Tuki must choose.*

*"Pung chao," she says. "Help him."*

*Delta reaches in her cloth handbag, pulls out a little cellophane packet of brown powder, puts it in a spoon, cooks it up over a candle until it is liquid. Then she sucks it up in a syringe, shoots it into a vein in his forearm. His body turns grey as death for a minute. His skin blooms to a pale, milky color as he falls into a deep sleep.*

"*Where are you getting that?*" she points at the empty packet and the syringe.

"*We prepare for the worst,*" says Delta.

"*We worry* pung chao *maybe you problem, too.*"

## THIRTY-SIX

It's two in the afternoon. The Tango is empty except for a couple of tables of guys, and Chivas is starting on the scotch and water. After his little interlude with Ruby, Michael is tempted, too. But he decides he is going to nurse his cranberry and OJ here at the bar, hopes the booze loosens the queen mother's tongue.

"She's a sick bitch, that one," says Chivas. "Full of venom. But Ruby sure knows how to throw a party. And sometimes I feel a little sorry for her. She's not even queer."

"Really?"

"A flaming fag hag. She loves the queens. She came on to Tuki, you know?"

"No!"

"Yes, counselor. Tuki told me the whole story. She was a little freaked out, if you want to know the truth. It was back in early July. Ruby conned Tuki into joining her on a three-day shopping expedition to Boston. Top shelf stuff. They stayed at the Four Seasons on Ruby's gold card. Their last night in town, the girls went clubbing and the hostess of Shangri-La got blotto on piña coladas. She nuzzled against Tuki's shoulder during the cab ride back to the hotel. And when they got to the room, Ruby attacked."

For some reason Michael can almost picture the scene.

"One second Tuki was sitting on the bed massaging a stiff calf, the next second the room was dark and she was on her back, pinned to the bed. Ruby was on top of her with her tongue down Miss Bangkok's throat. Tuki got free. Neither of them moved for about five minutes.

"After a while, Ruby started to cry. Then she told Tuki that she was in love with the Queen of the North Pole."

"Silver?" asks Michael.

"None other. And Ruby was feeling the distinct unhappiness of being second-string booty. Silver had hitched her wagon to the Great

One's star. Tuki was not only wigging out, she was starting to feel used. Like, she was Miss Drag Hag's surrogate Silver ... or maybe a means to make the Ice Queen jealous. Who knew at that point? But Tuki split and caught the next ferry back to P-town."

"Damn!"

"Ready for that drink yet?"

He nods. He'll take a sea breeze, light on the vodka.

"Let me get this straight. Big Al had the hots for Tuki. Silver wanted Alby. And Ruby had a thing for Silver. Is that right?"

Chivas slides him another sea breeze.

"We call it a daisy chain here in the Magic Queendom, honey. And things can get real interesting when you get everybody in the same place at the same time. Can you say J-E-A-L-O-U-S-Y?"

"Or murder?"

"Exactly."

"What's the story on Silver and Alby?"

"She was his girl. She lived, lives, in his house at Shangri-La—the glass jobbie. This was her fourth summer in a row. But this summer things got a little weird ... because Miss Tuki rolled into town shaking some tail feather. Next thing you know Big Al was two-timing his main squeeze."

"Dicey."

Chivas shakes her hand like she's flicking sweat off her brow.

"You have no idea."

"There's more?'

"Of course, cowboy. But information like this doesn't come cheap." She gives him a wink.

"So, what do you want?"

"How about a date?"

*It's the last week of July. Tuki steps from her outdoor shower at Shangri-La, wearing nothing but her robe to find Ruby waiting like a lost puppy.*

*Her gold necklace and perky little tube dress seem out of place with her pale, sad face. Tuki really has not seen her since their close encounter in Boston. And she is just fine with that. But now Ruby is tugging on her sleeve and saying they need to talk.*

*Suddenly, Ruby bursts into tears and settles into a deck chair on the porch of Tuki's bungalow. For a long time Tuki leans against the doorframe and stares out at the duck families paddling across the inlet. Ruby cries.*

*Finally, Ruby catches her breath and says don't shoot the messenger, but Alby is ...*

*Tuki fans the air with her hand as if to drive off a foul vapor. She does not want to hear that name. Every time it comes up, there is some new mess right in the middle of her life.*

*Ruby heaves a sigh, says that Tuki does not understand. Does she not know that her boyfriend is threatening Alby? The guy who looks like Jackie Chan. The guy from Bangkok.*

*Suddenly, she feels snakes racing through her veins. Last night, for just a second, she thought she saw a man who looked like Prem sitting in the audience at the Follies. She told herself then that it could not be him. She had blanked the picture out of her mind. An impossibility.*

*But it is true, says Ruby, he is here. In Provincetown. He was at Alby's office last night a little before the Follies show. He had a gun. He told Alby to stay the hell away from his girl, that he was taking you away. Alby told him to eff off, get out before he called the police. The next thing you know, he shot a bunch of holes in Alby's computer. Little flames rose out of the monitor.*

*Alby had a bullwhip hidden under his desk. When he started shooting, Alby grabbed his whip and zapped the guy right around the chest. Declared she was his property. And if this little prick from Bangkok came within a mile of her, he would kill his ass. Like don't fuck, Jasper.*

*Tuki says nobody owns her. Ruby shrugs, maybe so. But Alby wants to see her. Now. He says her immigration status could be at stake here.*

*Tuki can hardly believe her ears. Is she being threatened?*

*Ruby shrugs again. The man has a proposition. First, he wants to*

take Tuki to dinner after the show tonight ... and then he wants her to
move her things into the Glass House.

Tuki's mind starts sorting through pictures. She sees the jet to
Montreal and a gun in her face ... right beside some guy's chaang.

"No thank you, la," says Tuki. The Alby show is over.

Ruby's voice grows shaky, frantic. She says that Silver is going ape
shit. Right after the Bangkok cowboy shot up Alby's office, the Great
One told Silver that he was out-of-his-mind crazy, like heart and soul,
over the girl from Bangkok.

The news itself didn't break Silver's heart, but Alby is Silver's
sugardaddy. Not simply to the tune of a glass house to live in for the
summer, a sharp Harley to ride around town, and all of the costumes
a girl could dream of. He is her ticket to six figures a year. He owns the
loft in Soho where she lives in the winter. Gives her use of his townhouse
in Munich, a beach condo at Cancun. And he has been backing Silver's
film, TV, and video career to the tune of a half mil. One other thing,
the Great One is working a deal to protect all of his girls from the INS.
From deportation. Including Silver.

But Silver could not take the long view on her relationship with
him. Not now. She just hated the feeling that her hold on Daddy
Warbucks was slipping. She had thought that he was over his little
infatuation with Tuki. But now, because the old flame has shown
up, Alby is in meltdown again. Things are flying out of control in
Silver's life. She is pissed, jealous, not sure what to do next. Maybe
hurt somebody.

As some kind of payback thing, Silver invited about a hundred
people to Shangri-La to a party at the Lodge after the show on the night
Tuki's ex and Alby had their little showdown. The night the Great One
told Silver she was old news.

A lot of cocaine got passed around. People started doing crazy,
sick things. One of the dragon waitresses from the Follies got herself
smashed on margaritas and lost her virginity eight times on the day
bed in the back of the kitchen; three women stripped and did a girl-
on-girl thing in the hot tub. And Silver made Ruby get down on her
knees in front of the fireplace, pull up Silver's skirt, and lick a line of

coke off the ho's you-know-what. *The guests cheered Ruby on, while Silver did a lip-synch in the half-light of a flickering fireplace to "Do That to Me One More Time."*

*Tuki tells Ruby to forget Silver. But she just sighs and says she can't. It's complicated ... she just can't.*

*Ruby begs her to just pour water on this fire. Tuki is the only one who can. She must do what Alby thinks he wants. This once. Just go out to dinner with him. Jump his bones a few times. He has a crush on her. She is not the first. This kind of thing has happened before. Let it run its course, he will not hurt her. He only wants what he does not have. Then everything will be okay.*

# THIRTY-SEVEN

It is the seven-day gay fiesta called Carnival Week. The opening party is at the Slip. There is a talent show featuring P-town's working divas, followed by dancing. Now it is time for Michael to put the case aside for the moment and pay up. And Chivas is collecting. Tonight he is the one trading favors, not his client. He is her escort. And at seven o'clock in the evening, he is standing in the Tango dressed as the Sheik of Araby in one of Harry's old costumes.

Chivas makes her entrance looking like an aging, overweight version of Glinda the Good Witch from *The Wizard of Oz* ... in a gauzy white gown that you can kind of see through. But there is definitely something draggy about the look—maybe the way the eye shadow is way too green. Michael thinks he is out of here if anybody starts taking pictures. The last thing he needs is for a photograph of him tonight getting back to Filipa, his father, or Tio Tommy.

And a photo is a real possibility because he is not just stuck with the queen mother—she has invited Tuki to join them. She has to do a little number in the talent show, and she is dressed to take no prisoners. A sultry, Lena Horn look in a blue, rhinestone-covered evening dress that fits like a glove and slits way up the leg. Flame lipstick, hair pinned up off her neck, a fake diamond necklace, a pair of rhinestone heels. Patrons in the Tango whistle and hoot.

Chivas takes her dates by the arms. Out the door they go, arm in arm in arm, to the ball. Provincetown high society.

The sun has just about set over the bay. Shop lights are coming up in reds, greens, blues, yellows. All of Commercial Street is a runway. He has never seen anything like this. The crowd is so thick, the few cars that brave this narrow lane get swallowed in a herd of party animals. You can hear the buzz of the throng, the rustling of costumes, the rumble of disco and house up and down the street. The scents of Chanel and Obsession hang in the air.

A pair of identical twins—about six and a half feet tall—in black corsets, garter belts, and hose walk arm in arm. They look totally outrageous with their little blonde goatees and vinyl caps. Coming from the other direction is Eva Perón—dolled to the hilt like Madonna in *Evita*. Outside the Crown and Anchor, Oprah, Xena, Pocahontas, and Snow White strut their stuff for the crowd. At the intersection in front of the Governor Bradford, a Julia Roberts clone and two girls dressed like waitresses are reviving the *Mystic Pizza* thing and taking turns helping the policeman direct traffic.

And here come the drag kings. Everyone from Drew Carey and Jerry Seinfeld to Mick Jagger and Alan Jackson. For every king or queen whose character Michael recognizes, he sees ten other people in costumes that range from ballerinas to ostriches.

Maybe Prem is here, he thinks. What if he—

"Wave to the crowd, darlings. They love us," says Chivas.

After fours stops for toddies in friends' shops, Chivas is spinning out of control—tall men, short men, gay men, straight men, young men, ancient men. The old girl does not care. She passes out winks, wiggles, and kisses like it's Halloween and she is the treat.

Then, suddenly, Chivas groans. "Fuck. Smile for the King and Queen of S&M."

Coming out of the Pied Piper is none other than the Ice Queen of the Follies. Silver has outdone herself, looking more like Sharon Stone than Sharon Stone does. She is wearing a sexy white dress like Stone wore during the—sans panties—Michael Douglas/beaver shot scene in *Basic Instinct*. Silver looks all uptown and *Vogue*. She also has a dog leash in her hand clipped to a collar around the neck of a drag king dressed in a tux, trying to look like Brad Pitt. It is Ruby in a wig and drag.

Tuki is beaming a smile like a good little girl from Thailand should when Silver stops about five paces from them. She looks Chivas and Tuki up and down, and says to Michael in her skank British accent, "Hey love, where did you find this crusty relic of a three-dollar blow job and the juke joint ho?"

"Leave us alone!" says Tuki.

"Pardon me?" Silver, arching her eyebrow.

Out of the corner of his eye, Michael sees a crowd gathering to watch. Someone whispers "cat fight."

The fur on Tuki's back is up. "Find your DVDs, la?"

Silver's eyes flash. "Light any fires lately?"

Tuki smiles. "*Maeo mai yu nu raroeng.* When the cat is away the mice will play."

"Kiss my ass!" Silver shouts as she stomps into the throng on Commercial Street ... with Ruby at her heels.

"PMS," Chivas explains to the crowd gathered around them. "Every girl's secret shame!"


The talent show comes and goes at the Slip with both Tuki and Silver drawing raves from the crowd. Now everybody is down with dancing. Michael stands on the edge of the dance floor. He is tasting some champagne that Chivas has thrust in his hand. He realizes that the old girl has kept him laughing all night. So much so that he has almost stopped scanning the crowd for a Thai assassin.

A slow set comes on. The DJ spins a tune from *Pretty Woman,* a sexy cha-cha number called "Fallen." It played in the background of the scene where Julia Roberts first got transformed from a hooker into a stunning society girl. It is one of Filipa's favorite movies. She's made him watch it a dozen times. Now when he hears the music, he can picture Julia Roberts in her gauzy red dress with a quarter of a million dollars' worth of diamonds around her neck sparkling almost like Tuki's tonight.

He is listening to the song, having a little daydream, watching all the queens and kings dancing, when he feels someone grab his elbow. Tuki.

"Can I have this dance?"

He wants to beg off, lie. He says he is a lousy dancer. He cannot dance with a tranny. No way.

But her hand holds on. Suddenly they are dancing. She feels as light as a phantom in his arms. His feet are remembering eight years of dancing school in Nu Bej. "You can't call yourself Portuguese if you don't dance," his father used to say. So when a lot of the other kids were playing baseball or boosting bikes, he learned to dance, learned to love the feeling. It makes him sad sometimes to think how Filipa is clumsy, unschooled, exaggerated on the floor. They ought to take some lessons before the wedding.

But this, right now, is amazing. Tuki dances like a dream. He cannot believe it. So smooth, so light on her feet, so straight, so strong, so subtle. They spin together; they break; they move hip to hip, side to side, back and forward ... his right thigh grazing—spooning—the backside of her left leg. The blade of his hip slides against her soft rump.

He twirls her and pulls her back ... this time to his chest. The tenor sax moans. He is in trouble here: the song is only half over, and Lauren Wood is singing about how *erotic* it is to be back in the game. He wants to swear. This just cannot be happening to him. He cannot really be dancing like this. Not here, not now, not with this person. Straight men just do not do this kind of thing.

They are lying side by side in her bed back at Number Three. Talking. Talking about Asia again ... and New Bedford. Not the case. They talk like they are unraveling a giant ball of yarn in the moonlight. All the time they were dancing, she was noticing his gold ring with a small sapphire set in it. It is an engagement present from Filipa. He wears it on his left hand like a wedding ring. She cannot ignore it. She has to ask.

"Are you married, Michael?"

"Getting—" he chokes. "Getting married."

"When?"

"A couple of weeks."

"Oh, la." Her voice is just a whisper.

After a while she adds, "What is her name?" She reaches over and takes his hand. It seems an unconscious gesture.

Anita Baker is singing "No More Tears" in surround sound. Their bodies look like silver shadows on the moonlit bed. Ripples sparkle outside on the inlet.

"Would you mind a whole hell of a lot if we don't talk about it right now?"

He feels nasty. The nastiness of welcoming the scent of her freshly washed hair ... the flirting in her voice. The nastiness of giving in a little to the woman she appears to be.

But when she starts to unbutton his shirt, he catches her hand in his and stops her.

He says something in Portuguese—a person's name, a place, something else—she does not understand. His voice sounds funny. It's no longer warm and husky, kind of shaky.

"Did I do something ..."

He pulls away from her arms, sits up in the moonlight, leans back against the wall. She sits up beside him. He feels afraid.

It seems like hours go by before either of them says something more. Finally, he tells her he better go.

But he does not move. She presses her cheek to his chest.

He feels his skin tighten.

"I am sorry I am not what you want me to be." She strokes his head.

"Oh Christ!" he says and jumps to his feet.

She curls into a ball and braces herself for what she fears is coming next.

*It takes months and months, a private doctor, round-the-clock nurses, and a bundle of money, but Prem gets clean. His parents arrange everything. They send him to a famous hill station—a kind of mountain resort in Malaysia—to recover. He calls the club after two weeks. He says he is feeling better and he asks her to come. Please come.*

*But how can she? She has no passport. For the first time she truly realizes that she is an illegal, a person without a country. Even in Thailand.*

*"Hurry," he says. His parents have big plans for him. They want to change his life.*

*"What do I do?" she asks Brandy and Delta.*

*"Follow your heart," they say.*

So they arrange for her fake Thai passport, the one with the picture of her as a boy. Then she puts her drag in a suitcase, dresses as a boy, takes a second-class seat on the overnight train. It crosses the border at Hat Yai. In Alor Setar she pays a car and driver a string of pearls that Prem gave her to take her up into the mountains to the hill station. She has the car stop by a mountain stream and changes into the gold shantung sheath she wore on their first date. She puts on her makeup in the back seat. The driver watches in his mirror, but he says nothing.

When they reach the hill station, the air is cool and misty. The guard at the gate asks for her reservation confirmation number. She does not know what he means so she says she is a guest of Mr. Prem Kittikatchorn.

That would be impossible, says the giant Malaysian guard. He looks down his dark, broad nose at her and smiles. The person she speaks of has asked not to be disturbed under any circumstances.

"Mr. Kittikatchorn especially does not want to be disturbed by some filthy little Patpong trash. Go away. He puts a hand on the machine gun that hangs on a sling from his right shoulder.

She feels like a flea in the soft mud under the hind foot of a water buffalo.

# THIRTY-EIGHT

He is slipping into his loafers, trying to get himself out of Tuki's bungalow with a few shreds of self-respect, when the room suddenly goes white. He feels something hot on his back, turns to look. There are two figures shining flashlights in his face. He can see a man and a woman wearing dark ball caps. One of them has a pistol in hand.

"Please, come with us."

Some people say that bad things come in threes. He has never believed in this sort of superstition. He has always believed that you make your own luck. But now he is beginning to wonder, because here comes bad thing number three right on top of Chivas's tale of the daisy chain of jealousy infesting his case, coupled with whatever you want to call this misguided interlude with Tuki.

He and Tuki end up sitting in the living room of the Lodge with Ruby and Silver giving statements to four separate agents about who they are, what they do, and why they are here. The storm troopers are not the Provincetown or Truro Police, who are known for their tolerance. These are Gestapo in full battle gear—walkie-talkies and blue windbreakers with INS in gold letters on the back. There are state cops among them, too. And while the girls and Michael are giving statements, the storm troopers go through the Lodge and bungalows of Shangri-La bed by bed, drawer by drawer. Not only do they suspect that the girls are illegals, but they think they are keeping a disorderly house for immoral purposes. Michael, here, is some of the evidence. A John. Caught in bed with one of them. Not with his pants down. But close enough.

He has so much static in his brain he hardly remembers what he tells the female agent in jack boots who grills him for about two hours. But he cannot forget a few high points of the night. Like when an agent asks Tuki her name. She tells him, you know, Tuki Aparecio. And the agent comes out with, "Your REAL name, sissy boy."

A foggy dawn is settling over the Lodge and the inlet when Immigration makes their captives all strip together and bend over the dining room table. An agent who looks like Tommy Lee Jones snaps on a pair of rubber gloves, greases up his hand, and announces that he is going to "search all body cavities for incriminating evidence."

Michael is getting his rectal exam with what feels like a cattle prod, when another agent suddenly shouts like he has found the pot of gold at the end of the rainbow.

"Jesus H. Christ, help me out, Linda: this one has a pussy ... under his lil' pecker!"

Something begins to churn down in Michael's stomach. When he looks up, he sees that the person who has the vagina is not Ruby, who Chivas had told him was an actual woman, but who he can now see clearly has a dick.

It is Tuki. She has the plumbing of a what??

There she sits on the edge of the dining room table with her legs all spread apart getting a pelvic examination by a female trooper.

"Except for the IUD, this one is clean and just like god made ... him ...her?" The trooper sighs. She does not look even a little happy to be a part of this detail. "What is your game, sweetheart?"

That is just what Michael is wondering while he is bent over the table with some guy's fingers up his butt. Just when he thought he had Tuki figured out. His belly churns.

"I feel sick, bathroom, plea—" he shouts.

A green look begins to cross everyone's face as they picture what is coming.

"Fuck, go!" shouts an agent. "Run, man!"

"Run!!" shout about a dozen voices.

So he does ...

In the bathroom, after he empties himself, he has time to wonder about what has gone wrong with his nose for femininity. He misread Ruby as a biological woman. But guess what? It may be small and shriveled and almost buried in the biggest blonde bush you can imagine ... but he saw it. Her *chaang*. She has been keeping this a secret from everyone except Silver it seems. Jesus!

And Tuki? He thought he understood her. Thought her up-bringing in the drag houses of Bangkok had shaped her. Made a lost little boy named Dung crave the glamour of being a showgirl. But now this. Tuki really is a female. Well, sort of. Except for the *chaang*. If she has an IUD, then she must ovulate. Nature did this to her. It seems like such a cruel joke.

He has heard about hermaphrodites. Oysters are hermaphroditic. Some fish, too. But somehow the concept of a third sex has seemed a myth to him. Like something seen in cave sketches of a pagan god. Yet here she is. Like the Buddha, her mother had said. A holy child, a love child. Now he understands what Brandy and Delta must have been trying to tell Tuki when they spoke of the Buddha with breasts, when they spoke of old souls to her. And what she has been trying to tell him when she speaks of the Buddha and old souls. He sees that Brandy and Delta made a choice for her, to protect her. They somehow felt Tuki's essential femaleness. So they kept her in the drag houses because it was possibly the only place she could really live her life as a female and be accepted, and maybe find love. He cannot imagine what it feels like to live with a secret like hers. But he knows it has to hurt. Even if all your mothers love you. Even if you are an old soul. A child like Buddha. A holy child. Somewhere hidden beneath all of those smiles lies insecurity, maybe self-loathing. And anger. Probably anger. Maybe enough anger to kill. If he were Tuki, he might kill. Might do more than make a flamethrower out of a can of hairspray. The thought leaves him shaking.

By the time one of the troopers passes a robe into the bathroom, Michael has gotten enough color back into his skin to come out and face the public. Shangri-La looks like it has been hit by a hurricane. The troopers and agents are backing out the door with his ID, the girls' passports, everybody's cell phones, beepers.

"Clean yourselves up, and get this place back in order. You are free to go back about your *legal* business," says the agent in charge. "But do not try to leave this compound. We have guards at the gate.

You are all under house arrest until we can run some computer checks and make arrangements to ship the whole bunch of you off to a zoo. Have a good day!"

For about twenty minutes Ruby, Silver, Tuki, and Michael sit on the couches in the living room in bathrobes. Nobody says a word. They are all just sitting … staring at a pile in the middle of the floor of the assorted peculiar underwear of the trade … listening to the big stainless steel refrigerator humming in the kitchen. Michael is trying to imagine how he is going to explain this to Filipa, their families, and his bosses. He was conducting research for the case. It was the wrong place at the wrong time. He got caught in a sting and—

"I smell a rat," says Silver.

"Somebody out there doesn't like us," says Ruby. "Alby had the cops paid off."

"He's dead." says Michael.

"Thanks to your client and her ninja boyfriend," says Ruby.

Silver turns to Tuki. "Where the hell did Jackie Chan get to, love? I thought you'd be gone with him by now. Skip bloody bail. Wasn't he going to sweep you off to his golden cloud? What happened with that? Or does the dragon lady have the hots for her lawyer now?"

Tuki stands up, starts out the door toward her bungalow, hissing something in Thai.

"Wait!" He jumps to his feet.

# THIRTY-NINE

*Months after she was turned away at the hill station, she reads in the society pages of the* Bangkok Post *about his engagement and sudden marriage to the youngest daughter of a respected Thai silk merchant. Four times she pays a water taxi to carry her across the Chao Prya to Thonburi and ride down the* klong *past the River House.*

*Only once does she see them there—Prem and the bride. He is in olive shorts and a red polo shirt, cooking something on skewers over the charcoal brazier. She is arranging a bouquet of flowers on an outdoor table set with linen and silver and wine glasses for dinner. He sees her, she thinks. For a second he looks up and stares at her boat. And while he looks, a big fork drops from his hand. His wife turns to look at him when she hears the noise. He gives her a silly grin and shrugs his shoulders. Later, she reads in the paper that his wife is pregnant. She gives him twins. Little girls. After that day, she only crosses the Chao Prya River to Thonburi one more time.*

*When she comes back from seeing him in his new life at the River House, she does not get out of her hammock for two weeks except to go to the bathroom. A great tidal wave is rolling through her body with the speed of a turtle. She cannot eat. Her hair starts to fall out in clumps. Her legs turn to sticks.*

*Maybe AIDS, think Brandy and Delta. They are so worried they get a Buddhist priest to come to the apartment. It is late afternoon. The shadows are long and brown around her hammock hanging in the corner of the living room. He is a thin little man in a saffron robe with a shaved head, a lopsided handlebar mustache, and eyeglasses.*

*"Khawy thii nii dai mai?" he asks her mothers, pointing outside the door of the apartment. Can they wait outside, please?*

*When he is alone with her, he lights joss sticks all around the room.*

He speaks to her in Thai, tells her not to be afraid. There are things he must do to help her lift the weight of bad karma from her spirit.

"Open yourself to the Buddha. Buddha is the all. Buddha is the peace that passes all understanding."

His hand covers her eyes, and she feels his fingers brushing tears from her cheeks.

"Close your eyes. The soul cannot see with the eyes, only with the heart."

"I do not care about my heart," she says. "I wish it would die. I wish all of this life would die away soon. I want to be dust, la."

"Remember the teaching of the Buddha. Say with me again the lessons of the Buddha. Listen to the lessons singing in your heart, child. Will you do this?"

She nods.

"Life is suffering," he says.

"Life is suffering."

"Suffering comes from desire."

"Suffering comes from desire."

"If we eliminate desire, suffering will cease."

Her heart pictures desire, pictures Prem. Her chest heaves.

"We burn desire into nothing when we follow the eight-step path of the Buddha to happiness."

Her lips say these words. Her heart tries to sing with these words.

The priest talks to her about the Way of the Buddha.

In her soul she wants right understanding, right thinking, right speech, right bodily conduct, right livelihood, right effort, right attentiveness, and right concentration.

But her mind is stuck on those words, "we can burn desire." She feels the fire in her heart, wants to burn something. Burn desire.

## FORTY

"You're where?" Filipa's voice crackles over the phone line. "They booked you for what?"

He does not want to give her the bad news again. He is not really in jail. Yet. He is just sort of in detention at the state police barracks in West Yarmouth, having been arraigned in Orleans. But it looks like they are going to lock him up, until someone bails him out. He had expected just to be booked on probable cause for soliciting sex for money and be released on personal recognizance. That is the usual drill for Johns. But both the State and Immigration seem to have a burr in their butts about Shangri-La and the Sisterhood. So they have booked him on conspiracy, too. The charge will not stick, but for the moment it means the slammer, unless he can make bail. He tells Filipa this is all so stupid. A case of mistaken identity. He was just doing an interview for his case and there was this crazy raid ...

"Did you tell them you're a lawyer? That you were there on business? That you're going to sue the hell out of them unless—"

"That's not how it works, Fil. Trust me. The cops don't want to hear that kind of thing. It doesn't intimidate them. It just pisses them off. The time to fight this is at my hearing. I have to play nice until the dust settles, or they can make it real hard for me to get out of here."

"This is what you get for hanging out with all those ... those weirdoes."

He is silent. What the hell can he say?

"Michael. Michael, are you there?"

"Sorry."

"I'll bet you are. I'll just bet you goddamn are. I swear to god, if we didn't have the invitations sent out, the church rented, the caterer, and the band, I'd ... never mind. What do I do now?"

He tells her she needs to contact a bail bond person. Gives her the name of the folks that covered Tuki eight or nine days ago.

"I suppose you want me to get your client out again, too."

He takes a deep breath, knows what could happen to Tuki in jail.

"Well, it is the only safe solution for—"

"Wait. Can I ask how much this is going to cost?"

"Bail is $20,000 for me. $40,000 for her." As soon as he says "her," Filipa hangs up. He feels like a total fool. And for some reason he is picturing Vietnam again. The bar in Saigon, the girl dancing to a soul riff from Gladys Knight, the GI with his head hanging over a bottle of Bud.

His firm makes the bail for him and Tuki, but they are none too pleased. He tells the senior partners that he is making headway with Tuki's defense. He goes out on a limb and says she is clearly innocent. If ever there was a case in which the authorities have rushed to judgment, this is such a case. Tuki is a victim of racial, class, and gender prejudice. The hype sounds great. If only he can prove it. He has to. He has to come out of this a hero. It is the only way to redeem himself with Filipa, his firm, his family. And Tuki, too. So he better get down to business.

On the taxi ride back to P-town from the barracks, he tells her it is now or never. What is she still not telling him? He wants the naked truth. Even if she killed someone. He can deal with that, too.

"Don't worry. Just tell me everything. What is the big secret about Bangkok?"

*When she wakes, the apartment is dark except for the flash of the neon signs from the street. The priest is gone and so are Brandy and Delta. Five minutes after ten. Her mothers are at work. At the earliest they will be home by midnight.*

*She dresses as a market woman in black pajamas and takes the up-river ferry to the landing by the Royal Palace. A lot of the long-tail boats and river taxis tie up here. But at this time of night most of the boatmen have gone home, or they are out on the river carrying passengers. No one is watching these boats at the landing. She takes six full gas cans from different boats and loads them into one empty water taxi. She unties the taxi and drifts downstream with the current until she is away from the lights of the restaurant on the bank. Then she starts the engine.*

*She goes up the river almost a mile until she reaches the* klong *that heads to the River House. At the Royal barge sheds, she cuts the motor. The current carries her through the shadows of the stilt houses built out over the* klong *until she reaches the steps up to the deck of the River House. She can tell by the darkness and the stale dusty smell of the charcoal in the brazier that no one is here. Her cowardly lion and his family are safely sleeping in their Rama Road penthouse.*

*Maybe she is secretly hoping they might be here to stop her from going through with the plan. But now there is nothing to hold her back. She unlocks the door with the spare key from the flower pot. She goes inside and soaks the hammock where they used to make love. Then she wets down the bathroom, pours gasoline on top of the water in the big urn. She splashes gasoline on the dining room table, the living room floor, the cushions on the deck. There is a trail of gas between every place they ever made love. She saves half of the last can just for the steps down to the river. On the bottom step, she places two candles in a banana leaf and fills the cupped leaf with gasoline. She lights the candles, like they are on one of those little boats Thai people set out on the river as offerings to the gods and prayers for lost souls at the celebration of Loi Krathon. Then she starts the taxi's motor and slips out onto the dark river. And waits.*

*She looks back across the Chao Prya from her water taxi at the River House. Finally, when the candles have burned down to the level of the gasoline, there is a low thud that echoes over the water. In seconds the River House is burning from top to bottom as the sirens of the fire boats wail.*

*The fire nearly spreads to the Royal barge sheds.*

*It is the top story on TV news the next day.*

# FORTY-ONE

They are sitting across the table from each other on the porch of her bungalow. The afternoon is blazing with heat and humidity. Both of them are still wearing the jeans and T-shirts they wore to the lockup in West Yarmouth.

"Are we finished yet, Michael?" Her voice sounds frayed. Those last stories about Prem came with a lot of tears.

He hesitates. The story of her revenge, the story of her torching the River House, has hit him like a brick in the chest. The D. A. gets a hold of this, Tuki's case will be screwed royal.

"Can I go to bed?"

He wants to say yes, go to bed ... sleep your heart out because we are in a world of hurt. But he still has questions. And a hunch. Maybe he better go for it now. Who knows how soon Silver and Ruby will be out on bail and back here raising holy hell? And he is still not convinced Prem Kittikatchorn is totally out of the picture. Either in terms of the fire and murder, or now. Tuki makes it sound like the guy has crawled off somewhere to die. But who says he plans on dying alone?

"Just one or two more things, okay?" He fiddles with his water glass on the table. "You told the police you were with Prem when the security camera seems to have taken pictures of you stealing the murder weapon and Silver's DVDs. But you were here at Shangri-La weren't you?"

She tosses the curls back out of her face with her hand and squints at the ducks paddling across the inlet.

The way the sun is playing with her hair, lighting her golden skin, is unbelievable. After all the crap of the last twenty-four hours. He thinks this is the best he has ever seen her look. It is not beauty that he is seeing, he decides, it is peace. She looks like some weight is lifting off her heart as she starts to talk.

*This is the honest truth. The last time she sees Prem, it is the night of the fire, the murder. He has been watching her already for days. Now he says he wants to talk. It is important.*

*So she is with him again, walking barefoot along a dark and empty fish-boat wharf with her jeans rolled half way up her calves. His white cotton jacket is over her shoulders. The rain has stopped. As the sun sets over Cape Cod Bay, fog begins to swallow the pier. He is holding her hand and—she has to admit—looking very Jackie Chan in his rolled-up khakis and gray hooded sweatshirt. They are so alone. The water birds are only shadows, distant music.*

*She tries to avoid his eyes, cannot bear to see their glassy, faraway look. Tries not to think about the gun hidden in the pouch of his sweatshirt. But she knows it is there. Felt its weight when he hugged her. Does not know what she will do if he pulls it out. Say, shoot me, maybe.*

*"I'm going away tonight," he says.*

*She feels a faint trembling in his hand.*

*"You are using pung chao again."*

*"It dulls the pain."*

*"It kills you."*

*"Not fast enough."*

*"Would you give it up for me?"*

*He gives her a sad little smile. "It is too late."*

*She thinks back to Bangkok, her broken lover in the hammock at the River House. "It was always too late. From the start."*

*He shrugs. Maybe she is right. But now it is different.*

*"When I came here, I thought that if I found you again we could bury the past."*

*She says she wishes they could, but she knows that you cannot bury the bad without the good. All or nothing, it seems to her.*

*He says he can forgive her, but now he sees he cannot forgive himself.*

*That is how it is. It is the same for her.*

*"And now ... other things. Terrible things."*

*"What you have done to your family?"*

*He gives her a grim look.*

*"It is worse than you know."*

*Her heart feels like a tiny stone. For a moment she thought that just maybe this could work out. But now she sees there is no going back. And no going forward for the two of them. Not together.*

*"We could have had such a good time," he says.*

*"I did ... Didn't you?"*

*He looks at her like "Don't you know?"*

*But that is not good enough for her because a girl needs to hear someone tell her she is not alone with the things she is feeling.*

*"Please, la!"*

*He sighs.*

*"Anything I say will sound ... empty."*

*"Try me."*

*They shuffle along for minutes without saying anything. Finally she hears him take a deep breath.*

*"It hurts too much to be without you ... There I said it! Alright?"*

*She has to stop and swish her foot through a puddle on the pier before she answers him.*

*But she is out of words. There is a small furry animal stuck in her throat. She can feel her eyes start to overflow as he draws her to his chest, and lifts her chin with his hand to kiss her. His other hand is on the gun in the sweatshirt. She can feel it.*

*"Don't!" She presses her face against his neck ... "Just a hug ... please."*

*He takes his hand off her face, his other hand off the gun. Wraps her in his arms.*

*So this is what they have left. This is the end for her, she thinks. A very long hug on a foggy Provincetown pier.*

*Afterwards, he tells her what she guessed this conversation was leading to all along. He says that he is ready to die. That he is going to drag himself off like a sick cat now.*

*What can she say to this man staring at her with blank, watery eyes? She gives him a little kiss. Then she turns her back. Leaves him standing in the fog on the pier, and makes the slow walk toward Commercial Street.*

*She does not feel the first flames of anger until a limo pulls up alongside her, stops, and a drunk college boy in the back offers her a hundred dollars for a blow job.*

And yes. She was at Shangri-La too, that evening. If you must know.

The hurt and the anger are still rising in her when she hails a cab to take her back to Shangri-La. When she gets there, she tells the cabbie to wait and rushes down the path to Number Three. She has to hurry. Has to pick up some music, a costume. Has to get back to the Follies. She is running late. Forget the anger. It is showtime. She is not even noticing that the Lodge is lit up like Christmas—but nobody is around—when a shadow pops out of the trees in front of her.

She jumps about two meters.

"Tuki!"

A man's big hairy hands are grabbing her wrists. These hands are not Prem's. They are Alby's.

"Let me go!" She tries to pull away. She smells the cough syrup scent of raspberry schnapps on his breath.

For a second he holds her like she is in handcuffs. Then, suddenly, his fingers spring open. He steps back. She is free ... and out of here ... running down the path.

"Tuki!' he shouts. "Talk to me!"

"I have nothing to say," she murmurs ... and keeps on running. She was feeling a little dizzy before, but now things are even ...

"Please!"

"No, YOU please. Please just leave me alone!"

She hears running behind her. The next thing she knows, he has caught up, pushed himself in front of her to block the path. His neck is bulging. She can see that his forearms are all pumped up like he has just been working out.

"I'm sorry. This can't wait until tomorrow."

"It can wait forever. PLEASE ... just leave me alone!"

She tries to push past him ... but he is not moving.

"I can't do that," he says. "I know you have plenty of reasons to never want to see me again, but you need to level with me. You need to tell me the truth about where Silver's DVDs are. Really, I can help you with the Immigration people ... and this Prem guy if ... "

She thinks he is drunk or crazy. She does not yet know why he is asking her about Silver's DVDs.

"Tuki. He's just a weak little shit with a ... "

"You don't know anything!" she shouts.

He grabs her by the shoulders.

This is when she hauls back and swings. And leaves her hand print on his cheek ... with a very loud smack.

Suddenly she is screaming at him. Terrible names in Thai—and some in Vietnamese—before she turns tail. She runs right down through the woods to her bungalow, grabs her music, her costume, and sprints back to the cab. She wishes she had taken a steak knife from her bungalow. She knows he is coming after her.

## FORTY-TWO

Darkness is sinking over Cambridge when he buzzes Filipa's apartment from the entrance to the building. These are the dog days of August and the city feels gross. The air is like a thick syrup of exhaust fumes and rotting garbage. Traffic crawls along Massachusetts Avenue. In Harvard Square a crowd surrounds a twelve-year-old blind kid with a keyboard and speakers powered by a car battery. He is singing Smokey Robinson's, "Ooo Baby, Baby."

She answers.

"Hey, it's me. Can we talk?"

She says nothing. But she buzzes open the door. He is in, climbing the steps to the third floor, the top, with a dozen roses in his hand.

She meets him in the hall, her arms folded across her chest. All she has on is a Boston Celtics jersey and panties. It is that hot. But a wind is blowing from the open door to her apartment.

Huge floor fans, he thinks. She is the queen of cool.

"Fil—"

"You suck." She sweeps him into her apartment and slams the door. "You really suck, Michael. You know that?"

"Yeah. I do, Fil. I mean I REALLY do. I'd do anything not to have messed things up like this. It isn't fair to you or the wedding."

He is standing there like a statue in the middle of her tiny, very yellow living room. She is glaring at him. Not even a foot away. Big black eyes radiating heat. The sweat is pouring out of him faster than the gale from the floor fans can blow it away.

"What am I suppose to tell my mother? You don't think your little adventure with the police will make the *Standard Times* tomorrow in New Bedford? By this time tomorrow night, it will be all over southern Massachusetts and half of Portugal. Filipa Aguiar's fiancé was busted in a federal raid on a cat house full of transvestites. Perfect. Just perfect. Are you on some kind of drugs?!"

He rubs his eyes.

"Can we sit down? I'm kind of beat."

"You're beat? I just got off thirty-six hours in a pscyh ward. But you know what? In all that time I didn't see anybody who is as whacked as you. You know that, Michael? You're not just clinically interesting. You're certifiable. What the hell has happened to the man I love?" She waves at the couch. "Sure, sit down, make yourself at home. Want me to put the Red Sox on the TV for you? Anything else? How about some popcorn and a beer?!"

A door to one of the bedrooms creaks open just as she says "beer." Her roommate Callie makes a pained face, gives a little wave, and nearly sprints for the door to the stairwell.

"Gotta do the laundry," she says, then vanishes. No detergent or laundry bag in sight.

He sits. Stares at the boat moccasins on his sockless feet.

"Fil, I am so, so sorry. I admit it. I've gotten way too caught up in this case. I know it's stupid, but I feel like a whole lot depends on making a good showing here, covering all the bases. I want you to be proud of me. But I've been so afraid of mucking this up, I've lost all sense of what's important. You. You are my—" He almost says "shining star." Catches himself before the cliché pops out. What the hell is wrong with him?

She sits down beside him, still smoking him with those un-blinking eyes.

"Your what, Michael? What am I?"

He digs deep. "My joy." Not eloquent by any means. But honest. He wants to wrap her in his arms, but he can tell this is not the moment.

She lets out a little sigh. The heat from her eyes drops a few degrees.

"Show don't tell."

This is one of her favorites lines. She picked it up in a seminar somewhere. He hates it. The words come at him with some irrefut-able superiority, stealing every ounce of his energy.

"You're right. You're so right. I haven't been very good about showing you lately. But just give me a chance to make it up to you."

"How?"

"All I need is a few more days, Fil. A week or so at the most. Things are starting to break wide open in the case. Just a little more time. I swear. You won't have to worry about it interfering with the wedding. It won't go to trial. I won't let it. I'll put the whole thing behind us. I've got some new leads on—"

She jumps up, exhales with a deep chuff.

"Let's get out of here."


They've been walking for twenty minutes in silence on the bike path along the Charles River when she finally speaks. "Am I being a bitch?"

He wants to say that there is a new toughness, a determination about her in the last couple of weeks. She does not exactly seem like the carefree girl he has known for almost five years. But what is the point? Weddings stress everybody. And he has been no help. Worse.

"Does your silence mean yes? Am I the girlfriend from hell?"

He looks at the lights of Boston twinkling across the river.

"You're fine. It's me."

She stops walking, turns to him. They are in the shadow of the Harvard boathouse. So close he could touch the wooden walls.

"Are you gay? Is that what this is all about?" Her voice has lost its edge. It sounds softer, almost intimate.

Still, the question stops him in his tracks.

"Look, I'm a psychologist. I know these things happen. Guys who have been straight all their lives come up against some life-changing event like marriage ... and suddenly they start to short circuit. Come out of the closet with a bang."

He starts to walk again, takes her hand. Feels its warmth and its strength.

"Please. Just be honest."

"Okay. There have been times during the last week or so when I've wondered about myself. Wondered why this case has sort of taken over my life. I don't know the answer. At first, maybe my attraction to the case was the puzzle. A very strange puzzle. Tuki's world was so foreign to me that I found myself fascinated by everything about it. I felt like an explorer."

"So you're experimenting?" Her hand is suddenly sweating. He can tell that she is starting to freak.

"No. Jesus!"

"Then this is all about Tuki, isn't it?" She drops his hand, stands in front of him, searching his eyes.

"Look, Fil, I love you. I am going to marry you in two weeks. This case has me all tied in knots. Just give me a week to put this madness behind us."

"That's not what I asked. Are you falling in love with your client?"

"I don't think it's love," he says. The words just rush out of his mouth before he can stop them.

Her hands fly to her face. "Oh my god!"

He puts his arms around her neck and pulls her up against him. She feels soft and warm. Better than that. There is a kind of an elastic tension in her muscles that surrounds him. A hot, moist web. He wishes he could talk to her more about his attraction to Tuki, to this case. She is really smart about things like this, human relations. And right now he does not have a clue. But fat chance. The whole thing has gotten way too personal for everyone involved.

"I love you!" he whispers.

She pulls back out of his arms. "I need to be alone right now. Go do what you have to do."

"Just give me a week."

She runs the palms of her hands over her temples as if trying to hold in something that is bleeding from inside her head. "I don't know."

# FORTY-THREE

He is feeling shaky. He has been waiting at the prosecutor's office for most of Wednesday morning, hoping for a chance to see the D. A. When he was out with his father and Tio Tommy on the *Rosa Lee*, he could go for a week on almost no sleep when the cod were piling up on deck like cord wood. But now the fight with Filipa and two days without much shut-eye is killing him.

"You look like hell, Mr. Decastro." The D. A. is squinting across his desk at him with a skeptical look. He is a large, impatient man. "And you have ten minutes to tell me what's on your mind. Your client want to cop a plea?"

"Not exactly, sir. I've come across some new information that I think could break this case wide open. But I need your help. The state police have two queens named Ruby and Silver in custody at the moment for prostitution and imm—"

"I know all about it, counselor. I also know that we nabbed you and your client in the same sting. Get to your point."

"Both Silver and Ruby had pretty strong reasons to want the victim dead and—"

"If you are trying to deflect the heat off your client just because we picked up her fellow hookers, save it for court."

"I understand. But I think one or both of these queens knows more than she has said, is holding back on us."

"Us, Mr. Decastro? We are not on the same team here."

He feels his back starting to sweat under his suit coat.

"I just mean we are both trying to find justice in this case. The truth."

The D. A. rolls his eyes. "The truth is, counselor, we have your client on a surveillance tape stealing the murder weapon from the victim's bedroom just hours before the murder."

"It could have been faked!" He knows he's out of line here. But to hell with it. He suddenly feels a surge of adrenaline jolt his arms.

The D. A. looks astonished. Now he is rising from his chair. "I think we're done."

"No. Really, sir. Please. I don't mean to be belligerent—"

"Then don't. Calm down, man. You come in here looking half-cocked, full of piss and vinegar, like some actor on *Law and Order*. I won't have it!"

"It's just ... just that in my investigations over the last ten days or so, I've learned a lot about drag queens. They are the consummate actors. Female impersonation is their stock-in-trade. They have trunks full of costumes and wigs and makeup. If a queen can make herself look like Madonna, then why can't she make herself look like my client, too? Especially on a dimly lit, grainy security tape."

The D. A. settles back in his seat. He lets out a hoot. "You are really reaching, counselor, if this is your defense. Try this in court and the jury will be laughing at you before I'm done."

Michael feels his cheeks burning.

"Look, I know the victim was bullying your client in the dressing room at the Provincetown Follies. And I'm betting that he was using her status as an illegal to blackmail her into turning tricks. So here's what I'm offering. We'll forget about the videotape ... and the arson. Murder Two. And deportation. That's my offer. Take it or leave it. Some detective from Thailand has been calling me. Seems they want your client for arson back there, too. She's got a thing for fire."

He realizes he cannot fight this guy. Does not know how. And he is almost out of time here. He better try a different approach.

"Yes, sir, we'll take this under consideration. But I still think Ruby and Silver are involved or know a lot more than they have told us."

The D. A. is no dummy. He knows that what the public wants is swift justice. They want him to wrap up this case before summer ends. And they want to know that while life in P-town is not exactly mainstream America, it is safe from murderers, arsonists, and prostitutes. Maybe he can close this whole affair if he plays ball a little.

"Okay. What is it you want me to do, Mr. Decastro?"

"Keep Silver and Ruby in jail for a little longer. Just slow the paperwork when they try to make bail."

"Why?"

"So you can interview them separately. Get them to talk about the night of the murder and fire again. They've got a pretty stormy relationship. Maybe one of them will rat out the other if they think you might drop some of the charges."

The D. A. is trying to look like he is listening. But he is fidgeting with a ballpoint pen. Clicking it in and out.

"We've got hours of interviews with them from two weeks ago."

"Yes sir, I've read the material. But, with all due respect, I think what they told police before about where they were and what they saw at the time of the fire and the murder sounds pretty vague. They claim they were at a party in the East End. Lots of people saw them. But there were more than fifty or sixty people there. One or both of them could have slipped out, stabbed Costelano, set the fire, come back to the party, and ..."

The D. A. suddenly rises to his feet, extends his right hand across the desk to Michael. He has no choice but to stand and take the offered hand.

"I've got to hand it to you, counselor. You sure are giving this case the old college try."

"Yes, sir. But—"

"But the guy from the Follies, Richard somebody, already sprung the suspects in question, whose real names, by the way, are Steven Simmers and Ronald Polvey. Quite a pair. Two real fine ambassadors from Great Britain and Australia. That Richie fellow left here grinning like a pig in shit with the prospect of having them back at his little tent show."

"He's a thug."

"We know. We're watching him. But his sweethearts are clean. As far as the murder and arson go, we are way ahead of you. Our boys hammered at them all day yesterday. But they stuck by their alibi. And it holds up. We sent a couple of detectives to check it out. There is no chance either one of them could have stabbed Costelano or lit the fire."

"Why?"

"Because we've got about thirty people who say when the first sirens went off for the fire, they were standing in a circle watching Polvey, the one called Ruby, down on his knees giving his buddy a smoothie under his skirt."

"Again?"

"Beg pardon?"

"Never mind."

"Freaks pay to watch. A hundred dollars a head ... so to speak." He shakes his head, disgusted. "Unbelievable. The crap people will do in public these days. Discuss my offer with your client. If I haven't heard from you in two days, we go to trial. Think about that, counselor."

## FORTY-FOUR

He is not giving up on his theory about an imposter on the security tape. He wants to watch it with Tuki. If it is really her, maybe she will do something to show her guilt while she is watching ... especially if he surprises her with it. If she seems like she has been caught in the act, then he will bring up the plea bargain. If she seems innocent, then ... who the hell is the thief on the film?

And there is the other thing. Prem Kittikatchorn is lurking out there somewhere, just waiting to do mischief, or murder. Why would a man who has followed her all the way from Bangkok let her go so easily? Wouldn't he feed his hunger for Tuki, like his craving for *pung chao,* right down to the end? Haven't the two always been connected? He is still stalking her. You can bet on it. Unless there is someone to stop the bugger.

He figures it is too late to bring the cops in on this. Tuki has not filed a complaint. There has been no actual threat. And as far as the police are concerned, Prem is nothing more than Tuki's fictitious alibi.

He has to get out to P-town, take care of business. But this time he is not going empty handed. He has a pellet pistol tucked under the waistband of his jeans. Tio Tommy gave it to him for his twelfth birthday. He used to take it on the *Rosa Lee* to shoot the birds raiding the net when they were hauling back. It is not really a gun. Not a Baretta or a Glock. And it would not kill a man. But it might stop him for a while, if you hit him just right.

The traffic on Route 6 is hideous, and Michael does not get to the Follies until Silver is just wrapping up her act. The room is packed. But when Silver leaves the stage and the lights come up, a straight couple who have clearly seen enough of the lavender crowd vacates

a table. It is down front just two rows back from the stage. Michael
grabs it in a flash, before he has a chance to think things through. It is
one of the best seats in the house if you want to watch the performers.
But it sucks if you want to check out the crowd. They are at his back.
In the dark. He is not liking this. A killer could be hiding there.

When he sits down, he feels the barrel of the pellet pistol dig
into his hip. It does not make him feel any safer, and he wonders what
he will do if the shooting starts. Dive under the table maybe. Then
he thinks, perhaps, there is some truth to what Fil said about him
being certifiable. To hell with it. A double shot of tequila ought to
cure that. Make that two. By the time the lights go down, he thinks
he is ready for war.

The sound system hums for a second, then the music cuts in.
The song is Patti LaBelle's "Lady Marmalade," the story of one very
foxy lady of the night in New Orleans. After the first three bars of
the song, he can hear Lady Marmalade's sales pitch playing in his
head, lowdown and sassy: "Gitchi, gitchi, ya ya da da, gitchi, gitchi,
ya ya here."

The spotlight picks up Tuki making her entrance with a sexy
shuffle down the staircase. She has a look he has never seen on her
before. She is wearing a gold kimono stitched with little red dragons.
Her lips glisten bright crimson. Liner accents the Asian shape of her
eyes, her hair is pinned up in loose geisha folds.

Once again Vietnam is playing in his mind ... taking him back
to Saigon where the chorus of the song, "*Voulez vous coucher avec moi
ce soir*" echoed from the bars in Saigon twenty-four hours a day. He
imagines a bar girl named Misty, Huong Mei, singing to the juke box,
dancing on the bar of a Saigon dive. A golden-skinned goddess.

So what Michael sees coming down the stairs is not Patti or
Whitney or Janet. This next groove is spinning out from a lost little
lady named Misty, sending out the lala to the dark man in her life. A
private dancer coming at you straight from Saigon.

And she is smoking. Sashaying down the runway in that kimono,
kissing up to the mike, showing some leg. Bringing it down. Rocking
the poles. Working the steps.

The crowd is already howling. The sound kid at his panel is up on his feet, jamming, into the lip-synch with Lady Marmalade. But Michael is losing sight of all of this because he has been spotted, and the lady with the mike is homing in for the table-sex thing. He does not even know what is happening until she has him pinned to his chair with a lap dance. The humid air shimmers. Smoke in the spotlights.

But she has barely started. The kimono is still covering all of her surprises. So she struts away from him to sing the second verse ... and now she shakes her hair out in a wild explosion of curls. Misty's ghost struts. The shoes come off. The kimono is history. She works a pole dance in her black bra and G-string. Now she slips out of the bra and slinks back toward the new man in her life. Bump and grind. Like, eat your heart out, la. Her breasts are close enough to whisper in his ears, "gitchi, gitchi, ya ya here."

As she dances, as she sings, the air grows thick as fog in the room ... and in his mind. The golden spotlight flickers across her skin. He feels a moist heat. He smells a place he has never been. The incense and the opium ... the ginger and the charcoal fires ... the water buffalo and the rice paddies ... the river and the *plaa* ... the sweat of men ... the milk of mothers. Bangkok. Thonburi. The River House. Saigon—

Lights on.

The crowd howls. She bends over and kisses him on the mouth. He thinks this would be a good time for someone to take a shot at the two of them. Somewhere nearby, a waitress drops a glass. It hits the floor with a bang. He jumps up, hand going for the pellet gun.

# FORTY-FIVE

A thousand times before coming to America, he warned himself he might find a fallen angel. But seeing this lap dance, watching her rubbing and kissing the *farang,* is too much for Prem Kittikatchorn. She is shameless. He thought the escort service and her midnight rendezvous with the giant, the dead man, were the worst of her shame. But see how she humiliates herself here under the spotlights? Before a cheering crowd? This place is worse than Bangkok. She could teach a Patpong whore how to slither in sewer filth. He used to like the Americans. But look what they have done to her. Monsters.

His anger is beginning to tear at him, he is starting to care about something other than his dreams. Now he feels his hands starting to tremble slightly, and he knows that soon he will be crashing unless he shoots up more *pung chao.* But he left his kit twelve miles down the highway at a roadside motel in Wellfleet. And right now he has to save the queen of his heart from her shame. He thought he could swoop into America, win her back, and carry her off to a star where they could live happily ever after. This is the dream he always has when he feels the horse racing through his veins.

But since that night almost two weeks ago when he lied and said he was going off to die like a cat, the night of fire and death in Provincetown, his dream is cracking. Fading out. He had hoped that after the death of the giant, he would see a change in her. An opening for him to make things like they used to be. But there is no chance. Look at her. She is too far gone. He is too far gone. The only way to end their disgrace is the way he saved his wife and little girls from the humiliation of his queer cravings, his addictions. With bullets. Unlike heroin, unlike Tuki, bullets are forever. They taught him that in military school.

He has been lurking in the shadows, waiting for this moment of justice and redemption. Trailing her as best he can. Looking for his chance. But the *farang* lawyer has been in the way, the police and Immigration have been in the way. So tonight he has come out of the shadows. Brought himself and his gun—a snub-nose .357— right into the Follies. He will use this in front of more than two hundred witnesses.

But he cannot get off the shot. He was not much of a marksman back in military school, and he still is not. She is too far away. And there are people standing in his line of fire. He got here too late for a table down front so he chose this seat at the bar where his head and torso are above the crowd. He thought she would see him, could not miss him. Come to him the way she used to back in Bangkok at the Underground. Then, when she was a few feet away, singing just for him, he would put a bullet in her head. And his.

As she chants her Patti La Belle teaser, she looks right at him for a moment. Her eyes unblinking. But it is like she does not recognize him. He is just another John who would put dollars in her G-string. She is lost in her own dreams of Saigon, her mother, her father ... and maybe of this lawyer for whom she lap dances, her breasts in his face.

Suddenly the show is over. She slips off to her dressing room. The lawyer is getting up to leave. There is brusque purpose in the way he pushes through the crowd. The way a man on a mission moves. Maybe a man in love. He is going to meet up with the whore, to be sure.

Now the man from Bangkok leaves twenty dollars on the bar for his drink, slides off the stool, and follows the lawyer out the door.

## FORTY-SIX

What may soon be People's Exhibit A, the videotape from the security camera at Alby's Glass House, is rolling. It is almost one o'clock in the morning, and they are back at her bungalow at Shangri-La. He has popped the tape in the VCR while she is drying her hair after her shower.

"Is this it?" she asks, dropping onto the bed where he is sitting. She is wearing her blue robe, her hair is wild and fluffy.

"We're just getting to the part."

The focus is terrible. But it definitely looks like Tuki who they see on the screen, slinking into view on the deck outside Alby's bedroom in the same robe she has on now. Even though the face is shadowy, those curls sure do look like the ones he saw on her when she did her Whitney Houston thing onstage. A wig. Why? Unless this is not really Tuki who darts through the open screen door, takes two steps to the bureau, snatches up the DVDs, grabs the little jade-handled *dha* off the desk, splits like the wind. In the foreground, he can see the shadows of Silver and the master dancing a fugue on top of the sheets. Tuki lets out a sharp little cry.

"What's the matter?"

"I wish I had killed them right there."

He has a sinking feeling in the stomach. Is she confessing? He tries not to shout at her when he speaks, tries keeping a neutral voice.

"Why didn't you?"

"Because I was not there. That person looks like me ... but she does not act like me." She gets off the bed. Finds the remote beside the TV and shuts it off.

"I don't understand."

She sits down beside him again, her face a foot from his ... those soft, dark eyes of a child staring right into his.

"Would a girl who sees the man who makes every part of her

body vibrate like a temple gong *not look* when he is down and dirty with Silver? Like my archenemy *neung*, number one, la? No way, Joe. Right? I would look. But the thief in the film never looks. Does not bat an eyebrow. And those are not my earrings."

He snaps the tape into slow rewind. "What?"

There is only a second or so when the robber enters the room that you see a flash of an earring.

"She is wearing dark pendants of some kind. Not mine, la."

He is starting to think she is on to something here, wondering if she sees any hint of who is wearing her drag—

A shot rips though the picture window.

Shards of glass sting his neck. Blood blooms at her right temple and starts to run down the side of her face. Even as the glass is still flying, he snags her around the shoulders with an arm and pulls her onto the floor. They hit and roll on the broken glass.

Another shot cracks from somewhere outside, buzzes over their heads, and smacks the corner of the TV. Gray plastic splinters everywhere. Two more shots burrow into the bed with faint little thuds.

He lays with his body half-covering hers, the damp hair towel in his hand. He is pressing it to her temple, trying to stop the bleeding. Her eyes are closed. She feels limp.

"Christ, Tuki!"

"What happened?" Her eyes open, dart side to side as if she is just waking up.

He wants to tell her that she has been shot. But before he can push out the words, he hears hurried steps outside in the woods. Coming closer. A shot whacks the headboard on the bed.

A sort of growl comes from her throat. Suddenly she is shouting in Thai. The tones are not the sound of someone who is wounded or afraid. She is scolding like a frustrated, impatient mother. And she does not stop. Although the only light in the room comes from the small lamp on the nightstand, the room suddenly seems lit with spotlights.

Michael draws the pellet gun from his waistband, pumps up the pressure in its gas chamber. He does not know what kind of weapon the stalker has but the shots sound loud and heavy. He is guessing he's up against some kind of traditional revolver. Like the police use. The shooter must be just about out of bullets now. The trick is to get him to empty the gun. Then jump him before he can reload or pull another weapon.

Now he hears the scrape of sneakers on the porch. If the shooter comes right up to the blown out picture window casing, he will have a clear shot at them lying like fish in the glare of the halogen deck lights on the *Rosa Lee*.

He reaches up to the nightstand, grabs the lamp. Rips its cord from the wall and flings it out the open window casing.

The room goes dark. The lamp shatters with a crash on the porch outside as he pushes Tuki under the bed. He is rolling across the small room to the cover of the front wall when he hears a loud crack and sees the muzzle flash not even fifteen feet away at the window opening. As the bullet kicks up a little storm of glass from the floor, he hears the click of a hammer on an empty chamber.

There is no hesitation. He rolls up on his feet, pellet pistol in both hands. But before he has a chance to fire into the dark, Tuki starts shouting in Thai. A new note has crept into her voice. It sounds pleading. But more than that … tender.

Someone grunts. Then starts running. Michael can hear crashing through the bushes, heading away up the hill toward the parking lot. He takes up the chase. There is no moon and the starlight barely penetrates the woods. A fallen branch trips him. He goes down, the gun discharging when he hits. His knee hurts like hell. He is wondering if he shot himself, when he hears a motorcycle start and race away down the road.

For a minute or two all he can hear is the chirping of crickets, frogs, and night birds. Then Tuki calls his name.

By the time he limps back to the bungalow, she has turned on a light. She is looking at her face in the bathroom mirror, dabbing her head wound with a wet washcloth. But when she sees him limping, she drops the cloth and runs to him. She wraps him in her arms and says something in Thai. Just a couple of words.

They sound soft. Apologetic. Her body squeezes him to her until he stops shaking.

"This is bad, la."

"What?"

"He is not dead."

"Is he supposed to be?"

# FORTY-SEVEN

After he phones in the shooting, the police show up and immediately start to bust his chops about the pellet pistol, calling him Rambo. But the EMTs say later for that. These people need attention. It turns out neither one of them has been shot. She has a gash in her scalp from flying glass that the medics close up with some kind of fancy glue. He smacked his knee real hard on a rock when he fell, needs an ice pack and an Ace bandage.

"You two are lucky as hell," says a detective holding up the slug he has pried out of the floor with a penknife. "Do you know what this is? You know what one of these things can do to human flesh?" The bullet is spread out like a flattened, ragged mushroom.

"I don't know much about guns," says Michael.

The detective looks at the pellet pistol the patrolmen have confiscated, bagged on the kitchen counter. "No shit, counselor. But I'd say your visitor does. This is a man stopper."

He turns to Tuki, who is sitting at the kitchen table while the EMT finishes her job on the wound. "I don't like how this is getting to be a weekly thing. You and the law. Who the hell's been shooting at you, sweetheart? What have you got yourself into?"

"She doesn't have to answer that. She's the victim here, not the suspect."

The detective is a statey, a wiry Italian-looking guy, middle-aged. White short-sleeve shirt, baggy brown suit pants. He wheels on Michael. "If I want your opinion, I'll ask for it. But, see? I don't. I just want to know how Tuki here is feeling about almost having her gorgeous little self turned into Swiss cheese. Who did this, Tuki? Help me get this sick shit off the streets!"

Her mouth opens a little. There is a name on the tip of her tongue. Then she closes it a second before answering. "I do not know, detective. I did not see him." Her eyes flash a look at Michael. He cannot read it.

"Come on. Don't tell me—"

"Hey! Leave her alone, okay?"

The detective wheels on Michael, glares. "Fine, wise guy. Have it your way. I'm just the dumb cop. You don't want to cooperate, don't cooperate. Get yourself and your twiggy girlfriend blown all to hell. You think anyone really cares? But this is my crime scene. You can't stay here."

Tuki suddenly has a sick look on her face. "This is my home."

"Not any more, darling."

"But where will I ..."

The detective rolls his eyes at Michael. "Why don't you ask Rambo here."


When he wakes up on the couch, late morning sun is streaming into his attic. Tina Turner is singing, "What's Love Got to Do With It?" softly on the stereo. Tuki is standing at the stove wearing his powder blue dress shirt and pouring hot water into two cups of tea.

He does not think that he did anything weird last night, even though they both got a little toasted on Sambuca when they finally got to Chatham. He still has his boxers on. And there is no way she got on this couch with him. Thank god.

"I was having such a crazy dream."

She turns and smiles. "About me?"

He nods.

"Was I still alive?"

"Very. You were standing in a boat."

"You want to go out in a boat?"

He rubs his eyes. She hands him his tea and sits down on the couch. "Yeah, but ... but why didn't you want to tell the cops about your trigger-happy boyfriend?"

"No more police. They do not understand."

"He tried to kill us!"

"It is the *pung chao*. Not Prem. He needs help."

"Can I ask you why you want to protect him? Did he kill Costelano?"

She kisses him on the cheek. "Later, I promise. Right now it is a beautiful day. We are alive. And I love boats. *Sip bia klai mu.*" There is a shrill giddiness in her voice that he has never heard before.

"Pardon?"

"Now or never."


By noon they have bought and launched Michael's new boat. It is the Boston Whaler with a Johnson seventy and a trailer that Michael saw for sale down on Ryder Lane. He knows Filipa is going to have a fit, but he feels like he has scored big time. At this price the boat is a steal, even though both boat and engine are about twenty years old. And now he is taking Tuki on a picnic to Monomoy Island, the long, thin sand spit, the wildlife preserve, south of Chatham. She is so right. After last night, a little escape is in order. Damn, someone was trying to shoot him.

The tide is in so they are running along at 30 knots in the shallows on the west side of the island. He has heard that the southern tip of the island is swarming with stripers. So he has his casting rod, and he thinks that if they can get into the fish, maybe the thrill of a couple of bass on the line will take his mind off this madman with a cannon. He is going to love teaching Tuki how to lure, hook, fight, and land a couple of big fellas. She will just eat it up. Then when they are high on the ocean and the stripers, they will drop anchor. He will crack a bottle of Pinot Gri. They will graze on the lobster salad they bought for the picnic. And forget about the rest of the world. He had thought that he would be sharing all of this with Filipa. How things change.

There is a moderate breeze out of the southwest. Two- and three-foot waves are starting to crest, slap the side of the Whaler. He is standing, steering, not noticing that Tuki has the hood of her sweatshirt pulled up to shield her hair and is hugging his waist hard with her right arm to keep her balance. It is like the wind and waves are not even registering with him. His mind keeps replaying last night's shooting. He sees the blood running down the side of her face. Over and over again ...

He is watching it drip off the horn of her jaw when something like a haystack in the sea breaks right on the starboard bow and sends a sheet of water over the boat. It rips off his sunglasses and soaks them both. The fishing rod gets carried away. There is a foot of water in the boat. The engine coughs, groans with the new load.

"Shit. Just shit!"

"What's the matter, Michael?"

He looks at her. For a second he is seeing a double exposure. Her bleeding face overlaid with this other. The sweatshirt is pasted to her chest now. The hood torn back off her long curls. They fly in the wind. Water streams off her golden skin. But in a funny sort of way, she looks beautiful to him.

"I know better than to take a wave like that at this speed. Christ, my father would banish me to the fo'castle!"

"What?" She is hearing his words, but they make no sense.

He eases the throttle forward. The bow pitches up. Water that has been swirling around their legs races out the drains at the back of the boat. When it is almost gone, he adds more power and swings the boat in a sharp arch back toward Chatham.

"What are you doing?"

"Taking us home."

"Why?"

"I can't concentrate. I've lost my focus. I can't even run a boat anymore."

"I don't understand."

"I can't get my mind off you. Everywhere I look, I picture your face dripping with blood. Or I see someone who looks like you dancing in a dark bar. I have this terrible feeling that some really bad stuff is coming. And I only have about five days left to stop it. You've got to take me to Prem, Tuki. And you have to tell me why you are protecting him."

## FORTY-EIGHT

"You know a place called Nantucket, la?" She faces him over a table, toys with a glass of seltzer with lime in front of her.

"It's an island." His eyes skip away from her face, dart around the room to see if anyone is watching them. Then he swills on his bottle of Corona.

In P-town he does not think twice about being out in public at a restaurant or pub with Tuki. But in Chatham it feels dirty and wrong. It is not because she is a tranny. He has almost ceased to care about the details of her plumbing, or what people would think of him for keeping such company. It is just that now, since more than half the summer has passed, people around town recognize him. They have often seen him with Filipa. Some know he is engaged. That is why he has picked this roadhouse for their conversation. It is a little dive four miles from Chatham village ... away from prying eyes. And right now it is in the rarest of summer moods. Nearly empty. Almost the last of the lunch crowd has left. Bob Dylan echoes softly from the sound system at the bar, singing, "Lay Lady Lay."

He loves this song. But he hates this sneaking around, wonders if she knows why they are here and not at the Chatham Squire in the village. Nantucket? He bets he wouldn't feel this way if they were in Nantucket where nobody knows him.

"What about Nantucket?"

She stares at her hands.

"If you want him, he will be at this place Nantucket now. His family keeps a house there for vacations when they are in America. He always told me I would see it. Now, I guess I will." She gives a little grin. Nerves. He is learning to read the moods of her smiles. Lines of salt, left over from her dousing in the Whaler, crinkle at the corners of her eyes.

"Tell me the rest."

"What?"

"Why are you protecting him? I have to know, Tuki. Help me." His voice drills her. "That guy wants to kill us!"

Tears well in her eyes. Then she says, "That is why." Her voice is not much more than a whisper.

"I don't understand."

"I was ... I was trying to protect you. Not him."

"Me? I'm your lawyer. I don't need protecting. I—"

"You are getting married in two weeks. What would your girlfriend do if ..." She cannot continue.

He realizes that he has hardly thought about Filipa for two days. Tears have begun to roll down Tuki's face.

"Tuki? What's the ..."

She shakes her head.

"Nothing. It is just silly girl business, la. Go away. Do not look at me. I cannot stand ..." She flashes him a teary grin. Then she covers her face with her hands, gets up, starts racing for the women's room.

He catches her by the hand just as she reaches the restroom door. She flails at him with her free arm for a second or two. Before she melts against his chest.

"Everything's going to be okay."

"No."

"Why?"

"I told Prem."

"What?"

"I promised myself to him."

"That's all over."

"No, I told him last night I would come to him ... if he just let me have one more day with you. Now I have to go to Nantucket. He is dying."

Michael almost says, "Good. Screw Prem." But then he remembers the case. This guy could be the real killer, or a star witness.

"Do you think you can get him to talk?"

It is almost dark when the ferry from Hyannis lands them on Nantucket. Tuki has called in sick to the Follies. As if Richie cannot figure out that after all of the shooting last night, she may not be coming back for a while ... if ever.

"Now where?" He asks this question like she is his guide.

"I'm starving."

"You're kidding. What if he gets away?"

She gives him a look. *This is an island, la.* Then she takes his hand and squeezes it. "Please."

He understands what she is asking, feels it. She wants just an hour or two more with him, before who knows what. Their fishing trip was a bust. The stop for drinks was sick with tension. They both slept on the ferry trip over here. Now their time is running out.

He sees men and women in the throng on the street by the ferry dock eyeing her. He knows they are wondering if she is Halle Berry or Tyra Banks. She looks that good. Delicate leather sandals, pale yellow cotton slacks, baby blue boatneck cotton sweater. Her sun-streaked braids and curls pulled up in a ponytail. No makeup. Sapphire studs in her ears.

But it is her eyes that get him. They sparkle now as she looks at him, runs her hand up his forearm, and hooks him close to her.

"I would touch you forever, if you were my man."

He flinches.

He knows his way around Nantucket Town. Has come here a dozen or so times with his father and Tio Tommy on the *Rosa Lee* to find shelter from storms. But what he knows best are the bars like the Rose and Crown and the Atlantic Café. Finding a room or a place to stay is virgin territory. But they do not walk three blocks from the ferry dock before Tuki spots a vacancy sign on an inn called the Jared Coffin House. It is a Federal-style brick mansion. There has been a last-minute cancellation. Suddenly a room of colonial splendor is theirs for the swipe of a Visa card.

The desk clerk smiles at Tuki as Michael signs in. "Newlyweds?"

She smiles.

"We're wondering about a quiet place for dinner," he says.

"May I recommend our dining room or perhaps room service?"

Suddenly he is tired of feeling like a fugitive, or lawyer for the mob, when he is with her.

"What do you say we eat out?"


"Please, Michael. Take your time!" Her hand reaches over the table, grabs his as he lifts his wine glass for another swallow. The entrees have not arrived yet, and he has single-handedly downed well over half the bottle of Merlot. They are sitting near the storefront window of a quiet little restaurant called Black-Eyed Susan's. A soft violet light bathes India Street outside. Couples stroll the sidewalk, flickering in and out of the glow of the street lamps that have just come on.

"Sorry."

"You don't have to get drunk."

"How do you know?"

"I need you tonight. What is the matter?"

He puts down the wine and looks her square in the eyes.

"It's not worth talking about."

"Please, la." Her hand is on his again. "Do not shut me out. Not tonight. Just talk to me."

"You really want to know what's wrong?"

"I am so afraid." Her eyes stare at the flickering flame of the candle on their table.

"So am I, Tuki. That's what's wrong. I feel all torn up inside. I'm scared as hell. 'Face your fears and they will shrink to the size of bugs,' my father always told me. I have always believed him. But now I ... I don't know. This is too crazy."

"What?"

"I think I'm in way over my head."

"You want me to get another lawyer again? Want me to see the police? Tell them Prem is here. The shooter is here?" He hears a hitch in her voice.

"It's too late."

"Buddha says it is never too late."

"Buddha isn't getting married in twelve days."

"What do you mean?"

Something rises in his throat. He tries to swallow, but the words rush out. "I don't know."

# FORTY-NINE

He is the first to wake. He hears a raw wind whir around the eaves of the inn, smells the morning fog swirling over the island. Tuki lies on the far side of the bed wearing his Red Sox shirt. She has her head half-buried under a pillow. Her breathing is fitful, but she seems asleep. He does not want to disturb her. Knows what she has been through, fears what is still to come for her today.

But Jesus. This is crazy. He can picture the sneer on the D. A.'s face when he asks him to describe the sleeping arrangements for attorney and client in Nantucket. When he says, "We shared a bed out of desperation. I never touched her. We are not romantically involved." They will probably toss him off the bar. Filipa will send him packing. He cannot even imagine what his father will say.

Part of him wants to just get up and sneak out of here. But he has made her a promise. For her, and his own self respect, he has to see this through. Stand by his obligations. It is the only thing that feels right to him. He wonders if this is all about an over-developed need to please.

But maybe it is about something more basic. Something that he cannot put his finger on yet. One thing he knows for sure, it is not about physical attraction. Tuki is easy on his eyes, no question. But he has not gotten used to her touching him. He still cringes every time. Feels himself start to sweat, a lump forming in his throat, when she flirts. He thinks he knows what physical desire feels like, it is the lightning that shoots through his arms and legs when he is within ten feet of Filipa. There is none of that lightning with Tuki. It is something else, some other kind of bond.

He wishes he could understand it. But right now he has a more immediate problem. He has to find Prem Kittikatchorn and get him to explain how he killed the Great One and set the fire. Maybe he can still get Tuki, and himself, out of the spider's web once and for all.

There is only one Kittikatchorn in the Nantucket phone directory. On Madaket Road. The house is somewhere out at the west end of the island. By nine o'clock in the morning they are hunting for the place in a rented Jeep. Michael has a small tape recorder in one pocket of his khaki windbreaker. It is still foggy. Very foggy. The headlights of oncoming traffic come and go, phantoms in the thick mist.

"There!" she says, after they have been cruising back and forth between the beach community at Madaket and Nantucket Town for almost an hour. The fog has only lifted slightly, but now he can see houses, set back from the road along driveways. There is a motorcycle parked in one. "That is Prem's."

His first notion is to jam on the brakes and make a sharp turn into the driveway. But that would eliminate the element of surprise. Who knows what condition this guy is in? He might come out shooting with that cannon of his.

"I'm going to stop farther up the road, okay?"

She nods. Out of the corner of his eye, he sees that she has begun smiling like a crazy woman. This isn't good.

They park the Jeep in the public lot on Madaket Beach and decide to hike up the strand, approach the house from the ocean side. Even in the fog, it is not hard to find the place. It is a stilt house with two wings and an A-frame in the middle, its seaside wall is an array of sliding doors and glass. Stairs lead up to a deck that surrounds the main floor of the house. You can take the stairs leading from the driveway or another set from the beach.

They approach the house on a path through the beach grass. Their shoes are in their hands as they circle around among the stilts beneath the house, listening for signs of activity. The melody of Lionel Richie's "Stuck on You" seeps softly down over them. Tuki smiles, has a memory of a night in a limo in Bangkok. The River House. This is his music. His place. He is waiting for her.

Michael is getting a creepy feeling. When they retreat into the brush off to the side of the house, he pulls out his cell phone.

"What is that for?"

"I'm going to call the police. We've done our job. We've found him. Let them take it from here."

She grabs the phone away.

"*Rit luat kap pu.* You can't squeeze blood from a crab. He won't talk to them. He'll kill himself either with the gun or too much *pung chao.* Then what, la?"

He sees her point. Prem is the lynchpin in his defense. Everything has been leading up to this moment, getting a confession out of him. If the man dies, the case folds. She goes to prison for about twenty years ... or gets sent back to a death camp in Thailand.

"Let me go to him. Give me the tape recorder. He still loves me, he will talk to me. You go up to the deck from the beach side. I will get him to talk in the front room. You can watch us. If anything gets crazy, you call the police."

He does not like the strange, high-pitched note of confidence and urgency in her whisper. She is faking it. She is scared to death. But he does not have a better plan.

She holds out the phone to him, flips it open. "Come on, Michael. *Nam khun hai rip tak.* When the water rises, hurry and collect it."

He stares at the offered cell phone and scowls. This is bad.

Her eyes plead.

He turns his eyes away, takes the phone back, folds it closed, fishes in his pocket for the tape recorder, and passes it to her.

She leans toward him and kisses his cheek. Then she is just a silhouette in the fog mounting the stairs from the driveway.

He can hear them talking as he tiptoes toward the immense plate-glass windows and sliding-glass doors that look out on the deck and the ocean from the center of the house. Pressed against the wall at the edge of the window, he can see the back of Prem's head as he sits on a couch. But most of the room is blocked from his view. Prem is smoking. The scent of burning tobacco drifts out through a screen door. He can hear her voice perfectly, but he cannot see her or understand a word. She is speaking in Thai. *Damn.* He cannot tell how things are going ... or remember when he draws his phone, pointing the little antenna like the barrel of a gun.

For a while she speaks in soft tones. Her voice sounds tender, earnest. Maybe pleading.

Prem grunts, says something abrupt, disdainful, or sarcastic.

Tuki fires back at him with hot words.

He throws his lit cigarette over his shoulder with the whip of his arm. It strikes the screen door, leaves a smudge, falls to the wooden floor, and continues to burn. It is not ten feet from where Michael is hiding.

Suddenly Prem shouts something, just two or three words, then jumps to his feet. He comes around the couch. Starts jabbering again in fast short bursts. His voice rising with each new salvo. He looks as pale as a drowning man, scrambling for the fresh air as he heads toward the screen door, the deck. And he has a snub-nose revolver in his hand.

Michael presses himself back against the outside wall of the house, raises the phone in front of him, punches in 911. His right index finger is ready to press the send button.

Prem snaps the barrel of the pistol to his temple, closes his eyes.

Tuki shrieks. Just two words. *"Mai! Chi!"* Suddenly, she is at his side. Tears are running down her cheeks as she tears at the gun in his hand, hugs him, soaks his face in kisses.

Something claws at Michael's stomach. She's still in love with the man. Jesus Christ.

In the blink of an eye, the prick collars her around the neck with his free arm and presses the gun to her head. He is crying wildly as he pulls back the hammer of his pistol with his thumb. His face contorts like that famous photograph of a prisoner being executed by a Vietnamese officer.

Michael leaps—right through the screen door. His arms flailing. His body hitting Prem and Tuki with a loud slap. The gun discharges.

Now they are in a heap on the floor. He can feel a burning sensation shooting all the way up his left arm. But his right hand still holds the cell phone, and now he is shoving it up under the unshaven chin of Prem Kittikachorn like it is a weapon, screaming at this fucking asshole. The man is as limp as a sick child, and his breath stinks of tobacco and whiskey. His gun has flown from his hand, skidded away across the room.

Then it is in Tuki's hand, and she is standing over the men. She is pointing the gun at Prem. He weeps softly.

"Come on, Michael!"

He staggers to his feet, looks around for a pool of blood to see who has been shot. But there is no blood. *Unbelievable.*

While Tuki holds the gun on Prem with one hand, she looks him in the eyes and holds up the index finger of her other hand as if telling him to wait. She says something quietly to him in Thai. Prem closes his eyes, tears still flowing.

"He didn't kill Alby ... but he told me who did."

## FIFTY

*She is walking aimlessly on the sand flats by the cottages in the East End. It is just a couple of days after she gave that thug Joey his blow job in the back of a Lear jet. She is sick with shame. She's wearing nothing but a pair of daisy print panties, when here comes Nikki just about out of breath in her sweaty gray sports bra, pink shorts, and Nikes.*

*"Where did you come from, la?" she asks. Her voice full of Vietnam, Delta and Brandy.*

*"When you didn't show up for breakfast at the Lodge the last couple of days, I know something is wrong. So today I just came looking. It took me a while to find you, but I know how much you love water so ... here we are."*

*"Yeah," Tuki smiles, "here we are,* padruga." *She is almost brain dead at this point, but her heart is suddenly feeling big as a song.*

*The tide is out. They walk on the sand flats at the edge of the water all afternoon without seeing anything but crabs scuttling around, gulls digging for clams, sandpipers running back and forth ahead of little waves. Nikki peels to her panties, too. It is as hot as the beaches of Pattaya and Hua Hin. They do not have any sunscreen. So their bodies are just soaking in the ultraviolets. Tuki is starting to turn as black as her daddy, but she is not even caring.*

*She tells Nikki, unless some miracle takes place, she is out of here. Like on that midnight train to Georgia. Where ever Georgia is. After that she will regroup. Maybe head for Rio. She hears there is a lot of work for showgirls in Brazil.*

*"Don't leave me, padruga!"*

*"How can I not?" Her chest is already aching with the thought of leaving Nikki and the Follies and her nest at Number Three.*

*"Please don't take this the wrong way ... but swallow some pride, like the rest of us. Alby protects you from Immigration. And a lot more. Just swallow your pride."*

*She wonders what does a girl have if she does not have pride in herself? But right now she is thinking she swallowed every last drop of pride on the Lear jet to Montreal.*

*She knows what Nikki is talking about here ... the escort service that supposedly would make no demands on her when she bagged into Shangri-La. The escort service that just initiated her into the Mile-High Club. If anybody but Nikki hit her with this proposition, she might spit in her face. Tuki has been down this road before, and there is not much along the way that she does not spell "H-O."*

*But she thinks, maybe if Nikki can do it, so can she. And what is the alternative? A close encounter with Immigration and a swift trip back to Bangkok in handcuffs to face the mess she left behind?*

*She lets Nikki work out the details for the date. After the show a limo pulls up outside the Follies and honks two quick beats. The girls start down the steps in evening wear. They are not in show costumes, but they are still putting on the doll. Nikki is looking seriously seductive with deep plum lips and nails to match a long jersey dress of the same color. Black onyx pendants at her ears. She must be wearing four-inch heels because she is almost as tall as Tuki. And she has ditched her falsies from the show for a Miracle bra that actually gives her some cleavage. Her short hair is slicked back with gel, a racy look.*

*Simple elegance is the name of the game, and tonight Tuki has it in spades. She's wearing a green and red kimono left over from her M Butterfly days in Bangkok. Her hair is pinned up in a French twist with a golden comb to hold it all together.*

*Stepping out into the streetlights, Tuki scans the scene. The chauffeur opening the passenger door in the limo is, as usual, the brother Justin.*

*When the girls are in the back, Nikki presses the call button to speak to Justin.*

*"How much are they paying for this masquerade?"*

*"Four bones a girl."*

*Nikki whistles: "I guess they think somebody's going to get laid. Crank the jazz, Justin."*

"*Loud!*" *say Tuki, because she does not want to think about what is coming.*

*The men are waiting at a fancy East End restaurant that looks out on the bay from a little bluff above the beach. So maybe Tuki is a little impressed by the setting, half forgetting that this is a job until she see the dates.*

*They are not track-star types like Justin. But Jean—"Johnny"— Gauthier is about six feet five, thin, rangy, very sophisticated looking in a tux, with a deep tan, buzz cut, heavy two-day shadow, and one pearl ear stud. The guy gives off vibes like some kind of cross between Tommy Lee Jones and James Bond. He is in his late forties, and he kisses each of their hands when he meets them.*

*The second beau is Alby. All buffed up for a night of cheating on Silver.*

"*Oh no!*" *says Tuki.*

"*I swear I didn't know,*" *whispers Nikki.* "*But help me out,* padruga. *He's got me in a bind.*"

*Dinner goes by in a rush of Nikki's funny stories and laughter about escaping from Russia in a shipping crate. The next thing Tuki knows, a motorized launch is carrying them out into the harbor to a gigantic black sailboat named* Diana. *It is bigger than the Lodge at Shangri-La, with all kinds of cabins, acres of oiled wood, polished brass, and a sound system to kill for.*

*There is a Jacuzzi built right into the deck, and all four end up here at one thirty in the morning, wearing matching red bikini bottoms, compliments of the ship.*

*Alby has made it clear from his greeting kiss on her neck that he wants to make up. Let bygones be bygones. He still has a crush on her.*

*Everybody but Tuki is pointing out constellations in the dark. She is thinking this escort gig is way more loaded with danger than getting deported. When you lose to Immigration, you just get shipped overseas in handcuffs. When you lose at the escort business, no one ever finds your body. What the hell is Alby holding over Nikki? Why does she not just split? Take her chances with the INS?*

*And why is Tuki still here? She is ho-ing herself again and spitting in the face of everything Brandy and Delta ever taught her about personal pride. Is this about more than helping out a friend? Is this about getting even? Maybe. People in Bangkok know: she is not real good with betrayal.*

*She waits for the first time he leans close through all of the foam and tries to give her a kiss behind the ear before she strikes.*

*As soon as his nose breaks into her personal space, she swings her face around to catch both his eyes in hers and says, "Tell me about Silver!"*

*His hairy chest heaves. She hears him choke.*

*Nikki winces.*

*The French guy actually laughs.*

*"Did I say something wrong, la?" Her perfect little Miss Saigon voice.*

*Alby purses his lips and sighs, "Silver is a problem I came here to forget, Tuki."*

*"Sorry."*

*Nikki gives a desperate look like, "Chill, padruga."*

*Tuki says she is boiling, pops out of the spa, grabs a robe, scoots to the front of the boat. There is a light wind blowing here. She is letting it dry her hair while she fluffs it with her hands ... and waits to see if Alby will follow her.*

*He does, with champagne for both of them.*

*"I heard Immigration has been asking Richie some questions at the Follies."*

*"What?"*

*She does not like his tone of voice. It is sharp, sarcastic.*

*"Do not even start this, la. I need you to really listen to me, not be up in my face."*

*He sits down on the deck, cups his hands together, blows a deep breath into them. Then he pulls a big cigar out of his robe pocket, sniffs it, starts working it in and out of his mouth.*

*"Maybe I feel a little hurt right now, Starbright. You just tried to make a fool of me."*

"You took advantage of me."

"Like you had nothing to do with it? You made love to the idea ...
and then you made love to me!"

She feels something burst behind her shoulders like a dam.

"You had all the power. Always. The job, the house, the parties.
Maybe you even put something in my drink that first night when you
took me to your bedroom. And after you had your way with me, you
passed me off to your pal Joey. You big greasy puu jaa. You, you"—she is
searching for the English words—"stuffed crab!"

Then she is crying. And all of the time she is crying, she knows that
these tears are not really for what has gone down between Alby and her.
Or even for the game of cat and mouse she has been playing with the
INS for the last five years. She is crying for other things, things back in
Bangkok that her heart just cannot get into right now.

She leaves him sitting there sucking on his cheroot. Goes back to
the hot tub and tells Nikki she wants to leave. Forget the four bones. To
hell with his Brando voice, head massages from his magic fingers. His
lies about Vietnam.

"Are you crazy?" Nikki is straddling the French guy's lap. Her face
looks torn between pleasure and terror. Sex in the bubbles. "Don't do
this, Tuki!"

"I want to go."

"You have no idea what he can do. He can just squash us. Just tear
you up in little pieces and—"

"Ya ti ton pai kon khai."

"What?"

"I'll deal with the fever when it comes."

"But what about me?"

# FIFTY-ONE

"I cannot believe it was Nikki, la. Sweet Nikki. She is the last person to ever hurt ..."

"But he said he saw her?" The rental Jeep is winding its way back toward Nantucket Town and the Jared Coffin House. The fog still has not lifted. The air is cold and wet. Inhaling feels like drowning.

"That is what he told me. I have it all on the tape. He saw Nikki. He said he was standing outside the dressing room at the Follies after the show that night. Waiting for me. He could not accept that it was all over for us. He could not accept that I had turned my back on him and left him standing on a pier. But then he saw Alby go in the dressing room. Heard us fighting, my crying, my apologies, my kisses. It was too much, and he dragged himself outside in the alley to shoot up more *pung chao.*

"He was leaning against the dumpster, all but lost in a dream, when he heard me shouting at Alby. He saw me run out of the Painted Lady in my robe and disappear in the fog on the beach. That is just how it was. So he was there.

"A few minutes after he saw me disappear into the fog, Alby came down the alley from the Follies, swearing and kicking up clouds of dust with his feet. He went into his office. Turned on the lights. He started shouting. Like he was having a conversation with himself ... in different voices. Real angry. This goes on for about five minutes. Then Nikki shows up and goes into the office. More shouting. Smashing of furniture. Then the light goes out. Alby cries out like he is hurt. The next thing you know, the entire office just bursts into flames, la. The light is blinding, and Prem scuttles away to crash under a pier."

Michael takes her hand. It feels dry and cold. "You are still in love with him, aren't you? That's what you told him this morning. That's how you got him to talk. Just tell me the truth so I can have a little clarity."

"I do not know, Michael. I do not know if I still love him. I do not think it is love anymore. He haunts me. I cannot ever quite put him out of my mind. But this is useless to talk about. You saw him. You have touched him. You know. He is just skin and bones. He will be dead soon. It is what he wants. And it makes me so sad. All he wanted was for someone to love him, for his parents to ..."

She pauses, then adds something odd for her, something dark. "The Buddha is right. Life is suffering."

"Are you okay?"

She leans across the console between the bucket seats and puts her head on his shoulder.

"Please hold me."

He wraps his right arm around her and draws her body to his chest. "What were you two fighting about back there at his house?"

She raises her head and kisses his neck. "You."

He shivers.

Her eyes look up, trying to read his face. "Now what do we do?"

"Call the police," he says. He is not sure he is really answering her question.

Tuki draws back into her own seat and stares ahead into the fog.

"Do you think Nikki set me up?"

"We have to find her."

# FIFTY-TWO

"So now you want to talk. Now you want my help. It's Saturday, my day off, Rambo. If you weren't here, I'd be out fishing!"

He cannot believe it. What bum luck! Of all the cops who might get the nod on this, they have to draw the same state dick who was working the shooting at Number Three. The wiry, middle-aged Italian, Votolatto. And here at the West Yarmouth barracks, he is on his home turf.

"This is important. We know who the shooter was, we have proof that Tuki did not kill Costelano or set the fire. We have hard evidence."

Tuki pulls the tape recorder out of her handbag and puts it on the metal desk in the interview room.

"What's this?"

"It's a tape of the shooter's confession about his attack at Shangri-La the other night. More important, it tells what he witnessed right before Big Al took a knife in the gut and the fire started."

"No fucking way! How'd you get this?"

Tuki and Michael exchange looks. He gives her a nod.

"I went to visit him. His parents have a house on Nantucket Island. He talked to me. It is all here. He saw the killer go into Alby's office. He heard the fight. He saw the fire start, la."

"You can stop with this 'la' shit any time now, doll. It's driving me crazy. Who is this guy? The killer?"

"No. The shooter from the other night in Truro. His name is Prem Kittikatchorn."

The detective squints at Michael like, "Who's asking you, buddy?"

Tuki squirms in her seat. Stares at her hands in her lap.

"Long lost boyfriend from Bangkok."

"Oh, Christ! How long have you been here, Tuki?"

"Here?"

"The U. S. of A. Freaking America."

"About five years."

"I don't get it. Some guy from Thailand comes to see you after five years and just starts shooting. What the hell's he after?"

Michael pulls himself up to the table, assertive. "It is a domestic issue. Kind of complicated. He has been stalking her. I have the number of a detective in Bangkok you can call if—"

"Shut the fuck up, Rambo. I know about the Thai dick; I've been in touch with our illustrious D. A. I'm talking to the doll. Did you invite this shooter, Tuki? Did you call him to get you out of a scrape with Costelano? Did he whack the big guy for you, is that what happened? Now you going to give him up?"

She's wearing a sleeveless sundress, feels the air conditioner and the cop getting to her. Gives a little shiver. Smiles nervously. Shakes her head no.

"Then here's what I'm thinking. This turd Costelano got you roped into his escort service. You couldn't get out. He threatened you. You fought with the guy. Took him out with his own knife. Torched his place. Then when you get your ass in a sling with the law, you phone this old boy back in Bangkok, some kind of Thai wise guy. You call in the cavalry, so to speak. Because you got a lawyer who don't know shit from Shinola and—"

"Hey, hey! Watch yourself. You can't talk to us like—"

"Bite me, Rambo! This is my case. You come in here stirring up a hornets' nest on my day off with a lot of nonsense about a taped confession, an eyewitness account. You take what you get. Now, you're going to let your client talk to me, or am I going to slap you with obstruction of justice. Which is it, counselor?"

"Why don't you just listen to the tape."

"You. Didn't I just ask you to shut the fuck up?" He is pointing his finger at Michael, doing a kind of Robert DeNiro routine.

Michael raises his hands in front of him. Sits back in his chair. No problem.

"Now, Tuki, tell me, did the shooter get gun-happy the other night 'cause he saw you chilling with Rambo here? Is that how it was? You're still in love with the shooter, aren't you? That's why you wouldn't give him up the other night? So what's changed? College boy here poking you now? Is that it?"

Tuki is almost in tears, Michael is on the edge of his seat again. His eyes are burning holes in the cop.

"Jesus Christ, detective. She comes in here of her own free will to give you key evidence that will break this case wide open for you. You ignore the evidence and proceed to bully her. What kind of professional do you call yourself?"

"One who's not porking his client, counselor. One who is just trying to get a feel for the dynamics surrounding this miraculous appearance of exculpatory evidence. Get it?"

The detective picks up the little tape recorder on the table. Studies it for a few seconds, trying to figure out how you make the thing play.

"It's the green button," says Michael.

"Shut up, Rambo."

Votolatto pushes the button. For several seconds there is nothing but the sound of static. Then foot steps. A door unlocking. Door swinging open. A man's voice says something in Thai. The voice is haggard, faint. Tuki's voice responds. More Thai. Emotive. The sound of sighs, a hug, possible little kisses. Thai again. Him and her. The dialogue sounds like a soap opera playing from a distant room. You cannot understand a thing.

Oh hell, thinks Michael. He can feel his cheeks starting to burn. How could he have forgotten they would be speaking Thai?

For five minutes the tape runs on and on like this. Thai. The detective staring at the squeaking machine on the metal table.

Finally he clicks it off. "You're shitting me, right? This is the wrong tape? Gibberish."

"No. Prem. He is telling everything. He saw Nikki go into Alby's. Heard them fight. Heard Alby call out hurt. Saw Nikki run away and the fire."

"Who is this Nikki? Where is she now?"

Michael pulls a pink promotional flier for the Follies from his brief case. It has a picture of Tuki, Silver, and Nikki leaning back to back in evening dresses, flashing vampy, come-hither looks. He takes a pen and circles Nikki's face. "She left P-town about a week ago with her boyfriend, a bartender from the Follies named Duke. They were in a big hurry. We think they were heading for San Francisco."

The detective takes a look. Nods like he remembers her from the interviews that went down after the fire and murder. Fingers the tape player in his hand.

"This whole thing is in Thai?"

"You want me to translate?"

Votolatto rubs his temples with the thumb and index finger of both hands. "I hear my boat calling me! Get outta here. Go home, will you?"

# FIFTY-THREE

His father is lying back down on the floor of the wheelhouse in the *Rosa Lee*. His head and torso are inside a cabinet under the steering wheel. He growls as he rips out a bundle of corroded wiring to the engine instruments.

"Tommy?"

"No, it's Mo, Dad."

After the loneliest Saturday night he can remember—no Fil, no Tuki, suffocating heat and humidity, not much sleep—he has taken the detective's advice. He has come home. Home to New Bedford. New England's premier fishing port. A Portuguese colony on the fringe of America. He thinks that maybe, just possibly, he will find some answers here.

"*Cristo*, the prodigal son. Perry Mason. I thought you were my brother." The fisherman wiggles out from inside the cabinet, sits up. He is a man of spit and sinew with piercing black eyes. The Sox T-shirt and jeans give his taut body something of a James Dean look. Longish salt-and-pepper hair shags a bit over his ears. It takes his eyes a minute or two to adjust to the sunlight in the wheelhouse. "So?"

"So what?"

"So to what do I owe the pleasure of seeing the distinguished young attorney aboard my humble *barco de peixe*? You ready to come back out fishing?"

"Yeah, maybe."

"I heard about your problems."

"Shit."

"Sorry, pal. Nu Bej is a pretty small town. Word travels fast when a nice Portagee boy gets cold feet on the eve of his wedding."

"I need to talk about Vietnam."

"Because of that flit client of yours?"

"Hey!" He shoots his father a hard look. "Don't be like that! I came here for help, okay?"

Caesar Decastro gets to his feet. He sits down in one of the two swiveling captain's chairs that look out from the wheelhouse. "Take a load off."

Michael drops into the other chair. "I'm all screwed up."

"You want to level with me? You got a thing for this drag queen client of yours?"

"It's not what you think. She's from Vietnam. Her father was an American Marine. She is one of the boat people."

"So?"

"I don't know. I think about Vietnam a lot these days."

"You were never there. You weren't even born when—"

"But you were there."

His father's shoulders stiffen. "Yeah, so? You hear me bragging about it? You ever see me marching in any parades, hanging out at the Legion?"

"No."

"Well, I don't know what you got going between you and this client of yours, but leave me out of it. I've heard enough, buddy boy. You want to wreck your life and Filipa's, too? You ever think what she must be going through right now? You ever—"

He squeezes his eyes shut. "Stop! Just stop it, will you? Come on. Can we please talk without you getting up in my face and judging? I'm in trouble here!"

The older man rubs his chin, stares out through the windows at the harbor. Streaks of red are rising on the sides of his neck. He grabs a pack of Merits sitting beside the compass, taps out a cigarette, lights it with a silver Zippo. His hand is a little shaky.

"Dad?"

"Look, Mo, I've told you all of my stories of 'Nam a hundred times over. I didn't massacre anyone. I got no secrets. I was just a dumb kid in a soldier suit they told to watch out for our boys on liberty. I was an MP, for Christ's sake. In Saigon. And not for long. I never got up country or into the delta. Worst fight I witnessed was when a couple of drunk Marines thought they could whip a whole bar full of grunts."

"But you were there. You saw things."

His father takes a long drag, flicks the cigarette out the open door into the harbor. He squints his eyes and stares at Michael, trying to get a handle on the source of his son's uneasiness. And his own. "Look, I'm going to tell you the honest-to-god truth for once, okay, pal? 'Nam wasn't like those half-assed adventure stories I used to tell you when you were a kid. Not like the pictures you liked to look at in my photo albums. All those amazing temples, wise-looking monks with their shaved heads and orange robes. Not like those pictures of buddies hanging out shooting hoops in the sun on a ball court, or chilling with a cooler of brews on a beach. Smiling old men on bicycle rickshaws. Those pictures are a load of crap. Window dressing. Vietnam was one big cluster fuck from start to finish, Mo. You never knew what was going on there. Like nobody was accountable!"

His father's words come with such force that Michael squirms in his seat and wonders where this raw anger is coming from. Suddenly, he is sorry that he has come here, that he has started something that he cannot control. But he has to ask things. He has his questions. They have been burning a hole in the back of his head since he was just a boy. And now he cannot ignore them any longer.

"So why do you keep those photo albums? Why did you tell me about what a sweet place it was? About how, in a way, it reminded you of the old country, Portugal. What great people, what amazing people, you used to say. So loving and carefree. So simple. Why?" His voice is starting to tremble.

Caesar turns his head away, looks out at the lumpers toting boxes of fish off another trawler at the dock, loading them into a box truck. "I don't know. Because I'm a Portagee, Mo. Because Portagees are dreamers. I need to tell myself that it was worth going over there. Worth giving up two years of my time on Earth to the army. Worth missing the beginning of my only son's life. Worth all the trouble for our country. For everyone. Like your mother. I went over there and left her pregnant. And, damn me to hell, I knew. I left her without money or a wedding ring ... any kind of support. My god, she waited for me. How the hell do you explain that?"

"She's a great lady."

"You got that right! And I was a stupid little shit, who thought he was a badass. Christ, I enlisted. I wanted to go. Join the army and see the world."

He looks at his father's face. It seems gaunt, almost bone. And he feels a question that he has been avoiding most of his life tearing at his vocal cords.

"I looked at those pictures in the album so many times. There was a picture of a girl dancing on a bar in a G-string. And two other pictures of her. One in a red dress standing in some kind of native boat, like a big canoe, waving. I remember how dark the sky looked. The other picture she was swinging in a hammock in a room somewhere. She had on a Red Sox shirt. There was a little kid with curly hair in her arms. They were stuck behind some other pictures. They fell out one time. And I found them. She was Vietnamese. I always wondered ... Did you have a girl over there?"

For about thirty seconds his father does not answer. It is so quiet on the boat, you can hear gusts of wind whistling through the antennas overhead. When he speaks again there is a torn note in his voice.

"Her name was Meng. She was one of the Hmong people, the Montagnards. A refugee from the fighting in the hill country, a nursery school teacher. She had a place in Cholon. Up the Ben Nghe Channel. Chinatown."

## FIFTY-FOUR

*It is almost dark. The mist is starting to rise over the water. She is standing in a narrow wooden boat, nose to the landing on the river. The current sweeps rafts of flowering white water hyacinths downstream along with the muddy flood of the monsoon; egrets hitch rides on bits of broken houses, abandoned rice barges, the occasional body. Everything flows away to the South China Sea. The boatman sits in the stern in black pajamas, a paddle across his lap, staring at him with unmasked resentment.*

*"Come, la. I take you home now," she says.*

*He cannot remember how long he sat in the bar watching her dance to the ballads of Smokey Robinson, the Temptations, talkin' 'bout my girl. But he feels drunk now. His service shirt is unbuttoned to the waist, the MP chevron on his sleeve is stained with lipstick, rice whiskey, and Budweiser. There is a green beret stuffed in his hip pocket, a .45 snapped into the black holster on his hip.*

*He knows going into the boat is a mistake. There is a reason the army has guards posted along the roads to Cholon. On the bridges over the klongs, too. Navy swift boats patrol the waterways. Cholon is teaming with people, rats, vice, crime—off limits to GIs. But he knows. He has heard. This is how they go. His brothers ... with their women. By boat, in the dark, up the Ben Nghe Channel to another world, away from the killing, the savagery, the generals. To Chinatown. To drown in the wet, golden loins of Asia for a while.*

*She stretches out her arm, beckons him to the boat. He sees every inch of her body calling to him from beneath that red dress. It is nothing more than the thinnest veil. A film, really.*

*"This is bad," he says. "Are you sure ..."*

*"Quiet," she says.*

*The boatman is nervous. He says the army shoots the ferrymen sometimes.*

His eyes dart around, expecting to see the flash of a gun any second, the ambush beginning.

"Come." She extends her hand to him again.

In the distance he hears a harmonica whining, Bob Dylan singing "Like a Rolling Stone." The music seems to be rising from the river. Coming closer. Suddenly a swift boat growls out of the gathering mist and darkness from downstream, its search light flicking along the river banks.

She pulls him into the boat, onto its damp floor, her body molding to his. The .45 is in his right hand when the search light flashes overhead, then is gone with the last strains of Dylan.

"Fucking hell," says a faint voice on the swift boat. Who knows why.

The ferryman dips his paddle, backs his boat out from the landing. The current catches the craft and rushes it downstream. Coppery lights of charcoal cooking fires glow like fallen flares up and down the shore, wisps of smoke vanish into the violet sky of the coming night.

"Do you love me?" she asks. She says a name. It sounds like his father's. And his own.

The noise and energy of Cholon at night are tremendous. Even behind the concrete walls of this one-room apartment, he can picture everything: Throngs crowding in and out of the glow of kerosene lamps hanging over the tables of the night market vendors, the clucking shouts of auctioneers, the tables displaying sunglasses, counterfeit watches, tubs of steaming shrimp, live fish swimming in pickle jars. Beneath the shrill whistling of caged birds, music like the howling of cats echoes from tinny speakers. An ancient man with a long, stingy beard is on his knees in the street, dissecting a six-foot-long monitor lizard for a crowd shouting at him prices they will pay for the liver, the gall, the heart, the testes. The scents of charcoal braziers, curry, ginger, peppers, roasting peanuts, and frying fish filter through the wooden slats of the window shutters. The world is panting, sweating, selling its soul beyond these walls. Yet knows nothing of him in here.

"Everything be okay. Rest now." She lights a candle and a joss stick with a match. The room begins to glow. "You lie down." She nods to the large hammock hanging across the corner of the room from eyebolts sunk into the dirty green walls. She changes into a red satin robe.

The hammock is almost the only thing in the room except for a clothesline, a pole fan, a dresser with a carving of a Buddha with big breasts, a songbird in a wooden cage, and a console TV/stereo. In the center of the room is a Formica table with folding chairs. A dha with a dark jade handle lies on a counter by the small kitchen sink. On the walls are the faces of children. Scores of them—Vietnamese children, white children, black children ... beautiful children with huge, bright eyes. They are photos clipped from magazines, some snapshots too, taped to the plaster. He keeps thinking that this must all be a figment of his imagination. He is passed-out drunk. Dreaming. And maybe he is going to die here.

She puts her hands softly on his chest, slides his unbuttoned khaki shirt off his shoulders, presses him down into the hammock until he is sitting back, reclining. Half in, half out. Her legs straddle his knees.

He is burying his face in the black silk of her long hair when a back door to the room bursts open.

In an instant he has his .45 drawn, pointing.

She is off him like an explosion. "No shoot!"

Standing in the shadows is a child. Two or maybe a little older. A nest of black curls frames its beaming face. She scoops it into her arms, but its eyes never leave him.

He pops the clip out of his weapon. Then, for some reason he cannot understand, he rolls both pieces into his stinking khaki shirt and hugs the bundle to his chest.

"This is Dung," she says. "Dung, say hello to Michael."

Snap out of it, he thinks. Wake up, brother!

# FIFTY-FIVE

"I'm not proud of it. She was just a kid. So was I. It was a different time. The world felt like it was spinning out of control. We thought any day we would be sitting in a bar or walking down the street and a car bomb or a sniper would take us out. It happened to people all the time. We wanted to live a little before we died. Can you understand that?"

Michael pictures again the coppery lights of charcoal cooking fires, fallen flares up and down the dark shore of the Mekong. "Were you in love?"

His father leans back, rubs the back of his neck with the fingers from both his hands.

"Not like with your mother ... no. She was poor and homeless when she got to Saigon. Not there a week before the pimps were on her like flies, had her trussed up in a bra and G-string, hustling tricks for rent and food money in a bar called Wild Bill's. She had a kid, a toddler by another GI. So it was complicated. But I didn't care. He was long gone. And I missed your mother so much. I felt so bad about leaving her with you in her belly. I just wanted a woman to make me feel like everything was going to be alright again. And I wanted to take her off the street. She deserved better. That picture of the girl dancing on the bar. I took it the day I met her. So there. Now you know."

*The air smells of charcoal, roasting peanuts, pepper.*

"You lived together?"

"Just a few months. She had this one-room flat in Cholon. The army didn't feature that sort of thing. But they knew what was happening. There were a lot of couples like us in Chinatown. It had been going on for so long when I got there, you could see many Amerasian kids in the streets. They spoke English."

"What happened?"

"I got new orders. To the Philippines."

*Cage birds are whistling, shrill, staccato notes.*

"The war was going badly. There was all hell to stop it back home. Someone up top decided our fraternizing with the locals was out of control. The press had started to write about it (the hooch girls), and the army didn't like the heat. They decided to pull the plug on all the love nests. Coming off duty one night, a sergeant major grabbed a bunch of us MPs who were shacking up. He said, 'You got orders. Go to the barracks, pack up your gear, and get on the bus to the airport.' Just like that, we were history. No chance to say goodbye."

*The old man on his knees in the street is dissecting a monitor lizard, pulling out the liver, the heart, the testes with his fingers. Offering them up in his bloody hands.*

"You ever see her again?"

The fisherman gets a wet look in his eyes. "We always told each other live for today. We knew it wouldn't last forever. I sent her my checks for a few months. She never wrote. But I didn't expect her to. Writing English was hard for her. I felt the loss, unbelievable *saudade*. But I hoped she had found someone new. Someone from her own country who could cherish her forever, take care of her and the child. But really, who would have her with that half-American kid? Even in Cholon. I worried about her a lot. Then I heard from your mom that you were born. My only child, my son. I felt like I had been given a new life. A chance to start over. We named you after my father. And I never looked back."

"But sometimes you remember?" *Shadows of figures are crowding in and out of the lamp light in the night market. The hot, fetid smell of the river seeping through the streets, the open windows.*

"Yeah, kid. Sometimes it gets to me, if you want to know the truth. I'm not proud of myself for what happened with Meng. I should have been loyal to your mother. And honest with Meng. She never knew about your mom. But it's over. That was a long time ago. In another country. Nothing I can do about it. So I tell my half-cocked lies about adventure in the mysterious Orient ... And I try to let it all go. I suggest you let it go, too. Just quit this case, will ya? Give it up before it tears you to pieces."

"I can't." His words echo in the steel wheelhouse. They sound to him like bawling cats. He closes his eyes and sees a Vietnamese woman waving, beckoning from a small boat. And Tuki in a pink terrycloth robe. She sits on the ledge of a window, a chain-link screen across the opening. Her knees are pulled up under her chin, her dark hair falls in a ringlets over her shoulders and arms.

For a while no one speaks.

"Jesus. You know what?" Michael's eyes open, suddenly big as plums. He does not know where these words are coming from. "I was thinking that this trouble I'm having is all about Vietnam. But I'm not so sure anymore."

"Yeah?"

"Yeah. This is about a bunch of stuff."

*The boatman sits in black pajamas, a paddle across his lap, staring at him.*

"Like what?"

"I don't know. Honesty maybe. Helping people who need you. Loyalty. And guilt. A boatload of guilt."

The fisherman throws his arms up in the air. "Oh sure, that explains everything, buddy boy. Listen to yourself. You're talking nonsense. Guilt about what? When Nixon was carpet bombing the Viet Cong, you were just a baby."

He drops off his chair. Squints at his father. "Maybe that's the point. I'm not a baby anymore. I'm the son of a badass, a war vet, a fisherman, and a dreamer. So I've got some baggage. Maybe a lot more than I used to think."

"What's that supposed to mean?"

"I won't just abandon her."

"What aren't you telling me, pal?"

Something sharp and cold seems to pierce his chest. He sees her again. She is not a woman like the others in Bridgewater or even Provincetown. Backlit in silhouette by the blazing sun outside, she could be a child. In Saigon. In Cholon.

"Why not? Come on, Mo, talk to me!"

"Because ... because she could have been my ..." His mind considers her gender, gropes for words of relationship. He hears her voice: *Dung? Dung is my long lost brother.* "Blood," he says finally. *A holy child. A love child.* "Like ... all of those forgotten children over there. You know what I mean?"

His father sits frozen in his seat, staring at his hands folded in his lap. "Yeah, son," he says softly. "But what are you going to do about Filipa?"

# FIFTY-SIX

"I think we found them, Rambo." The voice on the other end of the phone is Votolatto's.

"Beg your pardon?" It is nine thirty Tuesday morning. Michael is still sleeping when the phone rings. Since he got back from Nu Bej on Sunday, he has been surfing the web almost full-time, checking out the drag bars in and around San Francisco for any sign of Nikki and Duke. But nothing is turning up except a whole lot of spam from porn sights. The buggers must get his address when he logs into the drag clubs. Filipa's going to love seeing this stuff.

"The infamous Nikki and her bum buddy. I think we know where they are, and it ain't San Francisco."

"Where?"

"The Vineyard."

"No shit."

"Yeah. No shit, counselor. Your client's tape checked out A-okay after we got it translated. So then we found your pal Kittikatchorn. What a mess, he was jonesin' bad as I've ever seen. But he talked."

"Really?"

"Confirmed what he said on tape to Tuki. Man, does he hate you, though. Anyway, we got some search warrants. Nothing comes up on the Russian queen. But we score on the boyfriend's bank records, debit card. Seems like he's been living the high life on the Vineyard, mostly Oak Bluffs, for the last ten days. Hotels, meals, freaking load of bar tabs, boat rides, clothes. Like the guy's on his honeymoon."

"Now what?"

"The captain thinks your client has a way with the gab. Thinks folks talk to her. Everything we got on this Nikki is circumstantial. Pretty solid stuff, but it doesn't totally get your client off the hook.

You hear me? How do we know it's not a conspiracy thing with your client and Nikki? We're thinking we want to send Tuki to them on the Vineyard wearing a wire. See what gets said."

Michael is not quite getting it. He can't see how you just plop Tuki into Nikki's secret love nest, uninvited, and expect anyone to say more than "Gee whiz, what the hell are you doing here?" But it sounds like the cops suddenly need Tuki. This is when the defense attorney says 'I want a deal.' He goes for the whole *paella*.

"She cooperates, we want all the charges dropped on Tuki."

"Tough guy, huh?"

"Just doing my job."

"Don't fuck with me, Rambo!"

"Immigration charges, too."

"You're out of your mind. What about the security tape, man? It's got her stealing the murder weapon."

"It's a fake. You're looking at an imposter on the tape."

"Says who?"

"Tuki. She says someone is wearing her drag. But they got the earrings wrong. They're not her earrings."

The dick is silent for several seconds. "I'm thinking, Rambo."

"Think about this. Tuki plays her scene right for you, she makes you a hero. You get the bad guy."

The detective exhales heavily into the phone. "I can't do any-thing about the immigration stuff, that's federal."

"You know people."

"I hope you are not asking me to tamper with a case, commit a federal crime?"

"She's not technically an illegal. She's the child of a U. S. citizen. Her old man was a Marine in 'Nam. There are laws to protect people like her. We just need some time, six months, a year would be better, to get her documented. See?"

"You're busting my balls."

"No. I swear to god. We just need to get a copy of her birth cer-tificate from Saigon."

"You've already been working this out in you head, haven't you?

The court's not going to pay you for immigration work."

He shrugs. "I do what I can."

"I gotta hand it to you, Rambo. Not many public defenders would hang tough with a case like this. They would just plead out the client and move on. What's your story?"

"When I used to fish with my old man and my uncle for ground fish on Georges Bank, we would sometimes have three, four, five days of heavy wind and seas. Couldn't fish. Could barely keep the boat afloat. Just jogging into it. One time I asked my father why we don't just turn tail and run from the weather. 'We came to catch fish,' he said."

Votolatto does not say anything. He is thinking about fishing. Thinking he should have known that the college boy came up in the fleet. Fucking tough Portagee. Bone for brains.

"Well, Vasco da Gama, are we going fishing on the Vineyard or not?"

"You going to drop the charges?"

"I have to speak to the D. A."

"Come on, you know you already did. You wouldn't have called me otherwise."

"She delivers, she walks. Fair enough?"

"On the immigration stuff, too?"

"You know what, counselor? You're a pisser."

"That's what my old man says. Help me out here. I need time to take care of the immigration paperwork."

"Maybe there's something I can do. But she's got to give us a top-notch show. You think she can handle it?"

"You ever see her onstage?"

"Naw, I don't go for drag."

"She's a movie star."

"So it's a go?"

"I'll tell her your offer."

"Don't be jerking me around, Rambo."

"This isn't my call. Tuki makes her own decisions. And one other condition."

"What?"

"I get to come along to watch out for her best interests."

The detective growls. "Can I ask you something? Does she give you a hard-on?"

# FIFTY-SEVEN

Wednesday there is a hurricane 150 miles east of the Cape. It is pulling in bands of heavy showers. Oak Bluffs—the square mile of Victorian cottages, restaurants, arcades, clubs, bars that Vinyarders call "Sin City"—clusters around a little harbor on the northern tip of the island. It is an old-school resort. There are scents of pizza and fudge, flooded streets packed with tourists of several races wearing Black Dog rain gear, trying to ride out the blow. Even though it is only three o'clock in the afternoon, the streetlights are on. It is that dark.

"How's that feel, sweetheart?" Votolatto smiles.

Tuki is sitting on a metal stool in the back of a plain white van parked by the harbor entrance. She is naked from the waist up, except for her bra. It looks like a sports bra the way the straps cross her back. She's got her hands up under the C cups adjusting her breasts.

"Cool, huh?" Votolatto says to Michael, who is also in the back of the van with a couple of techies. "Latest thing in transmitters. We figure these queens are all touchy-feely. Maybe Nikki or the boyfriend may try to hug Tuki. They might find a conventional wire setup, but no way, now. The mike, transmitter, and battery are right in the falsies. Even if you take the falsies out of the bra, you won't see the wire unless you know what to look for. Think of it. Tits with ears."

Michael nods. Never imagined such a thing. That is for sure.

"Okay. Showtime, everybody."

Tuki pulls on a pink cotton pullover and gray windbreaker.

"Don't forget your surprise, princess." Votolatto hands her a plastic baggie with something small and black in it.

"You want the umbrella or just go with the hood up?" Michael is asking. He is trying to be helpful. Sweat is soaking his brow.

Tuki gives him a little kiss on the cheek. "Everything is going to be okay."

"Yeah, Jesus, would you relax, Rambo?"

"Maybe she should take the umbrella. In case she has to defend herself, you know?"

The detective looks at the lawyer, like sit down and cut the shit. "Anything goes wrong, Tuki, somebody starts to get rough with you, five real tough guys are going to be in that bar in about three seconds. You drop to the floor and cover your head, okay?"

The bar and every table are full at the Bluefin Café on Circuit Avenue when Tuki walks through the door. She pulls the hood off her head and shakes out her curls. Somebody whistles. Maybe a charter boat captain or one of the house carpenters sitting in the corner. A Dire Straits song is playing on the jukebox. "Tunnel of Love." Duke is working the bar in a 'do rag that makes him look like the Jolly Roger. He is busy pouring off some beer and does not see her until she sidles up to the service bar.

"How about a Perrier with lime, la?"

He looks her way.

"Holy shit. Tuki! What? How ..."

She reaches across the bar. Grabs him by the strap of his tank top. Leans and kisses him right in the middle of his Fu Manchu. His tan face goes suddenly pale.

"I've missed you, la."

Even the techies, Votolatto, and Michael, waiting up the street in the van, know she is not lying. This is a good start. An honest icebreaker. She is shooting from the heart, not reciting a script.

Duke opens his mouth to talk. But she smiles and presses an index finger to his lips.

"We need to talk. Where is Nikki?"

"You on some kind of mission?"

"I don't have much time. I'm scared." Her words are still coming from her heart.

Duke asks a waitress to cover for him. He ducks out from behind the bar, grabs Tuki by the arm. Michael can hear a swinging door squeak on its hinges.

"Fuck," says Votolatto. "He's taking her out of the barroom."

You can hear the crackle of a grill, the clatter of plates.

"They're in the kitchen," he says into his radio. "I want a detail to get around to the back street. Let's go. On the double. Cover the kitchen door!"

"Hey, Nik, look who the cat dragged in."

Nikki is wearing a chef's hat, shaking a basket of fries with her back to the door. She spins on her heels as soon as she hears Duke's voice. When she sees Tuki, she drops the fries back in the frialator. They sizzle. With the heat and the humidity, the kitchen feels like Bangkok during the monsoon.

"*Padruga*. My god! Where did ..."

Tuki is on her friend. It is a big back-rubbing hug.

"You've got to get out of here. Like now, la. The cops are coming!"

"What I don't understand," Duke seems to be getting suspicious, "is why?"

"They want to talk to you about the fire and Alby."

"That a girl! Don't give them a chance to think this through. Jig the bait, sweetheart," says Votolatto in the tech van.

Nikki slides out of the hug, wipes her hands on her apron. "Why? I already talked to them for hours. If I could help you, you know I would do anything. I know you didn't do what they say. You didn't kill Alby."

"Yes, la. But things have changed. Everything is getting confused. You know my boyfriend from Thailand? The police got to him yesterday. I think he is the one. He killed Alby. Set the fire."

Duke and Nikki exchange a look.

"Really?"

"He is all messed up on heroin. He was jealous of Alby. And he saw what Alby was doing to us. So he just took things into his own hands. I know that is how it was. And you know what? I'm glad Alby is dead."

"He was a first-class prick, *padruga*." There is real venom in her voice.

"Nikki." Duke takes her arm, strokes it, tries to calm her down.

"Why are the police coming here?"

"Because he's lying to them. He told them he was outside in the alley by Alby's office when the fire started. He said he saw Nikki put a knife in Alby."

"Bullshit!"

"I know. But what if the police find us? Do you think they will let us walk this time?"

Nikki says something under her breath in Russian. Maybe she is remembering her last showdown at gunpoint with Immigration back in P-town.

"How did they find us? How did you … ?"

Tuki eyes Duke. "This morning I was in the dressing room. I heard Richie talking to the police. He told them to look for you at this bar. It was the place you were working when he first met you. He said it was like your old crib. You were from this island. I caught the first bus to Hyannis, then the ferry here. What do you think we should do?"

"Fuck," says Duke.

"Where can we go? We've got to get out of here."

"She's good," mumbles Votolatto. "She's got them by the balls. Now squeeze them, honey."

Tuki reaches into her pocket. "I almost forgot. I brought you this."

Nikki takes the baggie.

"What's that?" Duke can't contain his curiosity.

Nikki shakes the onyx pendant out into her hand. "My earring. I thought it was gone forever. Where did you find it?"

"On the floor in Alby's bedroom."

Suddenly, the kitchen is so quiet you can hear the fries crisping into hard little rocks in the frialator.

"Come on, Tuki. Set your hook, babe. Reel them in. It's do or die time!" Votolatto coaches from the van.

The do or die line gets Michael. He suddenly remembers that today marks the end of the week of grace he begged from Filipa. He has not talked to her yet. "Come on, Tu—"

There is talking again in the kitchen of the Bluefin. Nikki's voice now. "I don't understand, *padruga*."

"It means that you were there. In Alby's room, la. It means you wore my drag in there and stole his knife. You can see the earrings on the security tape."

"I just wanted the knife to scare him. I wanted out. I was sick to death of his telling me he was going to call in Immigration if I didn't fuck his friends. Sick to death of him threatening to tell Richie about me and Duke! I just wanted to go off and have a life with Duke. I swear, Tuki, I didn't want anyone to get hurt. I never—"

"But you framed me."

"I'm so sorry. I needed a disguise and your bungalow was open. I just borrowed some of your stuff. I didn't expect you to get in so much trouble."

"Nikki!" Duke's voice is booming. He's telling her to shut up.

"What if I go to the police with this? What if they are listening right now, la?" Something has snapped in her voice. Michael can hear it.

"Shit!" says Votolatto in the van. "I told her no threats! She's blowing this."

There is the distinct clang of cutlery. Like a sword being drawn.

"You won't have that chance! I'm sorry about this, Tuki."

Nikki screams. "Duke, don't!"

But it is too late. He already has Tuki collared with his forearm, squeezing her neck in a vice, with a carving knife at the top of her throat.

"Go, go, go!" shouts Votolatto to his SWAT crews.

Michael is already out of the van and sprinting down Circuit Avenue for the front entrance of the Bluefin when a loud metallic thud rings out from the kitchen. Five cops kick in the door.

# FIFTY-EIGHT

There is at least one body on the floor, smoke pouring from the frialator, when Michael gets into the kitchen. He is blocked by a swarm of cops in riot gear. Votolatto is already on his radio calling in an ambulance and EMTs.

As Michael tries to push through the crowd, his cell phone goes off. He automatically snaps it to his ear. A voice squawks his name. It seems far away, unearthly. And it is really messing with his concentration.

"Not now!" He stashes the phone back in his jacket pocket and bulls ahead.

When he finally catches sight of the bodies, the air rushes from his chest with a deep bellowing. Duke lies on the greasy yellow lino-leum. Out cold. His head cradled in Nikki's lap. She sits on the floor shouting for people to back away, someone bring her water. The left side of Duke's head and his ear are swollen and red. Michael cannot understand what happened ... until he sees the cast-iron skillet on the floor next to Nikki. She clocked him. Scrambled his brains. But what about Tuki?

He shouts her name over the crackle of cop radios.

"We already got her out of here, Rambo." Votolatto nods toward the open back door.

He can see the rain coming down in buckets. Then he is in it. Two women cops stand in the back street holding umbrellas over themselves and a figure squatting down on her haunches, arms locked around her knees. They have put a blanket over her shoulders, and now she is rock-ing back and forth like an autistic child at Bridgewater.

One of them catches his eye, reads his concern. "She's in a shit storm of shock. Where in hell are the medics?"

"Tuki," he says kneeling beside her in the rivulets, "It's all over. It's all over!"

She raises her head to look at him. Her eyes are black and wet and dilated. Her mouth opens to talk, but no words come out. Tears are rolling down her cheeks. Then he sees her throat. It has not been cut, but it is already one huge, purple-streaked welt. Duke all but choked her to death before he switched to the knife. She throws her arms around his neck, and they both fall onto the soaked pavement. He can feel her struggling for breath. He is trying to soothe her, just reeling off words to keep her from fading before the EMTs get there. She is trying to tell him something. But all she can manage is a high, faint whistle before she falls limp.

"Let her go!" shouts somebody. "We're losing her!"

Then three EMTs are on her with an intubation kit.


It is not until the next morning that Michael hears anything. They airlifted Tuki off the Vineyard to Mass General's trauma center in Boston. And they would not let him on her flight. So he found his way back to Chatham and got stinking drunk with a bunch of fishermen at the Squire. Now Votolatto is on the phone asking him if he wants the good news or the bad news first.

"Just tell me she made it."

"She made it. I guess it was nip and tuck for quite a while. But she damn well made it. Serious condition but stable."

"What do you mean?"

"There was a lot of damage to her larynx. They say it's going to be a while before she can talk right. Nobody wants to bet on whether she will ever sing again."

"Does she know?"

"I thought you might want to tell her."

"Christ!"

"Exactly. Look, Rambo. I'm sorry as hell she got hurt, okay? She put on a great show. Right up until the end. I'll give her that. Tell her we appreciate it. Tell her it was made for Hollywood. Tell her she is free and clear. I've spoken to the D. A. He's dropping all the charges. And it seems like Immigration has misplaced her file ...

So do your citizenship thing. This case is a wrap as far as she is concerned."

For a second he forgets to breathe. He just sits there on his bed in his boxers staring at the phone in his hand. He thought victory would make him want to run to the window and shout its name. But right now it feels like nothing at all. Just dead space.

Finally he inhales. "You got a confession?"

"The Russian, Nikki, and her pal talked. After he came back to life ... and everybody calmed down. You know, she really fucking clocked him with that frying pan. Major concussion. No doubt she saved Tuki's life. The D. A. offered them a deal, no worse than Man One to give it up. Maybe a lot less, especially for the Russian. And we said we might be able to help out with Immigration. So they spilled. You had enough or you want to hear about it? You sound pretty fried, counselor."

"Tell me, okay?"

"It's what you'd figure. The stiff, Costelano, has these queens blackmailed into working escort duty. Threatening to call in the INS on them unless they hustle their tushies. The Russian wants out with her buddy Duke."

"But why steal the fancy knife and the videos? Why frame Tuki?"

"Pretty much what Nikki told your client. The theft was an act for the benefit of the security camera. Tuki's drag just a convenient tool. Nikki thought if Costelano got all distracted by someone stealing his trophies, he'd plumb forget about playing the heavy with her. Seems she was a popular moneymaker for the escort service. The guy slapped her around sometimes to keep her in line. Anyway, nobody was thinking about murder, or framing Tuki, says the Russian. Just distraction. I tend to believe her, seeing as how she came to your client's rescue big time with that frying pan yesterday."

"So what went wrong?"

"Nikki and Duke made plans to run off on the night of the murder. But before they left, our boy Duke had an attack of machismo. He's a hothead, we saw that yesterday. And he'd had enough of Alby

whoring, thumping, and threatening his little darling. Forget stealing off in the night. It was payback time. He took the stolen knife
that Nikki gave him for credence and sneaked out from behind the
bar in the Follies. He got the key to the big guy's real estate office that
they keep in the register. He let himself into the office. Just waiting
to kick the shit out of Alby before splitting town with his honey. The
car gassed and ready to go as soon as Nikki packed her stuff into it
after work."

"But things got dicey."

"Next thing you know, here was Costelano coming down the
alley from the Follies after his close encounter with Tuki and her
flamethrower. He was swearing, kicking up clouds of dust. It's maybe
one in the morning. He went in his office. Turned on the desk lamp
and saw Duke sitting on the couch."

"A showdown."

"Basically. Duke flat out told him that he and the Russian were
history. The big guy was in total control-freak mode. This was not
his day. Having problems with all of his queens. The whole fucking
stable in revolt and at each other's throats. Tuki and Silver, like fire
and ice. Now Tuki was stealing from him. To top it off Richie was
raising holy hell because he suspected his main man of plotting to
run off to Neverland with the little Russian flit. 'Screw that shit, my
bald buddy,' says Costelano. 'I'm not going to drop a dime on your
girlfriend. If you two so much as think of splitting on the Follies
and me, I'm going to put her in a bag with a load of rocks and make
you drop her ass in P-town Harbor. Stay the fuck away from her. Get
back in there and tend bar.' Tough talk, see?"

"Yeah?"

"This went on for several minutes. Escalating when Nikki
walked in looking for Duke. Alby flipped out. Zapped her with his
bullwhip. Knocked the lamp over into a metal wastebasket where
it was sparking to beat the band. He tore into Nikki again with the
whip. Then he got on Duke. Real Lash Laroo shit in the sparks and
the shadows, I guess. He had Duke all wrapped up in that bullwhip
and down on the floor. Stomping the shit out of him when Duke

grabbed the stolen knife in his waistband and let Costelano have it in the gut. The wastebasket and a curtain burst into flames. And the whole office goes up."

"With half of Provincetown." Michael finds his water bottle and takes a long gulp.

Votolatto coughs.

"So it goes, counselor."

# FIFTY-NINE

It takes Michael the better part of the day to get his head together, zip out to P-town to collect Chivas, and drive to Boston. But by three forty-five in the afternoon, he and Chivas find their way to Tuki's bedside in Mass General.

She looks like hell. Her skin is ashen. Someone has combed out her braids and most of her curls so her hair falls over her shoulders like Morticia in the Addams Family. She has an oxygen mask over her mouth and nose. Her neck is a swollen mass of red and blue streaks. Her eyes are closed.

When Chivas sees all this, she turns to Michael and rolls her eyes. The old queen has on her version of a gypsy costume, complete with a red silk headscarf and monster hoop earrings. She thought the outfit might make Tuki smile, but now she just feels like a fool. A Halloween party leftover.

Michael can hardly believe this is the same person he met just three weeks ago in another hospital. But he tells himself, buck up, pal, it could be worse. *She could be dead.*

He moves close. Takes her hand. "Hey, I brought someone to see you."

Her hand rolls slowly into his. Squeezes a little. Eyes open three-quarters. They look bloodshot and drugged. Now her lips are spreading. Starting to move. Saying words as she looks into his eyes.

But he cannot read her lips. Not through the opaque plastic of the oxygen mask. And who knows if she is even speaking English. He feels something rising in his throat. He is about to gag when Chivas rallies, comes up right alongside the bed, bends, kisses Tuki on the forehead.

"What a girl won't do to get her name in the news, love. You are a scandal, you delicious little bitch! All the papers are calling you a heroine, an absolute superstar."

Tuki smiles a little, knows Chivas is bluffing, but does not care. She reaches up and runs the back of her right hand against the old girl's cheek.

"You're free," says Michael. "You broke the case. The D. A. dropped all charges."

Tuki does not seem to be listening. Her left hand is flailing around, searching for something on the nightstand next to the bed. He sees what she wants. There is a white erasable tablet, with a magic marker tied to it with a string. But it is just out of reach. He circles the bed and slides it into her hands. She blinks her eyes and mouths three words. "Thank you, la." He sees that.

She holds the tablet up in front of her, writing in big green letters.

WHAT IS WRONG WITH ME???

He tries to think positive thoughts. "You are going to be all right. It will just take a few days for you to get your energy and your voice back. You got a tough bruise on your neck."

Tuki scribbles something on the tablet, hands it to Chivas.

I WANT TO GO HOME.

"You're going to be out of here in no time, honey. We've already moved your drag to my place. We are going to throw a victory party for you at the Tango, the likes of which the Magic Queendom has never seen. And a welcome home parade down C Street. The only question is whether pretty boy here, or yours truly, will be your escort. Personally I'd go for age over beauty, but you ..."

There is a pained, urgent look on Tuki's face as she takes up the tablet and starts writing furiously. You can hear her wheezing through the oxygen mask. A shrill little alarm starts beeping.

FIND MY FATHER. PLEASE!!

"I'm already working on that, and I—"

"You have to leave!" A nurse has Michael by the shoulder, steers him and Chivas toward the hallway. "She can't take too much of this. She'll go into respiratory distress again."

An intern swoops into the room with a syringe in his hand and closes the door.

"Crap. Just crap!" Michael rocks back against the wall of the corridor.

Chivas eyes him like she knows that as of today, as of the D. A. dropping all charges, the court stops paying his salary. Anything he does now, including this visit to the hospital, is *pro bono*. "You going to keep your promise, good looking?"

"Are you?"

"The long lost knight returns from the crusades!" Filipa stands in the entrance to her flat in Cambridge, one arm braced against the door jam as a blocking maneuver. It is after six on this steamy summer evening.

"It's over. They dropped all the charges. I'm off the hook. Tuki's off the hook. I just have to make some calls, help her get documented as a U. S. citizen."

He searches her eyes for anger. But all he sees is sadness.

"We need to talk, Michael."

He inhales. Steadies himself for what he knows he has to say. "Yeah, we do. This isn't going to work out with us, is it?"

"I told my mother this morning to cancel everything. You can deal with the apartment."

A sack of rocks drops in his gut. "This is a little awkward, standing out here, trying ... Can I come in?"

"No. I don't think so."

"I don't understand. It doesn't seem right, after all these years to end it like this. Here."

"It was over yesterday. There is nothing more to say. You've already said your piece. I've heard it loud and clear. Goodbye, Michael. I'm all done crying."

"I don't understand." He is sinking.

"Your cell phone. Don't you remember? I called you yesterday. You shouted at me, 'Not now!'"

The rocks in his gut have turned to lead.

"You didn't shut off the phone. I heard everything!"

"It was chaos. Cops, victims. People out cold. Crying. Screams. I couldn't talk. I'm sorry. You wouldn't believe it. Tuki almost died. It was crazy."

"It sure was, Michael. Especially the part where you started talking to her. Did you even listen to yourself? 'Tuki, Tuki. Come on, sweetheart. Stay with me. Hold me. Look in my eyes ...' Jesus, Michael."

For a moment he wants to defend himself, say that she has misunderstood. Tuki was lying on the ground. In shock. Dying. Her throat swelling shut as he watched. He had no idea what he was saying. He might have said anything. He was just chattering, trying to keep her awake, alive, until help came.

"Just tell me, what do you see in Tuki that you don't see in me?"

He does not know what to say.

"Well?"

"I'm so sorry, Fil. This is not about you. You're an amazing person. You have been more than—"

"Just shut the hell up, Michael. And leave me alone!" She steps back into her apartment. Slams the door in his face.

For about five seconds he stands there staring at the aluminum numbers 302 screwed on the scratched and dented Luan door skin.

"I'm sorry," he says again. "I made a terrible mistake." He almost adds, *I was lonely, and I wanted to be like my father.* But he knows that this is no excuse at all. So he swallows the words. Then, he turns away and starts down the hall. His chest aches like he has just come up for air from the bottom of the sea.

# SIXTY

Saturday of Labor Day Weekend, the last hoot of the summer. Pangs of *saudade* are tearing at him. No more case. No more fiancée. No more wedding. And no idea when they will let Tuki out of the hospital. He talked to her once on the phone. Her voice sounded raw, stony. An octave lower. Depressed.

Since his big drunk at the Squire, he has been staying away from booze. Trying to keep busy. He has been working on Tuki's immigration issues. Learning buckets about the Amerasian Immigration Act of 1982, the Amerasian Homecoming Act of 1988, and new legislation in the works. He has found an advocacy group called the Amerasian Foundation online. Lots of links to other advocacy and support groups. A registry for children and parents searching for each other.

Tuki's father, Marcus Aparecio, does not turn up on the registry. But Michael has been in touch with advocates who have shown him how to use the web to find the guy. And last night he scored. Her father lives in Van Nuys, California. Runs a heating and air-conditioning service. Michael has the address and phone number.

But the research has not been all good news. Some sources claim there are more than 150,000 Amerasian children with American fathers, mostly former GIs, who have not been repatriated. Among this group, many are homeless. Few marry. Drugs, alcohol, and prostitution are common themes. The suicide rate among Amerasians is more than forty percent higher than the population at large.

It almost seems like Tuki is one of the lucky ones. But he needs to talk about all this with someone. Needs to decide how to present to Tuki all that he has discovered.

So at nine thirty in the morning he ends up on Chivas Regal's doorstep at the top of the stairs leading above the Tango. When the queen bee answers the door, he almost turns to run. Chivas is not in drag. What he sees is someone who looks a little like Danny DeVito with plucked eyebrows and a pink orchid-print robe, standing at the doorway. Bald. Wearing fuzzy white slippers.

"Don't you be eyeballing me all funny," Chivas says. "When you show up at this time of the morning, you have to take what you find, darling. So get over it ... I just look old and scary; *you* look like the victim of an airplane crash. Get in here before you catch your death."

P-town's Mother Superior hands him a mug, nods to a steaming pot of coffee in the coffee maker, and disappears to get into her uniform of the day.

He had almost no sleep last night. But after half a cup of Joe, standing out in the sun on a little deck overlooking the harbor, he is beginning to feel a bit of okay. The wind coming off the bay has a fresh, crisp feel. But it is definitely not helping his mood that Chivas has the soundtrack from *Pretty Woman* playing on the stereo. Could this be intentional torture? He thinks maybe he is going to throw his mug through a speaker if he has to hear "Fallen"—his old cuddle-dance song with Filipa—one more time.

"Just go ahead. Yell and scream, cute stuff!" She appears on the deck looking very Liz Taylor with a big black shag wig, killer blue eye shadow, a red satin pantsuit, black boa. And a little brown marijuana cigarette smoking from the end of a long gold holder.

"Let the thunder roll!" she says.

"Screw you," he wants to say. Because he knows that sometimes beating your chest and wailing is no solution at all. So he turns his back on the queen, leans on the railing, stares out at the last piles of wreckage from the burned buildings just a few houses away from here. He thinks about Bangkok for some reason.

"Try some of this, love. Sometimes it takes the edge off things."

She passes him the smoke. This is the first pot he has had since college. Dope was not his thing. He would never buy the stuff. But now he inhales and holds the serpent in his lungs.

He is still imagining Bangkok. Its golden pagodas, its teeming heat, its chocolate river. He feels wings spreading from the roots of his shoulders ... and wonders if this picture in his head is the place

Tuki meant when she wrote on her tablet that she wanted to go home. Or did she mean P-town?

A new CD comes on, *Graceland*. His mind is starting to smooth out into a jet stream of soft, warm air. He and Chivas lean on the railing of the deck and stare out at nothing. They pass the golden joint holder back and forth to the rhythm of Paul Simon singing about a road trip to Memphis, Tennessee.

After a long time, he speaks up. "I feel really low."

"I know," she says.

"I was supposed to be getting married today."

"Go ahead, blame me if it helps; it may well be my fault, love. I saw that you had it in you to rescue her. I promoted you. I took you to the ball. I didn't think about the cost to you."

He feels something hacking into the back of his neck. Someone is chopping off his head. Slowly. With a dull blade.

"You used me ..."

"She was in trouble. Terrible trouble. Like crashing and burning in that madhouse. And then, suddenly, here you come. Sir Lancelot."

"I've found her father."

"Of course, you can do anything."

"She wouldn't answer her phone so I left the address on her voice mail."

"That's one of the reasons she has fallen for you. You are persistent ... and you really care. But she knows it can never work out. Because, you know?"

There is a buzzing sound building inside his head, a tightening in his throat. Yeah, he *knows*. He is a little clearer about what he feels for her now. There were moments the night they danced together when he felt something tearing at his heart and deeper, darker places in him. But maybe it was just loneliness or something even more primal gnawing at him. He was far from sober and the longing died the moment Nikki came crashing into the bungalow streaming blood.

Still, he feels more strongly for her than he ever felt for Filipa. He knows that. Maybe he does love her. Maybe it makes his heart sing to know that she walks the Earth. But somehow all of the violence has twisted things in his chest. Way too much violence ... in Provincetown and in Southeast Asia. So he cannot love her the way his parents love each other. Like a fever. Like a drug. Like a miracle. This is not about his being straight or gay. In Tuki's world those labels cease to be relevant. It is what he told his father. For some reason, when all is said and done, she just plain feels like blood. And someone who has shared this outrageous nightmare.

"The girl is in agony, honey. She—"

"Christ! Just stop! Stop it, Chivas! I don't need to hear this! It makes me feel like hell. Why did I ever come here?"

She gives him a lip-quivering look, like go ahead and spit at me. "What did you expect from me?!"

"A saint," he mumbles. "I expected an absolute saint."

"Maybe you thought I was somebody else."

"Wonder Woman," he says, which is the first name that rises out of his mind.

"No. Wonder Woman would be the princess coming home from the hospital this afternoon."

# SIXTY-ONE

The organ music swells. The spotlight is coming up blue. She feels Percy Sledge in her chest, and then she is in after eight bars, singing "When a Man Loves a Woman." Her voice has changed. It has gotten lower, raspy. Sultry in a sort of Tina Turner way. She is not sure that she likes it. She will never do Gloria Estefan again. But at least she has a voice. At the moment, she can sing. But her vocal chords feel on fire. The doctor told her to speak in whispers for a month.

He watches from a table near the back wall of the Tango, not certain what to feel. He just knows he is glad to see her, glad to be here for her return. She struts a slow pause-and-go. The girl in black makes her entrance through the curtained kitchen door, singing about crazy love, blind love. She holds the mike like a torch to her lips, weaves among the tables. She does not see him. But that is okay. He is just trying to get used to her new voice. He is thinking it has claws. And as she sings, he pictures a seaside carnival. A Ferris wheel turning and turning and turning to the music.

The light-and-sound kid in the far corner is singing along, doing his own show for the shadows. And maybe she envies him because tonight, of all nights, the music is not carrying her into some private place. Tonight, she is searching, scanning her audience, hoping against hope that she sees the strong, dark, Portuguese face of the man who saved her life. The face that all but erases the smells of the River House and Prem.

But she still does not see him sitting back there in the dark. She thinks he is never coming to save her again ... could not save her even if he were here.

Her heart is having a hard time leaving its misery. He can see it. Everyone in the audience can. It is like they are all holding their breath for her.

The next thing he knows she is down by the bar sipping champagne and singing "Try A Little Tenderness." Otis Redding himself is now rising like stage smoke from that black dress.

The song starts out as a heartbreak hotel thing. But the tempo picks up with each new verse. Michael has seen the video of the Big O doing his thing to this number. The man is sleepwalking at the beginning of the piece. But by the end he is wailing and screaming, and the drums are banging. The horns blaring. Sweat is busting out all over. His shirttail is torn out. And his arms, legs, head are shaking. He is having a seizure. The audience is on its feet as the entertainer goes down howling "Gotta, gotta, gotta try a little tenderness ..."

Tuki, too, is sweating the song. The audience is clapping. She is jumping up and down on the runway, screaming. A dragon princess with the flames rising in her belly. Lifting her out of pain and proclaiming that she can still fly. Her vocal chords sizzling with their song.

Something takes over; it feels like the summer of 1966. A hot time in the Mekong Delta. Smokey Robinson and the Supremes ooze from the bars around Dong Koi Street in Saigon. Her *me* is still a schoolgirl in Cholon when Radio Vietnam introduces the Isley Brothers, the new soldiers' anthem—a special favorite for all the brothers out there like Marcus Aparecio. The song is "This Old Heart of Mine." What a tune! It is all about getting kicked in the teeth by love ... and getting up ... to love again. Violins backing up the Holland, Dozier, and Holland piano-of-soul. The song winds up like a merry-go-round ride.

It is the perfect song for a Saturday night of Labor Day Weekend, thinks Michael. Like the rest of the audience, he wants to hear that summer is not over. That summer and love will rise again. No stopping them. Just like the song.

And there is no stopping Tuki as she struts and sings her way right to the back of the room for a duet of bump-and-grind action with the light-and-sound kid, then back down among the tables to fall in love with a truck driver and his wife, for a verse or two. Before the song wheels into its last cycle.

As the crowd claps and sings along, she mounts the runway. She is free. This is her time, her moment to strut the boards, singing, bending to kiss the customers, plucking their tips like flower petals. Head high, chest out, hips swinging ... a sexy little kid from Cholon, a Marine's fantasy, a pair of Patpong queens named Delta and Brandy, a boat baby, a fugitive. A case cracker. A ball of fire. A girl who wears her heart for everyone to see ... for a man she will never have. She is all of these things, riding the wave ... until the music stops and the lights go out.

She wishes the scene would end here because she is feeling right with the night. And her vocal chords are ripping out by the roots. But she cannot stop. The crowd is pumped and shouting for more. She knew this would happen. Maybe hoped it would. She gave the light-and-sound kid a fourth CD to play for her encore, for a closer. But when he looks at it, she is sure he is wondering what she was thinking when she picked this piece. "The Crying Game." It is so dark, so blue.

She is violating just about every rule of cabaret by bringing the audience down from their high with this encore ... but too late. She picked her poison. And now, for the first time, she sees Michael sitting out their in the audience at his table in the shadows. Watching. All she can do is lock on his big soft eyes, listen for the music, and make her exit with style. Do what she has to do.

So she begins. The red spotlight catches her sitting on a stool at the end of the bar. She is in with the downbeat, afraid of where this song will take her. The words flow.

"I know all there is to know about the crying game; I've had my share of the crying game ..."

The backup is just a lounge piano, rhythm guitar, drumstick keeping time on a block of wood. Brushes on a snare drum. Like a lullaby. She is not even twelve bars into the number when her body starts thinking about sleep, beautiful sleep. She is really forcing now to get the notes out of her wrecked throat. Everyone and everything is getting hazy. The song is unraveling. And she is still sitting on a stool with her back against the bar ... paralyzed or something.

A video is doing a slow-mo waltz through her mind. She is dancing with her handsome young attorney, kissing his cheek in the moonlight at Shangri-La.

Her voice tells the story.

"First there were kisses ..."

Suddenly there is an echo in the room. "Then there were sighs ..."

That is not, *not* her voice singing this last phrase, giving her throat a break. *What is going on here?*

Something weird is happening. She is hearing applause. Slowly her eyes leave Michael. They follow the beam of an orange spotlight that is picking up a figure that has just appeared from the doorway to the kitchen. There, singing a call and response thing with her, is the Patron Saint of Drag herself. Wearing a floor-length, metallic-gold cape and a sparkling red and green turban. Chivas reaches her left arm out across the audience to Tuki. Her voice calls like Ethel Merman, strong and clear. Tuki's own voice calls back to her. She at last slides from her stool and begins to make her way among the tables toward the runway and stage. Toward her *pheuan*. Her friend.

They are singing to each other. The old queen draws Tuki to her like a child in the dark. They meet at the spot where the runway and the stage join ... and they end in harmony. They don't want any more of the crying game. Tuki's voice is shredding into a thousand pieces. Her eyes finding Michael one more time. Her knees going weak. She is smiling like crazy.

Chivas wraps her arm around Tuki's back. She can feel the hot rolls of the Queen Mother's waist in the cup of her left hand. She thinks of Brandy and Delta just as the song fades. Then the house goes black.

A minute later she is gone.

But nobody misses her until the next day.

# SIXTY-TWO

Monday, Labor Day, they go looking for her on Nantucket. Votolatto is there out of concern for foul play, and Chivas. Michael leads them to the place. He guides their little posse right up the stairs to the second floor and main entrance to the Kittikachorn vacation home. Votolatto rings the doorbell. Waits. No one comes. He rings the bell again, knocks hard. But still nothing. He tries to open the door. But it is locked.

"Tuki, honey." Chivas calls.

The detective pounds the door with his fist. "Is there another way in there?"

"Follow me." Michael is running as he starts down the stairs and heads around to the ocean side of the house.

The sliding door to the seaside deck is open. A pale green curtain whips in the afternoon sea breeze. Inside the room is empty. Ever so softly, Lionel Richie croons from hidden speakers.

"What's this?" says Votolatto. He is holding a red light-cotton hooded sweatshirt.

Michael says it is Tuki's.

Chivas calls her name again, sniffs the air. It smells like burnt sulfur. "What's that?"

"You don't want to know," says Votolatto. He is already following his nose down a hallway to the right. Michael behind him.

At the end of the hall there is a closed door. Michael grabs the nob, turns, pushes. But the door only cracks open, held fast by a security chain.

"Goddamn it!" Votolatto gives the door a sharp kick and it flies open with the cracking of wood.

This must be the master bedroom. Michael sees a king-size bed, raised about three feet off the floor. The champagne-colored comforter, the sheets, the pillows all tangled together. Clothes, a man and a woman's, make a trail across the white rug to a Jacuzzi. It sits, trimmed with a cedar skirt, on its own screened end of the deck looking out to sea. All but the corner of the spa is blocked from view by the high bed. Tuki's bra looks like a question mark, lying by the dust ruffle of the bed.

Chivas is just getting here when Michael sees the blood. Rusty swirls. Coiling, ebbing, flowing through the water in the hot tub.

"Aw, fuck!" Votolatto sounds like he wants to cry.

Stepping around the bed for a clear look, Michael sees the body. Nude, sitting on a bench seat in the spa. Back to them. Head buried in a forearm on the edge of the tub. For a second he thinks he is seeing a sleeper, or a person bent over in sorrow. Then he sees the hole, larger than a half-dollar, in the side of the head where the bullet came out.

The man from Bangkok, the lonely hunter, is dead. A thread of blood leaks from the corner of his mouth. The skin on his back looks the color of wax paper. Next to his left hand is a .357 magnum. Powder burns on his temple surround the purple tattoo of a gun shot.

"I feel dizzy." Michael falls to his knees next to the body. Something has sucked all the air out of him.

Chivas starts. "Oh, god ... oh, god ... Tuki!"

"Don't touch anything!" Votolatto jams his hands against the sides of his head, trying to restart his brain. His voice cracks. "He's been dead a while."

The detective stoops, puts his arm around Michael's shoulder. "Come on, counselor. I need you to hold it together for me, okay? I'm not doing so well myself. There's nothing you can do here. Take care of the old girl, will ya?"

Michael cannot speak. But he nods, turns his eyes away from the carnage, staggers to his feet. He had hoped that Prem Kittikatchorn would just disappear. But not like this.

Chivas is sitting on the bed with her face in her hands, sobbing. He drops down beside her. Gives her a big soft hug like he is hugging his mother. But it is as if something has woven a cocoon around him. He cannot feel her hot, wet breath or her tears on his neck. "Come on. I need a drink."

"She's gone," mumbles Chivas as they shuffle down the hall to the living room to look for the bar.

"I don't understand."

"Tuki. She was here. Her clothes are still here. He ..."

In his mind he hears her voice, low and raked with sadness. *I promised myself to him. I told him I would come to him ... if he just let me have one more day with you.*

The tears are rolling down the queen's cheek. "She's dead."

"Like hell!" he says. But he knows what she is thinking. Maybe it is true. Prem killed Tuki. Or she took her own life. He remembers the shooting at her bungalow, her scarred wrists from that night in jail. That the suicide rate among Amerasians is more than forty percent higher than the population at large.

"We've lost her."

His head snaps back on his shoulders. "She had her whole life ahead of her. She was free to start over."

Chivas stops walking. "That's not how she saw it." She pulls away from him, looks up into his eyes. They are standing in the living room now. The wind whipping the curtain, sunlight flooding the space.

"Why?"

"Everything she loved was behind her."

"What about us?"

"Us, too. I've got a buyer for the Tango. And you. You can never be the prince that she ..." Chivas has her face in her hands again. She settles onto a couch. "Can you just give me a minute, sweetheart?"

A web of darkness is spreading inside him. "I'll be outside." *If she is dead, let it be me who finds her. I owe her at least that much.*

When he gets to the beach, he tugs off his shoes and walks into the wind, thinking that at any moment he will see her crumpled on the sand leaking blood ... or floating face-down on the waves. But the beach is bare, and the ocean is empty.

Suddenly, he feels something tightening in his chest. All the air going out again. His legs shiver and freeze solid. He has to sit right here where the surf comes in and soaks his feet, his calves, his thighs.

His shoulders fall back against the cool sand and he squeezes his eyes shut. The breaking of the surf is ringing in his ears when he catches the first scents of the charcoal braziers, steaming curry, and roasting peanuts. Then he sees her in flashes, flickers. She is onstage, belting out "This Old Heart of Mine." The crowd is clapping to the rhythm as she works the runway, singing, strutting, bending to kiss the customers, plucking their tips. A love child, an old soul, a holy child like Buddha. With a nest of dark hair. A sexy little kid from Saigon, a GI's fantasy in a red dress. It is nothing more than the thinnest veil. Over heart and soul and blood. Her head is high, chest out, hips swinging. She is smiling when he loses her.

His eyes open at last, and he takes a long breath. He looks out to sea to the east. Rainsqualls are towering north of Georges Bank. The clouds look like violet pillars. Somewhere out there the *Rosa Lee* is hauling back. He can smell the pungent scent of fish caught in the web of the otter trawl. The birds wheel and dive after silver shadows. Mostly they come up wet and floundering and empty handed. They are fishers. They struggle into the sky. They spin and dive again.

# EPILOGUE

For a week there is some desire on the part of the Kittikatchorn family to pin the death of their son and brother on Tuki. But in the end, Votolatto convinces them that the evidence is too thin, and the coroner calls it suicide.

Tuki remains a mystery. After two weeks the detective reaches Michael by cell phone at home one night in Chatham. Votolatto say that the police still have not found her body. No calls on her cell phone. No sightings in Provincetown. No sightings in her old haunts on Silicone Alley in New York. No apparent contact with Brandy and Delta in Bangkok, according to Varat Samset. No sign of her on an internet search of drag shows. No credit card activity.

"It's like she just swam out to sea and disappeared," says Votolatto. "Left that clown dead, stripped out of her clothes, and headed back to the place we all come from, the mother of waters. It's a shame. She kind of grew on me. Amazing performance when we sent her in with a wire. I can see why you liked her. She had something. I don't know what. But some kind of vitality, I guess, made her larger than life."

Michael cradles the cell phone against the collar of his Red Sox shirt, stares around the dimly-lit attic, scratches the three-day growth on the heel of his jaw. He is sitting on the folding chair at his Formica table. It is empty now. Almost the whole apartment is. His personal stuff is packed in his jeep. *To hell with this place. To hell with Tuki Aparecio.*

"You still there, Rambo?"

"Sorry. I was just kind of remembering some things."

"Look, man. You've got to let her go."

"I just don't get it. I try and I try, but I still don't understand how—"

"You miss her, huh?"

Her knees are pulled up under her chin, hair falling in a thousand ringlets over her shoulders and her arms. She is a silhouette, a child. In Saigon. In Chinatown.

"Rambo?"

"Yeah?"

"Talk to me."

"Where the hell did she go?"

"Forget about it, will you? She's just gone, just history."

He does not know when Votolatto hangs up. But he knows that he listens to a dial tone for a long time before the earpiece starts bleating at him like a siren ... and he throws the cell phone at a wall. It bursts with a crack into a hundred pieces. They flutter to the ground, silver feathers in the dark room.

*When they tie up the* Rosa Lee *at the fish buyer's wharf in Nu Bej, Michael, his father, and Tio Tommy are bleary eyed, but grinning at each other. They have been awake for thirty-six hours fighting their way home from Georges Bank with the twenty-foot seas of a freezing November gale eating at their stern. But now they are here. Safe and sound. With a slammer trip of cod aboard.*

*The former public defender opens the hatch on the main fish hold. He is wearing a thick, charcoal fisherman's sweater and his yellow foul weather overalls, streaked with fish guts and blood. Flecks of snow swirl over the boat in the sharp northeast wind. "We going to be rich or what, Kenny?"*

*The fish buyer looks into the hold. It is nearly packed to the deck beams with ice and fresh cod. "Yeah, you can buy the moon. This must be your lucky day, Mo. DHL guy came this morning. You got a package in my office. You're not going to believe this. The tracking label says it came from Vietnam."*

*His father flashes him a squinty-eyed look.*

*He shrugs.*

*"Well, what are you waiting for?"*

*A minute later he is walking down the wharf with a package the size of a shoebox in his hands. He can see his father watching him, but*

*not watching him, as he and Tio Tommy supervise the lumpers unload-
ing gray totes of ice and cod. So he walks away from the* Rosa Lee *to be
alone with his hopes and fears. When he gets to the end of the wharf, he
drops down on a pile of nets. Sits and looks at the harbor, the hurricane
dike. The snow is coming thicker, starting to stick on the wharf, the
boats, the rigging as he tears at the thick cardboard of the box.*

*Inside the cardboard, beneath the tissue paper that carries away
in the wind, is a rectangular box about the size and weight of a brick,
covered in light green silk. He pushes open the small ivory clasps. Inside
there is something wrapped like a mummy in more tissue paper.*

*As he peels it away, he sees a face, then a torso, and finally legs.
They are folded in the lotus position. It is a statue. Made of some kind of
green stone, maybe jade. The Buddha. Its belly is round and full. And
so is the chest. The breasts of an earth mother. The eyes almost sparkle
in this face that spreads with a broad smile.*

*He is holding the Buddha in his left hand, trying to remember
what it was that Brandy and Delta told Tuki about being old souls,
about what old souls know, when his eyes see something that looks like
it may be a picture. It is lodged in the bottom of the silk-covered box.*

*When he pries it out with his fingernails, he recognizes the rich
colors of a Polaroid snapshot. There are a man and a woman in the picture. They are dressed in khaki shorts and white polo shirts, standing in
front of a large stone pagoda. The man is tall, slender, black. He looks
like Lou Gossett Jr. The person beside him is Tuki. Her hair is tied up
on top of her head in a gold and black fountain of curls. She is holding
the little green statue of Buddha in front of her in both hands like an
offering. And she is grinning, huge, just like the man.*

*He thinks it is an amazing grin, coming out of the blue the way
it does. Quite a pretty smile. It starts with her plum lips and straight
white teeth, spreads to her proud chin. Two little dimples bloom on her
cheeks as her eyes light up, full of discovery.*

*From somewhere in his chest, a voice sings about catching a mid-
night train. The snow now a warm rain on his cheeks.*